PRAISE FOR *NEW YORK TIMES AND USA TODAY* BESTSELLING AUTHOR ANNE FRASIER

"Frasier has perfected the art of making a reader's skin crawl."

—*Publishers Weekly*

"A master."

—*Minneapolis Star Tribune*

"Anne Frasier delivers thoroughly engrossing, completely riveting suspense."

—Lisa Gardner

"Frasier's writing is fast and furious."

—Jayne Ann Krentz

PRAISE FOR *THE BODY READER*

Winner of the International Thriller Writers 2017 Thriller Award for Best Paperback Original

"Absorbing."

—*Publishers Weekly*

"This is an electrifying murder mystery—one of the best of the year."

—Mysterious Reviews

"A nicely constructed combination of mystery and thriller. Frasier is a talented writer whose forte is probing into the psyches of her characters, and she produces a fast-paced novel with a finale containing many surprises."

—I Love a Mystery

"Has all the essentials of an edge-of-your-seat story. There is suspense, believable characters, an interesting setting, and just the right amount of details to keep the reader's eyes always moving forward . . . I recommend *Play Dead* as a great addition to any mystery library."

—Roundtable Reviews

PRAISE FOR *PRETTY DEAD*

"Besides being beautifully written and tightly plotted, this book was that sort of great read you need on a regular basis to restore your faith in a genre."

—Lynn Viehl, *Paperback Writer* (Book of the Month)

"By far the best of the three books. I couldn't put my Kindle down till I'd read every last page."

—NetGalley

PRAISE FOR *HUSH*

"This is by far and away the best serial-killer story I've read in a long time . . . strong characters, with a truly twisted bad guy."

—Jayne Ann Krentz

"I couldn't put it down. Engrossing . . . scary . . . I loved it."

—Linda Howard

"A deeply engrossing read, *Hush* delivers a creepy villain, a chilling plot, and two remarkable investigators whose personal struggles are only equaled by their compelling need to stop a madman before he kills again. Warning: don't read this book if you are home alone."

—Lisa Gardner

"A wealth of procedural detail, a heart-thumping finale, and two scarred but indelible protagonists make this a first-rate read."

—*Publishers Weekly*

"Anne Frasier has crafted a taut and suspenseful thriller."

—Kay Hooper

"Well-realized characters and taut, suspenseful plotting."

—*Minneapolis Star Tribune*

PRAISE FOR *SLEEP TIGHT*

"Guaranteed to keep you awake at night."

—Lisa Jackson

"There'll be no sleeping after reading this one. Laced with forensic detail and psychological twists."

—Andrea Kane

"Gripping and intense . . . Along with a fine plot, Frasier delivers her characters as whole people, each trying to cope in the face of violence and jealousies."

—*Minneapolis Star Tribune*

"Enthralling. There's a lot more to this clever intrigue than graphic police procedures. Indeed, one of Frasier's many strengths is her ability to create characters and relationships that are as compelling as the mystery itself. Will linger with the reader after the killer is caught."

—*Publishers Weekly*

PRAISE FOR *THE ORCHARD*

"Eerie and atmospheric, this is an indie movie in print. You'll read and read to see where it is going, although it's clear early on that the future is not going to be kind to anyone involved. Weir's story is more proof that only love can break your heart."

—*Library Journal*

"A gripping account of divided loyalties, the real cost of farming and the shattered people on the front lines. Not since Jane Smiley's *A Thousand Acres* has there been so enrapturing a family drama percolating out from the back forty."

—*Maclean's*

"This poignant memoir of love, labor, and dangerous pesticides reveals the terrible true price."

—*Oprah Magazine* (Fall Book Pick)

"Equal parts moving love story and environmental warning."

—*Entertainment Weekly* (B+)

"While reading this extraordinarily moving memoir, I kept remembering the last two lines of Muriel Rukeyser's poem 'Käthe Kollwitz' ('What would happen if one woman told the truth about her life? / The world would split open'), for Weir proffers a worldview that is at once eloquent, sincere, and searing."
    —*Library Journal* (Librarians' Best Books of 2011)

"She tells her story with grace, unflinching honesty and compassion all the while establishing a sense of place and time with a master story teller's perspective so engaging you forget it is a memoir."
    —Calvin Crosby, Books Inc. (Berkeley, CA)

"One of my favorite reads of 2011, *The Orchard* is easily mistakable as a novel for its engaging, page-turning flow and its seemingly imaginative plot."
    —Susan McBeth, founder and owner of Adventures by the Book, San Diego, CA

"Moving and surprising."
    —The Next Chapter (Fall 2011 Top 20 Best Books)

"Searing . . . the past is artfully juxtaposed with the present in this finely wrought work. Its haunting passages will linger long after the last page is turned."
    —*Boston Globe* (Pick of the Week)

"If a writing instructor wanted an excellent example of voice in a piece of writing, this would be a five-star choice!"
    —*San Diego Union-Tribune* (Recommended Read)

"This book produced a string of emotions that had my hand flying up to my mouth time and again, and not only made me realize, 'This woman can write!' but also made me appreciate the importance of this book, and how it reaches far beyond Weir's own story."

—Linda Grana, Diesel, a Bookstore

"*The Orchard* is a lovely book in all the ways that really matter, one of those rare and wonderful memoirs in which people you've never met become your friends."

—Nicholas Sparks

"A hypnotic tale of place, people, and of Midwestern family roots that run deep, stubbornly hidden, and equally menacing."

—Jamie Ford, *New York Times* bestselling author of *Hotel on the Corner of Bitter and Sweet*

FIND
ME

ALSO BY ANNE FRASIER

DETECTIVE JUDE FONTAINE MYSTERIES

The Body Reader
The Body Counter
The Body Keeper

THE ELISE SANDBURG SERIES

Play Dead
Stay Dead
Pretty Dead
Truly Dead

OTHER NOVELS

Hush
Sleep Tight
Before I Wake
Pale Immortal
Garden of Darkness

NONFICTION (AS THERESA WEIR)

The Orchard: A Memoir
The Man Who Left

FIND
ME

ANNE FRASIER

 THOMAS & MERCER

Text copyright © 2020 by Theresa Weir
All rights reserved.

Published by Thomas & Mercer, Seattle

www.apub.com

Amazon, the Amazon logo, and Thomas & Mercer are trademarks of Amazon.com, Inc., or its affiliates.

ISBN-13: 9781542005623
ISBN-10: 1542005620

Cover design by Damon Freeman

Printed in the United States of America

FIND
ME

CHAPTER 1

It was dark by the time Cathy Baker took off along the Southern California trail just outside the town of Redlands. She knew about the missing joggers. In fact, she'd been called to work one of the cases, which was why she was jogging by herself tonight, hair pulled back in a ponytail, running shoes, mace tucked into the waistband of her shorts, a survival whistle hidden inside her shirt to alert nearby backup.

She deliberately matched the victim profile.

It was called Operation Mousetrap. Not a very original name, but concise. Ten trained women from police departments around Southern California had agreed to be bait for the Inland Empire Killer. Top secret, carried out in various locations. Cathy Baker had extensive self-defense training and felt confident about being able to fight off an attacker.

Ten minutes into her jog, she spotted something on the trail. She was already tense, but now she was on high alert. She felt for the mace, pulled it out, and hid it in the palm of her hand, releasing a confused breath when she got close enough to see a crying child on the path. A little girl, barefoot, no jacket or sweater even though the night was chilly. Her auburn hair was straight and chin-length.

Cathy crouched in front of her. "Are you lost?"

The girl, who looked to be maybe five or six, sniffled and wiped her nose with the back of her hand. "Can you help me find my mommy?"

How had she gotten there? Had she wandered away from home?

The girl pointed away from the trail. "She went that way."

Ah, so her mother was nearby. Relieved, Cathy stood, tucking the mace back into her waistband. Didn't look like they would be catching the Inland Empire Killer tonight, but it was a good thing she'd been out. She hated to think of the poor kid spending the night in the dark and cold. She took the girl by the hand. "We'll find her."

"If we don't, can we go to your house?"

Strange words for such a young child. "Of course. What's your name?"

"I'm not supposed to tell."

"Why not?" They walked deeper into the woods.

"Names aren't part of the game, are they?"

"What game?"

"The game. The game we're playing."

At the child's unsettling words, Cathy slipped her fingers back inside her waistband and felt for the mace.

From somewhere, a man's voice shouted, "Run!"

The child ran.

Cathy was struck in the head and knocked to the ground. The container of mace fell from her hand. She rolled to her back, knees to chin, kicking hard. Blood running in her eyes, she grabbed the mace and jumped to her feet, all the while wondering where the girl had gone, trying to make sense of what was happening. Was the child part of this? Or was it just a coincidence?

She aimed the container at her assailant's face and pressed the trigger. Nothing happened. Just a sputter.

The man knocked her down. A knife flashed and she felt red-hot pain as he sliced her throat. She made a gurgling sound, saw the blade again as his arm moved high above her head.

"Daddy, no!"

Daddy?

The man looked up, surprised. Then his weight was gone and she heard running footsteps fade.

Cathy put the whistle to her lips. No sound came out.

The child had returned and was standing nearby.

Cathy tugged hard on the whistle, breaking the chain from her neck. With one hand pressed to her bleeding throat, she held out the whistle to the little girl. The child didn't move. Cathy urged her close, nodding and motioning for her to take it, trying not to show her own fear. The girl stepped closer. With hesitation, she took the whistle. Cathy lifted her own hand to her mouth, pursing her lips to mime a blowing action.

Not taking her eyes off Cathy, the girl slowly lifted the whistle to her mouth. Cathy nodded in encouragement.

The girl blew. Once, then again, the sound exploding, shooting up to the stars.

Cathy's hand dropped away from her throat. She heard sirens, and at one point she opened her eyes and saw the girl standing over her. Then, like the man, the child ran off as Cathy felt her life slip away.

CHAPTER 2

Present day

Homicide detective Daniel Ellis entered San Quentin, California's only death-row prison for male inmates. He was grateful for the shade and the blast of air-conditioning, while at the same time mentally preparing himself for what was to come. He'd been summoned (*summoned* was the only way to put it) by inmate Benjamin Wayne Fisher, also known as the Inland Empire Killer. It had taken Daniel eight hours to make the drive from the Homicide Department in San Bernardino to San Quentin. He was hot and traffic-weary and suspected this was just another instance of a death-row prisoner in need of company, even if that company was a cop. It happened a lot. He was going into it hoping for more but expecting nothing.

He checked in at the front desk, where he was issued a special photo ID. As he unloaded his pockets for the metal detector, then stowed his belongings including his gun in a locker, he allowed himself to fixate on the high percentage of serial killers with the middle name of Wayne. Someone had even gone to the effort of keeping a running tally, and so far there were 223 killers on the list. It was just another one of those odd things that made no sense in a sea of things that made no sense when it came to compulsion-driven killing. The phenomenon even extended to non-serial murderers. Proponents of "the Wayne Theory," as it was known, had determined that 0.41 percent of convicted murderers had the middle name of Wayne.

A guard escorted him through a series of doors that opened via an intercom system operated by controllers who sat behind monitors in a central hub. The system had been implemented after a bloody riot in which forty-two people were injured. Now, if a guard was accosted, the doors would remain locked. All inmates knew this, but they still occasionally tried to kill someone in an attempt to escape.

In prison, surfaces reflected and magnified sound. And every face, whether prisoner or guard, reflected an acute awareness, along with a commitment to fight to the death if conflict broke out. It was a place where most people were one uninvited glance away from a meltdown, and the need for hyperawareness took a toll on guards and prisoners alike.

Prisons had a smell unlike anything Daniel had ever experienced. It was instantly recognizable; even blindfolded, he would have been able to tell he was in a prison. In this bleak ecosystem of little natural light or fresh air, beneath the canned odor of industrial cleaning products that didn't quite cover up the scents of urine and feces, lurked the caged breath of dead men. It was like moving through the moist exhalations of infamous prisoners like the deceased Charles Manson and Sirhan Sirhan. The odor got in your clothes and hair, and Daniel fully expected it to be a part of him for the next several days.

He'd never met the Inland Empire Killer, but he probably knew more about him than anybody in the country. Daniel had been a kid when he first heard of Fisher's crimes, but they left an imprint on him that had changed the course of his life. He'd spent much of his time at George Mason University studying the case, and he'd even written a paper on Fisher. Odd that he was the one meeting with him now. Life was strange.

He was shown into a narrow room with beige concrete-block walls and no windows, a place too bright for even the faintest shadow to live. Fisher was already there, sitting at the table. The man hadn't aged well.

Everything Daniel saw and heard and smelled reminded him that this was the most unnatural place on earth, while he grasped with uneasy empathy that the occupants would be here until they died. A wasted life was a tragedy however you looked at it, and the idea of living behind these walls forever was a heavy thing to think about.

Fisher still had an aura of professor about him. He was one of those people who could look nerdy and intellectual, or crazy creepy. Daniel had been told Fisher was the go-to guy for inmates suffering from emotional issues, doling out advice like a resident guru. Fisher had taught psychology on the outside, further proof people went into certain fields in order to try to figure out their own psychoses.

Daniel took a seat across from Fisher, trying to control his reaction to being in the same room with a man who'd occupied so much of his brain for too many years. He pulled a pack of fruit-flavored gum from his pocket and slid it across the table. Fisher's favorite. Or at least it used to be.

Fisher dug into the pack, offered it to Daniel, who shook his head, then popped a piece in his mouth, leaned back, and closed his eyes, chewing and savoring it for a few moments before looking at Daniel again. "I used to coach girls' softball. They loved to chew this gum. The smell and taste of it really takes me back."

That hadn't been Daniel's intention, and this shared moment made him feel a little queasy.

Fisher got down to business. "Thanks for coming." He sounded as if he were meeting a business associate or getting together with a colleague for afternoon coffee. But instead of a tweed jacket or a sweater with elbow patches, he wore an orange jumpsuit, heavy handcuffs on his wrists. He wasn't shackled to the floor or secured with a belly chain, proof of his elevated status within the prison.

California had the death penalty, something that came as a surprise to many who thought of the state as being too liberal for such a measure. But even before the current capital punishment moratorium, the death penalty hadn't been implemented that often. In fact, the last lethal injection had taken place at San Quentin in 2006, so the chance of Fisher going anywhere soon was remote. He'd most likely die of natural causes behind prison walls. And even if executions had been more popular in the Golden State, Fisher wouldn't get the needle until he shared where he'd disposed of his victims. Daniel always figured that was his long game, the missing bodies his insurance.

People wondered what it was about California that produced so many serial killers. It had the inauspicious distinction of having more serial kills than any other state, and also some of the most notorious killers. Maybe it was just a numbers thing—California was a big state and had the highest population. Or maybe earthquake tremors and fault lines had people subconsciously on edge. It was especially perplexing considering how much sunlight the state got; it was sold and embraced as the land of happy people. Maybe in gloomier states people were too cold and depressed to act upon their violent obsessions and fantasies.

"I was hoping to meet with Franco," Fisher said.

Franco, the detective who'd handled the case from the beginning.

"He's retired," Daniel told him. "I've taken over his job."

"You look like you should be working as a barista somewhere while you try out for the occasional TV role. How old are you?" As happened with smells in a confined space, the room had taken on the sweet and fruity scent of Fisher's gum. Daniel knew right then and there he'd never chew gum again, especially fruit-flavored.

"I'm old enough." He wanted to say he was older than the women Fisher had murdered, but he managed to keep his mouth shut.

"You don't look like you've really experienced life or dealt with people like me," Fisher said. His words were an example of how narcissists, with their lack of empathy, didn't think others were impacted by life in the same way.

"Listen, I can go away and come back in five years. We'll both be older then." The snarky comment slipped out before he could stop it, and Daniel gave himself a mental kick. He didn't want to do anything to lose the guy.

Over the years, Fisher had requested many visits from Franco. They'd always started out promising, with Fisher talking about plans to tell him where the bodies were buried, but Franco had been old-school and had refused to bend to any of Fisher's demands. Daniel, by contrast, planned to bend like hell to get what he wanted. He'd been after this for far too long to let it slip away now. And there was no denying who was in control here. Fisher was the only one who had the answers they needed. He had nothing to lose. Daniel's goal was to make sure the conversation didn't stop.

One side of Fisher's mouth quivered with the hint of a rusty smile. "Consider this an interview. I want to find out if you're qualified to work with me, so I'm going to ask you some questions."

Daniel let Fisher roll.

"Do people call you Dan or Danny?"

"My mother was the only one who called me Danny."

"Past tense. Is she dead?"

Daniel looked at him, taking in his bloodshot eyes, the broken veins in his face, the skin that had an unhealthy pallor from living years inside. Without blinking, he said, "Yes."

"My condolences. I lost my mother while I was here in prison. It's tough when someone you love dies and you're inside."

"I'm sure it is."

"She was a homesteader in the desert. My father up and left one day and she had to raise me all alone out there. You know, back then you had to farm the ground for seven full years or lose it. Somehow she did it."

It was interesting to see he seemed to admire and care about her. From Daniel's research, she appeared to have been a good role model, but public perception could often be false, and he'd never been able to find much information on her.

"You married?" Fisher asked.

"Divorced."

"Being a cop's hard on a marriage."

"That's right."

"What about kids? Got any?"

"My personal life doesn't belong in this conversation."

"That must mean yes."

Daniel shrugged. "Doesn't mean anything." He didn't mention the dark and twisted relationship that had existed between Fisher and his own daughter.

"Here's an interesting thing about prison," Fisher said. "When people come in from the outside, you can smell the world on them." He inhaled deeply.

Daniel relaxed a little with the shift in conversation. "What do I smell like?"

"The interior of a car that's been sitting in the sun. The freeway. Like exhaust fumes and diesel. Were you stuck in traffic?"

"It's California. The interstate was backed up in several places."

"Does that café outside Santa Clarita still exist? They had the best peanut-butter pie. Have you ever eaten peanut-butter pie?"

"I think I know the place you're talking about," Daniel said. "It's been overrun by cool kids, but it's still there."

"I'd love a piece of that pie."

Daniel's strategy was to give in to every demand Fisher had as long as it wasn't impossible. "I can arrange it." Whatever it took to find the young women he'd killed so the families could have closure. Everybody needed closure. "Better yet, you could actually go there," Daniel added. "Smell the freeway, maybe even catch a whiff of the ocean if the wind is blowing hard from the right direction." Highly unlikely unless part of California finally fell into the ocean, but salt air added flair to his offer. And there was always the chance a big chunk of the state would be gone tomorrow.

Fisher was interested.

"I could arrange it." Daniel wasn't sure how, but he'd make it happen. Close the place down, fill it with cops, let Fisher eat his damn pie. "If you tell me where the bodies are."

Most of Fisher's kills—at least the ones they actually knew about, because Daniel was convinced he hadn't confessed to them all, if he could even remember them all—had taken place in an area between Los Angeles and the Mojave Desert known as the Inland Empire, thus his nickname. He was caught because one of his victims had escaped. The targeted victim had been a petite young blond woman named Gabby Sutton, who now appeared to have a normal life, at least from a casual bystander's perspective. *Life goes on.* For some. If you weren't murdered.

Fisher chewed his gum, not looking professorial anymore. "Not *tell* you," he said. "*Show* you."

Daniel hoped the hammering of his heart couldn't be seen through his shirt. *So close.* "That's possible," he said slowly. He didn't want to appear too eager.

"But I have stipulations."

This was where things tended to fall apart. Franco's theory was that Fisher just wanted company and he never planned to share the body locations. Not really a surprise. Things got lonely in prison. And now Daniel had promised him a ride down the freeway. There was a good chance Fisher would string this along until he died, leading Daniel to one false grave after another.

"Before you tell me no," Fisher continued, "let me make it clear that I would never be able to find the locations on a map. I have to physically go there. In a car. And even at that, I can't promise we'll find them all."

Day trips. A death-row tactic not unlike visits to medical clinics. Daniel didn't blink. "Can you give me a general location?"

"The Mojave Desert."

A big place, stretching from Los Angeles County all the way to Utah, Arizona, and Nevada. Over forty-seven thousand square miles. If they went, they'd most likely drive around and not find anything. Fisher would say he couldn't remember, and they'd take him back to prison. Somewhere along the way he'd say he needed to go to the bathroom, and he'd try to escape.

"I can arrange it," Daniel said.

"One more thing." Fisher reached into his shirt pocket and pulled out a small plastic packet. Daniel recognized it as the kind of insert that used to come with billfolds, almost obsolete now that everybody had smartphones. It was a reminder that time had stopped for Fisher.

Fisher unfolded it and placed it on the table between them. Photos, five in all, had been slipped into the sleeves. Daniel leaned closer.

The images were discolored and faded, with edges curled and soft from hours spent in Fisher's hands. They were all of the same person, a child with straight auburn hair, bangs, and a sweet, innocent face from another era.

Fisher tapped the table next to the photos and pushed them even closer to Daniel. "I want my daughter to be there."

Daniel's heart sank. He was not in the business of family counseling. "Not a big deal." He managed to keep any sign of tension out of his voice.

"It might be. She won't talk to me."

"When did you last see or hear from her?"

"When they arrested me thirty years ago."

Hope fell hard. Ben Fisher was not only trying to manipulate his daughter, he was using Daniel to facilitate it. "I've heard she isn't in the best of health," Daniel said cautiously.

Most detectives knew Reni Fisher's story. She'd joined the FBI and had lived out east for a while. She was so good at profiling she'd guest lectured at Quantico. But two or three years back, there had been rumors of a breakdown. She'd quit the FBI or had taken a leave of absence, and hadn't been heard from since. An agent would know how to hide. And even if Daniel could track her down, she probably wouldn't want anything to do with this. He understood.

Daniel offered Fisher something else. "We can come up with more perks so she doesn't have to be involved. I'm not sure she'll cooperate even if I could find her."

"Kids can wear you down. They beg and beg, and you finally give in."

"I don't understand."

"She used to beg to come with me. On our little family adventures. The apple doesn't fall far from the tree. Reni, or we don't have a deal."

He seemed to be saying Reni Fisher had been the reason for the murders. That was unlikely given her age at the time, but Fisher wasn't the only person to have proposed that theory. It popped up from time to time on online crime boards. Still, as far as Daniel was concerned, Reni was the real victim here. When she was a child, her father had used her as bait to lure young women to their deaths.

CHAPTER 3

The Mojave Desert didn't appeal to everybody. In fact, it didn't appeal to most people, which was why Reni Fisher liked it. But it wasn't the only reason. The desert had been a part of her life as long as she could remember. Long before she'd become an FBI agent.

She'd moved away, to cities out east, but now she was back, and she wondered how she could have possibly forgotten her love of the place. On her good days, the scent of desert flowers and creosote bush was all the therapy she needed. On her bad, it was still a steadfast reminder that the landscape had been a comfort yesterday and would be again tomorrow.

Sometimes she couldn't help but feel she'd been a terrible friend, abandoning a place that had meant so much to her at one time. And yet the desert didn't seem to care about her thoughtlessness. It remained the same, continuing to turn sunrises orange and sunsets red. It continued to sit quietly under fast-moving clouds and thunderstorms while allowing the wind to carry its sand away, lifting the grains high, taking them far beyond the desert. It had never waited for her to return, but it had always been there.

It was spring now, one of the best times of the year in Reni's opinion, fall being a close second. Summer, on the other hand, could be unforgivingly hot, especially during monsoon season when the humidity kicked in, making the swamp coolers unusable. People would pull curtains tight and huddle inside until the sun and temperatures dropped.

Many of the outsiders who ended up in the high desert came because their souls were wounded and they wanted to start over or hide or forget or pretend the past had never happened. Reni Fisher could claim all those things and more. But the desert could only do so much. And often the people seeking comfort left after a while, going back to where they'd come from, a little healed, or a little more damaged by solace unfulfilled. Others stayed, claiming they were home and would never leave. Reni fell into the latter category.

Her place was located twenty miles from Joshua Tree and a couple hours east of Los Angeles, but much further in the sense of geology, weather, traffic, and life in general. Going from city to desert dwelling was like taking a trip from the earth to the moon.

It wasn't easy to find. The dirt road was rutted and climbed steadily to an elevation that bothered some but not others. Her small cabin was situated on a steep rise that afforded a view of Goat Mountain in the distance and a flat basin below. On a clear day, Reni liked to think she could see all the way to Nevada. Maybe she could.

Because her place was so removed from civilization, she felt safe and secure. And because she had the reputation of being distant, not wanting company, people didn't bother her. So the last thing she expected was a visit from the world she'd deliberately left behind. When she heard a car, followed by a knock on the door, she wasn't inclined to answer. Let them think nobody was home. Maybe it was the investigative journalist who'd shown up a couple of weeks ago. The young woman had left her card in the door. Carmel something.

Another knock, this one more aggressive.

Putting an eye to a crack in the heavy curtains, closed now to block the sun, Reni was able to make out a man in a black suit. Nothing good came in a suit. You had your funeral directors, your FBI, your lawyers, your detectives.

Holding her breath, she moved away from the window and stood very still in front of the locked door, intensely aware of the stranger on the other side. She could feel the dark world he brought with him. It seeped through the cracks of the old cabin. She no longer carried a gun, or even owned one. Guns were not a part of this life. That proved to be a good lifestyle choice because right now her fingers were twitching as she imagined the comforting weight of a weapon in her hand.

The persistent annoyance knocked again.

Once again, she didn't answer. She was sure he knew she was inside even though the only hint of present occupation was her battered and rusty white truck parked out front. That didn't mean she was home. For all he knew she might have gone somewhere with someone. Closer to reality, she might have been hiking, but not at midday in temperatures that were hot for April.

The dark and shifting shape of his shadow moved against the curtains. Moments later, she heard the slam of a car door. But that sound wasn't followed by an engine turning over or a car driving away.

She peeked through the curtains again and saw he'd found a sliver of shade and was sitting on the ground, arm resting against a knee, back against the shed that housed her kiln. His jacket and tie were gone, his sleeves rolled up. Without his suit he didn't look as threatening. Just hot and tired. Human.

Was this about her old partner? Her old job? A cold case? Worse, did someone need her? She was surprised to find she had any curiosity left in her.

She opened the door wide and shouted to him, asking what he wanted.

"A drink of water would be nice."

City folk. Funny thought, since she'd been "city folk" not long ago. But people came here to slough off that skin, and it happened quickly. "Only an idiot drives into the desert with no water." People died in the desert all the time, dehydration and disorientation hitting them before they knew what had happened.

"How do you know I'm not from here?"

She made an exasperated face anyone with the least bit of emotional intelligence would understand.

He heaved himself to his feet with an agile yet stiff movement. Ground sore. When he was close and they were finally face-to-face, he appeared a little taken aback. Maybe because he'd been expecting the person she used to be. Polished and professional. Not some long-haired, barefoot hippie with clay dust on her hands and jeans.

"You're hard to find," he said.

"Apparently not hard enough."

She was surprised her voice didn't tremble. She gave herself points for that. And since she rarely spoke, she was equally surprised her voice worked at all and wasn't just some croak pretending to be words. "This is private property. Who are you, and what do you want?"

"I tried to call first."

She checked her phone, then turned it around so he could see the latest blocked number.

"That's me. My name is Detective Daniel Ellis. I'm from the San Bernardino County Homicide Bureau. I'm here about your father."

She placed a hand to her chest and felt the rapid flutter of her heart through her T-shirt. Dry mouth, shaking. This was the emotional earthquake she'd spent so much time trying to avoid. *This* was why she was in the desert.

There weren't any self-help books for the children of serial killers. It would have been an extremely niche market. Hopefully. But in an attempt to understand why she couldn't shake her past, she'd read books on dealing with trauma. She'd tried to understand why her yesterdays came rushing back even when she thought she was managing and coping and had put them behind her. In retrospect, she should have seen this coming, but when your walls were up, surprises hit harder.

As a diversion from the colliding thoughts in her head, she forced herself to zero in on the man in front of her, cataloging him, profiling him. Tall, looming, a young and too-serious face, a head of dark hair.

16

In a gesture that almost seemed affected but might have been a move of politeness, he swept off his sunglasses. His brown eyes held caution. People tended to look at her that way nowadays.

He seemed familiar, and she struggled to place him. She'd blocked a lot of things. It was the only way to survive. Where had they met? George Mason University? Quantico?

In case she doubted his introduction, he flashed his badge and asked if he could come in.

People always left a little of themselves behind once they were gone. There was DNA, yes, but for her it was more of an energy that could take days to wear off. She did not want him in her home. Who knew how long it would take to purge him once he was gone. But it was hot out, close to ninety. She couldn't refuse someone water and respite from the midday heat. She stepped back and let him inside.

The swamp cooler was chugging away on the roof, blasting air through vents with enough velocity to stir hair and ruffle clothing. Once he was inside, she sensed his relief at being somewhere cool.

"Have we met?" she asked, struggling to recall the world beyond the desert, while at the same time shying away from unwanted memories. She was unprepared for someone to bring her father into her safe space. Not his physical body, but rather thoughts of him, words of him, the ugliness of his life and all he'd done, floating freely about the room, touching everything. Her clay, her pottery wheels, even her dog's ashes. Nothing was safe or sacred.

Her guest glanced around, giving her place the detective once-over. Probably mentally labeling it as bleak and rife with despair. More workshop than living space, something monastic and sparse except for the shelves of pottery in various stages of production, some recently removed from the wheel, others glazed and waiting to be fired. He took in everything in the open space, from the cinder-block walls to the concrete floor covered in clay dust just like her.

"Quantico," he said. "You visited a profiling class I was taking."

Ah, she'd been right about a connection to school. She remembered him now, along with his part in the brief introductions that had circled the room.

"You asked if I felt complicit in my father's crimes even though I'd been a child at the time."

He winced. "Sorry. That was out of line and too personal."

He was sweating, and she remembered his initial request.

She retrieved a container of cold water from the refrigerator, poured, and handed him a glass. "Don't apologize for digging deep and getting personal. It was a good question. I don't remember my answer though."

He took a long, grateful swallow. "You said no one should feel guilty for the crimes of others. Especially not a child."

Her scripted reply. She'd put together a lot of those over the years. But the answer was true even though a minute never passed without her feeling guilty. More of that day returned. "Didn't you have some crazy marksman skills?"

"Good memory."

For some things.

"I don't make it to the firing range as much as I'd like, so my proficiency isn't what it used to be." He finished the water and set the empty glass on the kitchen table. Then he rudely wandered around her workshop, visually examining her pottery wheels, glaze buckets, pug mill, tubs of clay, and shelves of pottery. He seemed especially interested in the designs requiring an intense-heat process that involved bird feathers. He paused in front of a map that covered half a wall. The Mojave Desert. He took note of the areas marked in red.

She came and stood beside him, hands in the front pockets of her jeans. "These are the places I've searched for my father's victims." Some of her searches had taken place on what had once been her paternal grandmother's property, now her father's, an area so vast it would take a crew years to cover every hidden gulley and wash. Out there, a person could drive for hours and not see another car. That's how remote it was.

As the years passed, the chances of finding anything had become more unlikely. In a land of loose sand, rain washed many things away, even bodies.

And yet, she kept looking.

Other people spent their free time going to movies or going out to eat or visiting museums. She looked for the women her father had killed, feeling an overwhelming need to find them.

"Interesting," he said. "I've gone over the files we have on your father, and most searches were conducted closer to his home in the San Bernardino National Forest outside Palm Springs. A small team spent only a few days on your grandmother's property."

She was impressed to find he knew so much about the case considering it was so old. Odd, really, but then many detectives had their pet cold cases they liked to pull out and fixate on now and then. The popular theory was that her father had disposed of the bodies closer to their Palm Springs home, in the area of Greater LA known as the Inland Empire, but she'd always felt the desert might have been the place he'd buried them. The desert promised seclusion for a killer, and the heat brought about rapid decomposition. A perfect dumping ground.

"Why the extensive focus on the Mojave?" he asked. "It's hours away from the known locations of the most likely missing persons cases. He had much quicker access to wilderness closer to home. If he buried his victims in the Mojave, he would have had to transport them a long distance in the heat. Plus, detectives found no sign of anything at your grandmother's cabin. And back when she was still alive, she stuck with the story of never seeing anything suspicious."

That was all true. "He loved the desert and he was very at home here," Reni said. And yet that link hadn't tarnished the desert for her. Or maybe the desert hadn't allowed itself to be tarnished.

"That's not enough of a reason. And maybe no reason at all, because killers don't typically want to taint the places they love."

"Nothing you learned in any profiling class at Quantico or in the field applies to Benjamin Fisher," she said. "He cared about me, I have no doubt about that, and yet he had no qualms about using and tainting me. In fact, I would guess it was part of the pleasure he derived from it all. Mixing me up in it, his little father-and-daughter outings of death."

Her bluntness seemed to make him uncomfortable, yet he was the one who'd started this, who'd brought Benjamin Fisher back into her headspace. What had he expected? It had to be a struggle for him to know just where to push and just where to hold back. He might have even forgotten for a second that she was Benjamin's daughter, and that this wasn't a detective brainstorming session.

Looking around, he asked, "How long have you been making pottery?" He seemed to be trying to shake off the awkwardness of the situation.

"Off and on, several years." She was happy to talk about something else.

Making pottery was an escape of a sort. She got up in the morning and cut bubbles from the clay by pulling it through wire strung between frames. She'd work it and slap a piece on the wheel and focus her energy on that piece, on keeping it centered and keeping it smooth and keeping it from going wrong, because one small error, one small distraction, and she'd have to start over.

When she threw a pot, she never thought about the past; she thought about the repeated wetting of her fingers in the can of water, the steady and even pressure applied to the clay. She thought about the way the sun felt streaming through the window, hitting her back. She never thought about her father. She would not allow him to be a part of her art, of the clay, and the creation. Her goal, which she'd somewhat succeeded at until today, had been to keep him out of this healing space.

Her pottery provided income too. The area got a lot of tourists due to the proximity to Joshua Tree National Park, and her tranquil and oddly delicate pieces that echoed the layers of sky and mountains were unique enough to take off.

Daniel picked up a bowl from a workbench and turned it over to reveal her potter's stamp. "What's the logo mean?"

"Just an image from a dream." A crude stick bird, something a child might draw. Or in this area, something that could have been a petroglyph. "It has no real meaning. I couldn't come up with anything. I had a dream and used it."

"I wouldn't tell people that." He put the bowl back on the shelf. "It's a bit underwhelming."

She laughed. It was a sound that didn't come out of her very often. "I'll try to drum up something better."

"You don't practice at all anymore? Detective work? Teaching? Seems a shame with your insight and skill."

"I've taken a few cases over the past several months. Mostly missing persons. None that ended well, but they brought closure."

"You look different," he said bluntly.

A long way from her Homicide days and a closet full of black suits of her own, all of which she'd given to Goodwill. The calendar would show that she'd only been gone three years, but it felt like ten. Definitely another life.

After the breakdown, it hadn't taken long for her to realize she needed to escape everything, mostly herself and the thoughts she couldn't turn off. There was one obvious way out, one way to make everything stop, but she refused to go that route. First because of her dog, and second because she couldn't do that to her mother. It was her own personal joke that the dog had come first. So she made the decision to pack up her truck, load up her dog, and hit the road with no plans or goals. Because on the road, every day was an escape as the highway unfurled in front of you and rolled up behind you and you just kept moving, focusing on the needs of the day. Where to stop for gas, where to walk the dog, where to camp for the night, always moving toward or away from sunsets.

But her old dog got older and she began to feel guilty about dragging him on her journey even though he never complained. And when he reached the point where it was time to let him go, she realized she had no home for his ashes. So she returned to California less than a year ago and bought the tiny cabin and put his ashes and collar on the mantel above the fireplace. She made it livable but not too livable, because she didn't deserve that. Years before, she'd been pretty good at making pottery, taught by a long-ago college boyfriend, so she picked up a used pottery wheel on Craigslist and began making pots again.

And the healing began.

"I hope you didn't come here to criticize my life choices," she said.

"No, but it's a big leap."

He seemed concerned. Her mother often wore that same expression.

"This is me now," she said. "Creativity is healing. You should try it. You have a high-stress occupation. Pottery is very meditative and calming."

"Not really into that stuff."

"Everybody should create something."

"I think the last thing I made was—" He stopped abruptly, obviously changing his mind, and said, "some kind of macaroni art in grade school."

She wondered what he'd almost said. "That's a shame. But I know you didn't come all the way here from San Bernardino to talk about crafts." Hand on a hip, she asked, "I'm ready to hear what you have to say."

"Let's sit down."

Sit down. This was not going to be good.

Her father was dead. That was it, she decided.

She'd waited for this day for so long, and now she felt a surprising threat of tears. She'd never gone to see him in prison. Just couldn't do it. And as far as she knew, her mother had gone only a couple of times. And now if the news was of his death, she found herself feeling guilty about not visiting him. How stupid was that?

The sun was setting, so she opened the curtains and they sat down at the kitchen table. Daniel seemed to struggle for words.

"He's dead," she said.

"No, in fact he's very much alive."

She was both relieved and disappointed. San Quentin was eight hours away, more if the traffic was bad, but still too close. Could his very proximity pull her back into his orbit of decay? "Interesting," she said calmly, going very still. Not a knee shake or the turning of a hand into a fist. She didn't clutch at the denim of her jeans. She didn't blink or raise an eyebrow.

"Five days ago he contacted me and offered to show us where his victims are buried."

Promising, but also something her father had said before. "That's excellent news. The victims' families deserve closure." She glanced at her shelves of pottery and suddenly felt Daniel's earlier sense of displacement. The pottery, this house, the ancient truck outside, waiting to go somewhere else that wasn't here. This area, her clothing, all seemed foreign now, the work of someone else who was strong and centered. "Thanks for letting me know."

He had to leave. She needed to be alone. She sucked in a wobbly breath and nodded so he would think she was okay, but the nod was jerky. She probably wasn't fooling him. "That's good. That's very good," she added. He'd most likely come as a courtesy, so she didn't hear the news from somewhere else. "I'll tell my mother."

"That's not all," he said.

What else could there possibly be?

"He had one stipulation." He looked down at his hands, then back up. He had a small round scar near his eyebrow. Chicken pox? Piercing scar? Piercing.

"He won't lead us to the burial sites unless you come along."

Reni's brain shut down and her gaze highlighted objects, trying to draw her away from the pain in her chest. The vivid yellow in a painting on the wall, the glass her guest had drunk from. She would have to get rid of that. It would always remind her of this moment.

"I can't." She hadn't seen her father since the day he was taken away in handcuffs, calling her *baby girl* as the cops led him off. Thirty years. That's how long it had been. "That's impossible."

"I thought you'd say so." His voice was soft. Did he use that voice when interrogating criminals? It was a good one, with just the right tone. "I get it."

People often asked what it was like to be the daughter of a serial killer. She didn't blame them for being curious. Sometimes, in order to stop further questions, she just told them it was awful. One word and done. Other times, when she was feeling especially generous and in the mood to share or maybe even try to put her feelings out there in the world so they weren't such a weight to carry, she gave them the short version of the truth. It had to be short, because no words existed that could adequately convey the damage to her soul and the empty yet painful pit her father's actions had left in her belly. The best she could do was chip a piece from the multilayered truth. Sometimes, depending on her frame of mind, she would suggest they imagine the thing they cherished most in the world, something that made them feel safe and loved, and turn that upside down. The arms that encircled you becoming a monster. The mouth that read to you at night and gave you a good-night kiss becoming a wound of lies, a dark cavern of crawling bloatflies.

But it was much more complex than that because the heart still remembered the love that went both ways, that flowed in and out. And the bond between father and daughter was unique and special. It pulsed and generated love on a cellular level. And the evil deeds, no matter how old she got or how many lives she lived in order to step out from under his shadow, couldn't drive out the memories of the person she'd known and loved. So now, even at the age of thirty-eight, when she thought of him, it was still with a familiar ache of the soul as she mourned the loss of the man she'd thought he was, and not the man he'd become. And she continued to find it impossible to come to terms with the fact that those two conflicting people still resided in one body, that he was still alive, rotting away on death row, passing the time until his final goodbye.

Daniel was quietly waiting.

How could she possibly see her father again? How could she possibly keep herself from shattering? Her entire life since his arrest had been trying to move on, pretending he was dead. Trying to get him out of her heart when he once *was* her heart. She wasn't sure she could live through even a short encounter.

"What does he want?" she managed to whisper.

"I don't know. Just to see you, maybe?"

"There has to be more to it than that." She picked up a tube of lip balm from a pottery bowl on the table. The balm smelled like lavender. She got up and threw it away. She grabbed Daniel's glass and threw it in the trash too. The whole house would have to go, and she would have to burn her clothes and move far away to a place that was nothing like this. Mars maybe.

"You've got time," Daniel said. "Day trips for killers on death row don't come easy. And we'll have to get the prison staff to sign nondisclosures; the last thing we want is media presence or onlookers increasing the potential escape risk. Your father won't be told when the excursion will take place, just in case he has someone working on the outside."

She had to give him credit for not mentioning the glass.

"So unblock your phone. Wait for my call. I'll start the paperwork, and if you decide to do it, this will give you time to talk it over with your mother." As an aside, he added, "Just so you know, he didn't ask to see her."

"It will bring the families closure," Reni said, trying to convince herself.

"It might bring you closure too." He blinked a little too slowly, as if tamping something down as he went for a positive spin. A few more years and a few more murders and that kind of thinking would be burned out of him.

She noticed with a shock that the sun was going down, filling the room with a pink glow.

Her father had loved sunsets. It was one of the things she remembered most about him. He would take her hand and they'd stroll to a special viewing spot on her grandmother's property. The sun would hover in the sky for so long, she sometimes thought maybe it wasn't the sun at all, but something he'd convinced her was real. Twisting reality, making her think and see what he wanted her to think and see.

Everybody talked about criminal profiling. She'd taught classes around the country on it. She was supposed to be an expert. She used to be the person they called when a horrendous crime took place. But he'd never fit. A man who loved his family, loved nature, loved sunsets and animals. A man who'd given her the perfect childhood and had adored her. A man who loved and was loved.

And yet he was evil. Maybe the worst kind of evil, because it had hidden right in front of her and tricked her child's heart. And later, when she began to suspect, when she tried to expose him, her mother didn't believe her, and Reni began to doubt everything she knew.

But even now she missed him. That was the danger of seeing him again. She missed how he said her name. Reni, an old family name, spoken softly, with the hint of a southern accent. He was in prison and she was here, in the desert, safe from him and his control. But she was afraid that if she saw him she would love him again.

"I'm sorry," Daniel said, as if he understood what she was going through. But nobody could understand. She didn't expect them to. Or want them to.

"This is just another notch in your belt," she said. "When it's over, you'll be the guest speaker at Quantico. But this is my life, my mother's life. I don't want it sensationalized. I don't want to find out you've sold the story to some podcaster for a ten-part series. I don't want press on-site. I don't want to see the story from your perspective anywhere."

"I completely agree. I have no plans to achieve fame or fortune from this."

"Oh, come on. At least fame among your peers. I know how important that can be."

He shook his head. "Not interested."

He could deny it all he wanted, but something was driving him. She got the sense he had a little more skin in the game than he was acknowledging.

"Some people actually just want to do the right thing," he said.

She glanced at the map on the wall and knew there was only one answer. And if her father actually took them to burial sites, maybe it would undo the sense of complicity Daniel had asked her about that day at Quantico. "I'll do it."

CHAPTER 4

Three years earlier

Rosalind Fisher's volunteer work with abused women had conditioned her to expect phone calls in the middle of the night. Physical abuse, often fueled by drink and drugs, tended to happen after dark. So when the ringing phone woke her, she expected to hear the voice of her contact at Safe Home. Someone needing immediate shelter, because Rosalind always had a guest room waiting. Always food and clean sheets and towels. Bandages and ice packs and pain medication, if needed.

This call *was* from a person in need, but not a stranger.

"Mom? I need your help."

Nothing was as sharply painful as that jolt of a mother's fear. It cut deep.

Rosalind turned on a light and sat up in bed while wishing Reni wasn't so far away. She'd felt the extreme distance had never been a good idea, but she always tried to support her daughter no matter what decisions Reni made, even if they were bad ones.

"Tell me." Rosalind struggled to keep her voice calm, collected, with no indication of the panic she felt. That would help no one.

"It was dark. My partner and I were working a case . . . and I thought I saw someone who really wasn't there." Reni's voice was thick and a little slurred. Drugs? Alcohol? This wasn't good.

"Are *you* okay? That's what I want to know."

"Yes."

Rosalind let out a tight breath. Everything could be fixed. Everybody could be made to feel better if a person used the right words. "Where are you?"

Reni told her. She was calling from a hospital. That was reassuring. She'd admitted herself, medication being the reason for the thick tongue.

Reni had always been a handful. That was the truth. As a newborn she'd cried nonstop for days, and Rosalind had reached a point where intervention had been necessary. She hadn't been worried about herself or her lack of sleep, but an infant couldn't continue like that. It was a bad situation. Out of desperation, Ben took Reni to his mother's cabin in the desert. And, as the story went (although Rosalind doubted the speed of Reni's turnaround), she stopped crying immediately and began drinking formula and sleeping like a normal baby.

But Reni remained a sober and melancholy child, always watching, thinking, but often keeping her thoughts to herself. A bond between them never really took hold, not the way it should have. Sometimes Rosalind wasn't sure if Reni liked her at all. It was hard to mother a child who didn't like you. Ben always said Rosalind was imagining it, but she didn't think so.

Maybe that was why Rosalind had opened her home to abused women. It partially made up for the strained relationship she had with Reni, and it provided an excuse for Reni to spend more time with Ben. But once he was in prison and Reni's grandmother died, it was just the two of them, and Rosalind stepped up to take care of her daughter. And for the first time in their relationship, Reni responded.

"I'm sorry, honey. Maybe it's the stress of your job." Reni had the softest heart, too soft for her own good.

"I don't know."

Rosalind sensed she wasn't getting the full story. "Things happen in high-stress situations," she said, trying to reassure her daughter. "And in the dark . . ."

"There's more."

She sounded so upset, so unlike her collected self.

"I've never drawn my gun on anybody," Reni said. "I'm good at keeping a level head. But my partner's face in the dark . . . it changed. I saw somebody else."

"Who?"

A long pause. "Daddy."

"Oh, honey." What words of comfort could she give to *that*?

Rosalind had been waiting for something like this. For so long she'd started to relax and think it might never happen. She'd studied grief and complex trauma, both in college and later alongside Benjamin. Odd to think he'd been an excellent teacher, but he had.

The day after Ben's arrest, when the truth came out about what he'd done, Reni retreated into her stoic, quiet self. It wasn't until later, when detectives questioned her, that her part in the murders was revealed.

"I'm going to catch a plane first thing in the morning," Rosalind said. "We'll figure this out together."

"You're coming?" Disbelief and relief.

"Of course I'm coming."

The next morning, Rosalind caught a flight from Palm Springs to Boston. At the hospital, she spoke with the doctor caring for her daughter.

"I don't think she should go back to work, at least not right now," he said.

"I agree. She's coming home with me."

"I'm advising her to take a few months off. If she isn't seeing a psychiatrist, I strongly suggest she find one. She needs medication. She needs to be away from stress. She might have had a post-traumatic flashback. Honestly, this isn't unusual. I think most of our military and police force should be getting some form of psychological support and learning self-care and stress management. I'm sure she's going to be glad to see you."

Rosalind wasn't prepared for how bad Reni looked. She calculated how long it had been since she'd seen her. Just a few months. Not long enough for her to be so thin, with sunken cheeks and protruding bones and dark circles under her eyes. This hadn't happened overnight.

"Everything's going to be all right," she told Reni. "We're going to go home." She could see Reni wondering about the word *home*. "California," she explained.

Probably not the best idea to take her to the house where the bad things in her life had started. But it was also a place of comfort, or at least it used to be.

"I'd like to go to Grandmother's cabin."

It had always annoyed Rosalind that Beryl Fisher was the person who'd been able to care for Reni as an infant. "Oh, Reni. I hate the desert. You know that."

"You don't have to go."

"There's no electricity there, and even hauled water is hard to get. No cell service. That's not the place for you right now. Let's just get home and we can talk about that later. Okay?"

Reni nodded.

Rosalind helped her get dressed. The nurse handed Rosalind a bag of medicine and scripts. Outside, they took a cab to Reni's apartment. While Reni sat on a chair in a stupor, Rosalind tossed clothes and toiletries into a suitcase. Then she noticed the dog dishes on the kitchen floor. Damn. She'd forgotten about the dog.

"Where's Sam?"

"A neighbor's watching him."

He wasn't one of those pocket puppies. He was a big Lab. Change of plans. They'd have to drive clear across the country. Rosalind knew even a heavily drugged Reni would not be okay with cargo-shipping the dog. Rosalind wasn't comfortable with the idea either.

"What about my fish?" Reni pointed to a bowl containing a purple and red betta.

Rosalind tracked down Sam's location, luckily in the same building. She traded the fish for the dog, passing the bowl and food to a man wearing workout clothing.

"My daughter's been wanting a fish," he said.

"Great."

Back in the apartment, they boxed up everything for a permanent move. Five days later they were in California and Reni was resting in her old room, Sam next to her on the bed.

CHAPTER 5

Present day

It was always hard returning to the house where the police had hauled her father off in handcuffs. Normally Reni went out of her way to avoid stepping inside those familiar walls. She'd strongly considered calling to tell her mother about the deal Benjamin was trying to cut. It would have been easier over the phone. But in the end she felt she owed her mother, who'd done so much for her recently, a face-to-face.

So, hand on the wheel, a booted foot removed from the gas pedal as the elevation on the four-lane dropped, she drove the hour from the high desert to Palm Springs, watching the outdoor temperature increase with each mile. It wasn't unusual for it to be twenty degrees hotter in the low desert.

Three days had passed since Daniel Ellis had shown up at her cabin. Since then, she'd attended a craft fair and had sold enough pottery to get her through another month. She wasn't sure if she'd ever return to the FBI, but she'd used up all leave-of-absence pay long ago and was living hand to mouth, the pottery the only thing keeping food on the table and her small mortgage paid. She was okay with her current state of affairs, and actually liked the ever-present threat of immediate collapse. Everything could be gone tomorrow. Or not.

Her mother had offered to help out financially, but Reni declined for more than one reason. Rosalind Fisher could be controlling, and Reni didn't want to be at her mercy. And unlike the rockiness of the past, their current relationship was decent. Not strong, but better. She didn't want to risk disturbing it.

She hit town and cut through the tourist district.

Palm Springs felt like a coastal California city, but it was located a hundred miles from any beaches, on the edge of the Inland Empire. People were always commenting about how they thought the ocean should be just one street over, or just around a turn. Nope. *Keep driving.*

She'd been born and raised there, her view too close as a kid to really have a solid take on the place. It had just been the town where she lived. But in later years, Reni had come to understand Palm Springs was like a glossy magazine someone had left open in the sun by the pool. The desert city was famous as the birthplace of the mid-century modern movement. That influence could be seen everywhere, from coffee shops and hotels to private homes. Located two hours from Los Angeles, the city had also been the playground to the stars, and palm-lined streets with names like Gene Autry Trail and Frank Sinatra Drive reminded visitors of old Hollywood. The airport even had a concourse named after Sonny Bono.

When temperatures in the Coachella Valley got too intense, an aerial tram carried people up and away from the heat to the San Jacinto Mountains, while highways provided smooth car rides to and from lower and higher elevations, past fields of iconic giant white turbines lazily stirring ozone that had drifted down the valley from LA. The ozone usually came with air-quality warnings and at the very least a headache. If that wasn't exciting enough, both the San Andreas and Walker Lane faults lay deep and hidden a few miles out of town. There had been some fairly big quakes in the past, but everybody was still waiting for the big one. Specialists said it was a matter of when, not if.

Bring it on.

Feeling a deep and familiar dread, Reni turned at a stop sign and drove down a wide, smooth street to the cul-de-sac where she'd grown up. Her family home, built in the fifties, was about as classic as it could get, with a butterfly roof and white breeze blocks and giant palms. A perfect example of mid-century modernism meets Desert Modernism. It had even been part of a few home tours over the years, something her mother was proud of. Reni figured people just wanted to see the place where the Inland Empire Killer had lived.

She hadn't given her mother any advance warning about her visit, and as soon as she stepped inside and dropped her bag on the low couch, Rosalind Fisher began her purging ritual, which was what they'd both started calling it.

It had taken a while, but Reni had come to realize that odors were big triggers for what had eventually been diagnosed as complex trauma. The smell of the house was a blow to her no matter how prepared she was or how much time had passed. Even though the walls had been repainted and there were no family photos on display anymore, even though she'd lived there for years after Benjamin's arrest, going away for any length of time and returning had a way of reawakening a response that made her curl her hands into fists until her nails cut bloody half-moons into her palms.

Even now, so many years later, as her mother moved from one spot to the next, lighting candles and turning on an essential-oil diffuser, Reni could smell the dark childhood she hadn't known was dark until later. The place where your life changed in a moment, where your reality turned upside down, could never be hidden or covered with paint or artwork or the cloying scent of a million candles. Rather than becoming something new, overwriting what had come before, the candles and art merely merged with the past.

Her mother, with her jingling gold bracelet, black cigarette pants, and crisp sleeveless white top with the collar arranged just so, looked like a cross between Audrey Hepburn and a tall and younger Sally Field as she dashed away to reappear with a bottle of air freshener that she held high and pumped.

Something new added to the repertoire.

It smelled like evergreens, and Reni's stomach churned for a moment before she got it under control. Halting the physical response was a trick she'd been working on. If she could freeze it, back it up, the emotional jolt stopped along with it.

She didn't tell her mother the spray bothered her. Because just as Reni hid her deeper feelings, her mother battled the past with things she could spray and melt and light.

Elegant and polished, with dyed hair, never any roots, never left the house without makeup, went to yoga classes and paint classes and ate healthy, heavily influenced by her location and her philanthropic life as a supporter of the local arts and artists, her home a refuge for women in need of a safe place and a bed. That was Rosalind Fisher.

"You should have told me you were coming." She set the spray aside and with a flick of the thermostat turned on the air-conditioning to circulate the scent through the house. "I would have aired things out for you. I know how sensitive you are. You and those headaches."

Reni had explained it all away as migraines. Easier than saying scent-triggered flashbacks. What happened would always be a cloud over them and between them, but by silent and unspoken agreement that reached back years, neither talked about it. Even now it didn't seem real. It would never seem real. But she tried not to let her mother see how much it had damaged her, maybe because Rosalind had suffered enough, maybe because Reni didn't want her fussing over her. Yet knowing she'd be seeing her father soon made Reni acutely aware of how raw she herself was.

As a child, her world had revolved around her father. Their home had been her safe place, her family often boring. But even the most boring people could harbor deep and ugly secrets. She'd found that to be true in her profiling work too. Serial killers weren't typically interesting in real life. Fact. Her father had been a respected psychology professor with a counseling business on the side that he ran from their home. Her mother had played the role of upper-class Palm Springs wife who wasn't rich enough to run with the rich but did so anyway because she was a force. Some might be inclined to think her charity work was a way to soften the sting of her husband's misdeeds, but Rosalind had been into humanitarian work before she'd met Benjamin Fisher in college when taking the same psychology course. As it turned out, Benjamin had a sick urge to cause pain. Rosalind had an urge to stop it.

"I need to talk to you about something," Reni said. *Might as well get this over with.* She headed for the kitchen, a room that should have been inviting, but one she found no less disturbing than any other part of the house due to the sliding glass doors that looked out to a small pool where her father had taught her to swim and had tossed her in the air while she shrieked in delight.

She closed her eyes, wishing the earth would swallow her, imagining jumping into the pool and releasing her breath and letting herself drift to the bottom, away from everything. At the same time she thought about her cabin an hour away. She thought about the can of ashes on the mantel and the way sunlight fell through the windows. She would be back there very soon. That was her promise to herself.

When she opened her eyes, she was still in the place she didn't want to be. A place of evil and sick secrets where Reni had watched from her bedroom window as the police took her father away, wondering when they'd come for her.

Later, when things died down and she returned to school, children whispered about her behind their hands while avoiding her. And most of the kids she'd grown up with never spoke to her again. There had been a petition to get her removed from the school, the reason being that she was "a disruption to the educational environment." They lost, but Reni left anyway, because, as her mother put it, "They were disrupting *her* ability to get a good education."

No amount of time would lessen the guilt Reni felt over her role in her father's sick game. Yes, she'd tried to tell her mother, but she'd presented it as something vague and easy for an adult to brush off as a child's paranoia or even a dream. Because Reni didn't truly understand what was happening, and deep down she hadn't wanted to get her father in trouble. She hadn't wanted to cause friction between her parents.

"Daddy likes to play games," she'd told Rosalind all those years ago.

"I'm glad you have a daddy who plays games with you."

"Daddy takes me to the park at night."

"Darkness isn't a reason to stay inside. Darkness isn't anything to be afraid of."

"Daddy acts funny."

"He sometimes drinks too much and that can cause a grown-up to act funny."

Now, in the kitchen, arms crossed, Reni quietly told her mother about the deal Benjamin wanted to strike.

"He's made these bargains before," Rosalind said, always so practical. "And they went nowhere."

"This seems different." Mouth dry, Reni filled a glass with tap water and settled into a chair at the table with her mother.

She'd sat in the same spot as a child.

Why had her mother kept so much of the furniture? Even the bed she'd shared with Benjamin? Reni would have dragged the damn thing outside and set fire to it on the front lawn. Years ago, Reni had even tried to talk her mother into selling the whole place. At one point it seemed Rosalind was on board with the idea, but then she changed her mind.

"I like it here," she'd said. "I don't want to move. And I don't know what I'd do without Maurice. Or what he'd do without me."

Maurice, their friend and neighbor, had been a constant in their lives, sitting with them after her father was arrested, never pulling away like so many people had done. He'd taken them to movies and out to eat, and he never cared if people stared and whispered. She was pretty sure he'd been enamored with her mother. And still was.

Reni also recognized that for her mother to leave her home would only mean her father had caused even more damage to their lives. And she understood that what her mother had done was brave. She'd remained and had held her head high And, after a time, people quit reacting to seeing her in public. The whispers and glances had stopped years ago. New people moved in, and many didn't even know their history. And now Rosalind was even being honored with a community service award for her volunteer work. She deserved it.

"I think he might be serious this time," Reni said. "I've never been part of the equation before. I just wanted to warn you."

"Who is this detective?" Rosalind asked. "Are you sure he's legitimate? Maybe he's someone looking for a story. You know how reporters have popped up throughout the years. Someone was here not long ago and I sent her away."

"She might be the person who showed up at my place too. The detective's name is Daniel Ellis. I checked out his department page. He's legit."

Her mother pulled out her phone, typed awkwardly with one finger, scrolled, then turned the screen around. "He's just a baby."

Reni smiled. Rosalind had done a Google Images search of him. There was Daniel Ellis in a tuxedo, standing next to a woman in a green gown. Oddly enough, the tux made him look even younger, like a kid dressing up. "He's got one of those faces," Reni said.

"He should grow a beard. Something well-trimmed. Nobody's going to take that face seriously."

"You'll have to tell him that if you two ever meet." It would have been easy to find Rosalind's comment annoying, but Reni had learned to take what she said in stride. Rosalind had opinions and suggestions for everyone. She just wanted to help people.

"I found his number. I'm going to call him."

"Don't. I'm not twelve."

"I don't think you should be involved in this. You're too fragile. Go back to the desert and work on your pottery."

"Do you realize how patronizing that sounds? Like telling me to go play with my toys."

"I'm sorry, honey. I'm just worried. And you have an amazing talent, a talent that has helped you navigate these past couple of years. Don't undo that. I'm all about supporting artists. You know that. So please, tell him no. Call him right now. Why, even if Benjamin took you to the bodies, it won't bring the dead people back. All it will do is make things worse for us. It's been thirty years. *Thirty years.* It's over. I don't want to go through all that again. Press vans will be parked on the street. I won't be able to go to yoga without a microphone shoved in my face. Tell him no." The last part was a command. Rosalind didn't seem to realize Reni was an adult and no longer had to obey her.

"It's not over for the victims' families," Reni said. "They still need closure. Time makes no difference." She wouldn't mention that she needed it too. Her mother knew she continued to search for the bodies, but Rosalind had no idea how much or how often.

Her mother took her coffee cup to the sink. "I know, sweetheart, but it's not just me I'm worried about." She turned around, hands gripping the counter behind her. "Doesn't he know you've had a hard time lately? It makes me mad that he'd even bother you. It's thoughtless of him. You've been doing so well, and I would hate to see this undo all the progress you've made since, well . . ." She didn't say it. She didn't have to.

The breakdown.

The room seemed to shake a little, then stop. Her mother didn't react, so Reni wasn't sure if it was a tremor or a wave of dizziness. Neither was good, but she was hoping for a tremor.

"I'll be fine." She wouldn't. But closure for everyone was more important than her mental health.

"You have to stop feeling guilty," Rosalind said.

"The guilt will never go away. In fact, I don't want it to. If it stops, it'll mean I've forgiven myself. I can't allow that to happen."

"This business with Benjamin is not going to be healthy for you. Think about yourself for once."

"This is part of me, Mom. You've never really faced what happened." It had been hard to deal with her mother's behavior after Ben's arrest. Rosalind had been in denial for years, and sometimes Reni felt as if she were shouldering all this by herself. Of course, Rosalind hadn't been involved in any of Ben's kills, which probably made it easier for her to move on. But that was also part of what made things harder on Reni. She felt a little betrayed by Rosalind even though she knew there was no justification for that emotion. What happened wasn't her mother's fault.

"I'm realistic," Rosalind said. "My life is important, more important than his, and I refuse to allow him to ruin the years I have ahead of me. It's as simple as that."

Reni had felt very alone after her father's arrest. Her mother's attitude had seemed to invalidate Reni's struggles, and so she'd pulled back and closed up. She had to remind herself that she'd been a child and her mother might have simply been trying to protect her. And yet she couldn't help but say, "You weren't involved, though."

"How can you say that? Don't you think I've wondered why I didn't see any signs? You were a child. I was an adult. Of course I heard him leave the house sometimes. I thought he was having an affair with a student."

Reni was beginning to wish she'd never told her mother about the bargain her father was seeking. It gave her father power from his cell, and now she and her mother were arguing. "You're right. It might never even happen." It would be just like him to torment them, then change his mind. Another of his games. Maybe he'd never planned to take them anywhere. Or more likely he would never actually take them to any bodies. He would just get a little day trip out of it.

"Well, I for one am not going to let him impact my life again." Rosalind nodded as if coming to a decision. "I'm going to buy a dress for the upcoming award dinner. And I'm going to get my hair done and get a facial. How would you feel about going? Do you own a dress anymore?"

This was her mother's way of coping. Her social life. Her charities. "I can get one," Reni said. Maybe she could find something at a thrift store in Joshua Tree.

"You seem a little uncomfortable about the idea. You don't have to go."

"It's just that people are accustomed to seeing you, but not me. I don't want the focus to be taken away from you and your accomplishments. I don't want people talking about your freak kid."

"That's ridiculous. I'd like you to be there. You're my daughter and our family has had enough harm inflicted upon it. Get something formal. You never wear colors anymore. Red would be nice with your olive skin."

"That seems a little too flashy for me, but I'll think about it." The less attention she drew to herself, the better. Black would be her choice.

"Whatever you do, don't wear black." Rosalind made a sad face. "Black is depressing." She moved behind Reni and lifted her daughter's thick braid. Her hair had grown, not out of a desire to have long hair, but out of neglect. "You don't have any gray in your hair. Isn't that something? I started going gray in my thirties. Your hair is still the color mine used to be. Such a shiny auburn." She finger-combed loose strands. "How about a haircut?"

Not such an odd and out-of-context question. Rosalind used to cut Reni's hair way back when, a childhood memory that made her feel vaguely uneasy for no real reason. *Go get my scissors, Reni.*

"Maybe."

"You could give it to Hair for the Children."

It was just like her mother to always think of others.

"Let's do it right now." Rosalind sounded excited. "Don't look at me like that. I'll do a good job."

Reni's phone didn't ring very often, so when she felt it vibrate in her pocket, she jumped a little before checking the screen. *Daniel Ellis.* "I've got to take this call." She stepped out the back door so her mother couldn't overhear.

"We're ready to launch," Daniel said.

No. *Too soon.* "That was fast."

"I'm surprised too."

From the adjoining backyard someone shouted at her. "Hey there, Little Wren!"

It was Maurice, dressed in baggy white shorts, a big straw hat, and sandals with knee socks, something of a signature look among the older men in the area. He was filling his hummingbird feeders.

Little Wren was the nickname he'd called her ever since she could remember. Proud of his play on words, he'd once explained that *his* name for her was spelled with a *W*. He was a nickname guy and had one for almost everybody, but hers seemed to give him the most satisfaction. She'd never bothered to remind him of her father's bird obsession, and that continuing to call her Wren was a little tone-deaf after all that had happened.

Reni waved back and pointed to the phone in her hand. He nodded, pulled out his own phone, mouthed the name Rosalind, and answered. She was probably calling to tell him about Benjamin.

"When?" she asked Daniel.

"Tomorrow."

Her stomach dropped. "Where?" Her next thought was that it had gotten her out of a haircut.

"You were right. We're going to the Mojave Desert."

CHAPTER 6

"It's time," the guard said.

Benjamin Fisher tore a sheet of paper from the tablet, folded it several times, tucked it into his pocket, and got up from the desk where he'd spent so many hours of so many years. He paused to run his fingers across the spines of his psychology books. He looked at the stacked journals that amounted to decades of writing. On a high shelf were shoeboxes of letters from women he'd never met, most wanting to marry him. None of the letters were from his daughter. Some were from their neighbor, Maurice, but even Maurice's had become more infrequent over the years, effectively cutting off written information about Rosalind and Reni that he could revisit again and again.

He'd miss this place. It had been his home for so long. He'd gone through many changes here. Some men, when they got out of prison after being behind bars most of their adult life, couldn't handle the outside and they'd commit a crime just to get back in. He understood that. They came from such a small world and weren't equipped to cope anymore. Prison was like a safe womb. A noisy womb, but a womb all the same.

The guard unlocked the door.

They were in what was known as East Block. It housed over five hundred death-row inmates. Ben's cell was on the third floor. Directly outside his door was a recent photo of him, along with a sheet of paper listing the type of restraints he required and the jobs he was allowed to do. Talk therapy, with the proper restraints, with prisoners who had special benefits. He liked to think he'd done a lot of good here.

"Let's go," the guard said, hands on his belt. Ben would be taken to another room where he'd be put in more restraints. Would Reni meet him there? He'd rather she didn't. Outside would be better. In the open, away from the prison walls.

As they moved down the walkway with curled razor wire above and a cement floor three stories below, men shouted.

"Where ya goin', lady-killer?"

"Live man walking!" someone else shouted. Several people laughed.

Thanks to their current governor, there was a moratorium on executions in California. That had inmates hopeful, but there were those who'd told Ben they wanted to die. Ben understood that too. And there were others, some who'd been his friends, who'd managed to kill themselves. But right now, the death chamber waited for no one, and he'd heard it was going to be dismantled. Of course, that didn't necessarily mean the moratorium was forever. It could be reversed.

The thing he wasn't going to miss was the noise. Every surface was hard, and every sound was amplified.

"When you comin' back, lady-killer?"

"Soon." He wanted to say *never*, but he couldn't risk the truth even presented as a joke. He didn't plan to ever come back.

Outside the building, but not outside the perimeter, Detective Ellis and two guards waited for him next to a white prison van parked under bright lights. Ellis was wearing a dark suit. "I hope you brought more practical clothing," Benjamin said. "We're going to the desert."

Ellis didn't answer. He certainly had the cool detective persona down.

With guards on each side, Ben shuffled to the van. Nobody inside but the driver. Ellis and the guards climbed in. "Where's Reni?" Ben asked. "This isn't happening without her." It gave him a powerful feeling to think that everything they wanted was in his brain and he could decide when and where to let it out. But they weren't playing right.

"We'll meet her at a rendezvous point."

"This isn't what I planned."

"This is what you're getting," Ellis said. "You didn't specify that she ride with you. It's five hours to the off-road point." Ben had shown Ellis a map, with the explanation that it was only partway. He certainly wasn't going to point out the target.

"It wasn't easy to get her to agree," Ellis continued. "So if you push any harder, this might be over right now, and you'll be led back to your cell."

"What about the pie?"

"I haven't forgotten. We'll stop on the way back."

Ben considered that. "Let's go."

Ellis spoke to someone, instructions were relayed, and the gates opened. Another van followed them.

It was strange to see the prison from the outside. It was beautiful, he thought as it shrank into the distance. Like a castle. This would be the last time he ever saw it.

As the drive continued, he tried not to let Reni's absence ruin the trip. He was no longer behind walls, he'd seen a sunrise, and he was currently staring at a beautiful sky. Most of all, he could see *so far*. The change from the very near of prison to the very far of the desert hurt his eyes because he was so accustomed to focusing on close objects. It was like someone had removed blinders from his face. At times he had to wipe away a tear with his sleeve.

Several hours later, after a well-planned bathroom break and refuel and food on the go, the vans pulled to a dusty stop in the middle of nowhere. One of those lonely rest areas in the desert. And there she was, stepping out of a white pickup. His heart almost stopped beating, and he actually did stop breathing for a moment. He hadn't seen her since the day he was arrested, and the last memory he had was of her face at the window as he was pushed into the back seat of a patrol car.

She was regal.

He would have expected no less. That shiny auburn hair, those strong brows, and strong cheekbones. And so tall. She'd gotten that from Rosalind, because he was not a tall man. The way she carried herself, head up, back straight, with no shame, made his heart swell with pride. And the signature way she walked, with a long stride and a hip roll, her weight hitting the balls of her feet in an unintentionally lanky and almost smart-ass casualness, gray sweatshirt tied around her waist . . . That was his walk. She was doing his walk and didn't even know it.

Here she was, grown and proof that she was his, that she'd always been his, flesh of his flesh, his DNA, his girl, child, woman. Through the window glass, he smiled and lifted his hand in greeting.

She paused and stared, brows furrowed.

It took him a moment to realize she didn't recognize him. She was trying to figure out who was in the van. He caught his faint reflection, enough to see the gray hair, the baldness, the sagging skin. He wasn't the good-looking guy he used to be.

It was harder for beautiful people like him to get old because they had so much further to fall and so many adjustments to make, going from a world where things came easy because you were so damn dazzling, to a world where you had to fight to prove you were even average.

He saw the moment she realized who he was. Her face changed. There was a flash of horror, and then a quick downward gaze as she resumed her walk to the second van.

CHAPTER 7

Two years before Benjamin Fisher's arrest

Reni's father woke her, finger to his lips. In a soft whisper, he said they were going on a secret adventure. He gathered her in his arms and tip-toed from the house, closing the door quietly behind them and putting her in the car. The world was dark and hollow and mysterious. And he didn't even make her wear a seat belt.

"You're getting better all the time," he told her as they drove away. She could feel his excitement. "You like to play the game."

Reni liked being trusted with a secret, and she liked spending time with him, but she didn't like playing the game. Not anymore. It made her feel funny, and she hated leaving her warm bed. But the game was something fathers and daughters did together. Daddy said so.

Both her mother and father told stories about how, when she was a baby and wouldn't sleep, they'd drive her in the car. Even now, at age five it still worked. On this night, like many of the other nights, she tried to stay awake but couldn't. She only woke up because the car slowed to a stop. She peeked out the window and saw trees.

There were always a lot of trees. And trails for walking and running. It looked like the park by their house, but it wasn't. And it was colder here than Palm Springs. It smelled like Christmas. She hugged her stuffed rabbit closer and said words she knew she shouldn't say. "I wanna go home."

"I drove all this way for you," he told her, elbow over the seatback, his face in shadow. "So we could play the game. Don't be a baby. You aren't a baby, are you?"

Her lips trembled and her eyes stung. "No." She was a big girl. She could write her name and tie her shoes and almost ride her bike without training wheels.

"Save those tears for the game." His voice was gentle, but she knew he wasn't happy with her. "We don't want you to dry up." He chuckled, and she thought about rain puddles and other things that dried up.

"Can I put my coat on? I'm cold." Her legs and feet were bare. She stretched her nightgown to cover her knees as she tried to get warm.

"Not now. A coat and shoes are not part of the game. You know that."

She tucked her chin to her chest and swung her feet, once again trying not to cry.

"Do you remember your new lines?" he asked.

She recited them. "Can you help me?"

"That's right. What else?"

"I'm lost."

"Good girl. And?"

"My mommy went that way. Can you help me find my mommy?"

"You point in my direction, okay?"

She nodded, pointing like she would do once they were outside.

He seemed satisfied, and they got out of the car. Like always, he left the trunk and doors open, engine running. He swung her up into his strong arms and carried her through the woods, his breathing loud in her ear. He was warm and smelled like soap and sweat as she clung tightly to his neck, not because he might drop her but because he made her feel safe, so safe that her head began to bob. She was sleepy again.

She woke up fast when he slipped her down his chest so her feet touched the cold ground. It wasn't as dark here, and she could see lights from faraway buildings. Trees made scary shadows, but these trees didn't have hands like the ones where her grandmother lived. There was a picnic table and a bench and a trail that led to houses. People lived down there. They weren't really in the woods at all.

"Is the girl coming?" she asked, talking about the other player.

"She'll be here soon."

There was always a girl in the game. Reni never knew their names, and it was never the same girl.

Her father pulled her back into the shadows. "Remember the rules. Don't talk to anybody but a girl by herself. She's the only one playing the game. She's the only one who knows what she's supposed to do."

"Okay, Daddy." She shivered.

"I hear somebody coming, so I'm going to hide."

She didn't cry. She wanted to, but she didn't. She had to save her tears for the game. It would be over soon, and she'd be back home in bed.

Her father vanished into the trees and she watched the path, listening for the slap of running shoes, waiting to see if it was the girl playing the game.

It was.

She was pretty. He liked the pretty ones. This girl was wearing a pink sweatshirt and pink sweatpants, her hair tied back in a ponytail. A lot of them had ponytails too.

Better to grab them with, her daddy would say with a laugh.

Sometimes at home he would brush Reni's hair and put it in a ponytail, but neither of them said anything about the girls. They'd just look at each other and smile, knowing they were both thinking about the same thing.

She waited the way she'd been taught.

When the running girl was close, Reni stepped out of the shadows and began to cry. *Turning on the faucet,* her father called it.

Sometimes her tears were fake, and she'd make loud sobbing sounds and rub a fist against her eye like her father had taught her, but tonight she really cried. No sound came out, but her shoulders shook, and she felt her face doing terrible things, mouth open in a silent wail.

The girl stopped.

They always stopped.

Just the girl's presence made Reni feel better and not as scared. She pulled in a couple of shaky breaths and was finally able to talk, speaking the words of the game. "Can you help me find my mommy?"

The girl knelt in front of her and took her by the arms. "Oh, you poor thing!" She looked around. "You're freezing! And your feet are bare." She sounded confused, maybe wondering how Reni had gotten there. "Did you come here with your mommy?"

A big nod and a sniffle, this one fake. Like Daddy said, she *was* getting better at the game.

"Don't worry. We'll find her." The girl stood up and took Reni by the hand, smiling down at her. "Where'd she go?"

"That way." Reni pointed in the direction her father had gone.

Together, hand in hand, they walked into the woods. It was darker there, and there was no trail. Just dirt and leaves. Both of them almost fell down, tripping over a big root.

"Are you sure she went this way?"

The girl sounded worried, not as friendly and happy as she'd been under the lights. Like maybe she was thinking about something else. Reni really wanted to go back where they could see the houses from the trail. She thought about turning around, but she didn't want to ruin the game for her daddy or the girl. They were counting on her to be brave and do what she'd been told to do.

"Yeah."

"Okay, just a little more. If we don't find her, I'll take you home and call the police."

A lot of girls said that. It was part of the game too.

Reni smiled. This was the right girl. She'd started to wonder. And while the ponytail girl looked at Reni, a dark form appeared in front of them. It was her daddy, but he never seemed like her daddy in this part of the game. He seemed like somebody else, somebody scary.

He spoke his one word in a weird voice. "Run!"

Now it was time for her to hurry to the car.

She turned and ran back the way she and the girl had come, rocks jabbing her feet. She finally reached the path and ran toward the headlights and the sound of the car engine, her arms pumping, her head roaring like a fan turned all the way up. She climbed into the back seat and grabbed her stuffed animal, tucking her freezing feet under her bottom, curling up on the seat, covering her ears the way she'd been told.

And waited.

And waited.

Where was he? He usually came soon. That was part of the game. *Don't worry. I'll be right behind you.*

She was never supposed to look. It was one of the most important rules.

But this time, because he didn't come, she sat up and peeked out the window. Then she got out and called for him.

She heard a scream and other weird noises. Did he need help?

Scared, but concerned for her father, she tiptoed back down the trail and into the woods, stopping to listen. More than once she thought about turning around and running back to the car. But her daddy might need her.

And then she saw them, her father on top of the girl. It looked like he was slamming her head with a rock. That was the weird sound she'd heard.

Words that didn't belong to the game came out of her mouth before she could stop them. "You're hurting her!"

Her father looked up, his face shadowed and ugly, like the mean wolf in a book. "Go to the car!"

She didn't move. Couldn't move. But she could still talk. "Don't hurt her! Stop hurting her!"

"It's the game!" the wolf snarled.

The girl on the ground was quiet now, and something dark was crawling out from under her head. That was good. She wasn't screaming. She wasn't in pain. Just the game.

"Go back to the car!" Her father's voice was high, like a lady's.

She turned and ran, not thinking about anything but his weird voice. She climbed into the back seat and covered her ears.

Her heart was beating as fast as hummingbird wings. *Everything's going to be all right. Just close your eyes and take a little nap.*

She felt a bounce and heard the trunk slam shut. Keeping her head down and her eyes closed, she heard her father slide behind the steering wheel, breathing hard like a dragon. Without a word, he drove away fast, tires squealing. Later, as the car took them home, he reminded her: "Just a game."

She was afraid he was going to yell at her, but he suddenly started laughing. He laughed for a long time, then blew out a breath and said, "Wow, that was exciting. Almost as exciting as the time you went off-script with the whistle."

That had been long ago, and she barely remembered it. He didn't get mad at her that time either.

At the house, he tucked her into bed and gave her a kiss. "Go to sleep."

He was shaking and he smelled funny, like sweat and something else, and his hand, when he smoothed her hair, was red.

"I'm sorry, Daddy."

"That's okay. You were just doing what most humans would have done."

"You mean behavior? Like the birds?" He'd told her how some birds were bad. Some birds would push other birds' eggs from nests and break them. But there were good birds too, ones that sat on nests in terrible storms to protect their babies. She wanted to be a good bird.

"Yes, behavior. A big word for a big girl. We're all just behaving the way nature designed us to behave. You should never be sorry for that, and you should never be sorry for having a good heart."

"I just wanted to help the girl."

"I know, little bird. That's why I love you so much. But the girl was never in danger. I told you that."

"She's a good actress?"

"That's right."

"With fake blood?"

"Yep."

"Will we play the game again?" She didn't like what happened tonight, but the game was their special time. She didn't want that to end.

"I think you might be getting too unpredictable. I might have to find someone else to play instead of you. Maybe a grown-up."

"Please, Daddy?" She started to cry. "I still want to play. I'll be good. I won't get out of the car."

He looked at her for a long time, no longer the scary wolf he'd been in the park, but her daddy. "We'll see. I have to admit things have been getting a little stale and boring. Your response adds something to the night."

That was almost a promise.

She smiled and snuggled deeper into the covers. He gave her a kiss and left the room. She heard soft conversation as he and her mother talked in quiet tones, then the house door closed and the car drove away, just like always when they played the game.

Reni used to believe everything her father told her, but lately she found he didn't always tell the truth. Now, deep down, she wondered if he was telling her the truth about the girl.

CHAPTER 8

Present day

At the rest area, wind so strong it drove sand between her teeth, Reni climbed into the second van and sat in silence while trying to control her shaking, her heart pounding after the accidental eye contact with her father. She'd imagined being the one with the upper hand, but he'd caught her off guard.

She hadn't recognized him. He was so *old*.

Daniel slipped inside to sit on the bench seat beside her. Black suit, white cuffs, black tie. He slid his dark glasses to the top of his head. She left her glasses in place, feeling safer behind them.

"You're not equipped for the desert," she finally said. His clothing was a safe place to focus on right now.

A flicker of reaction. "So I've been told." He said more things she wasn't calm enough to completely absorb, something about his riding in the other vehicle with her father, her van following behind. Something about a two-way satellite communicator he planned to use once they were out of cell-service range. If a body was found, they'd need to get a crime-scene team out there to process the area.

He wasn't as unprepared as he appeared.

He said something more. She nodded. He seemed okay with that response, and he left. One of the guards climbed into the driver's seat. He asked if she'd like to sit up front.

"No." She was calming down now, enough to note the uneasy glance he gave her over his shoulder before the two-vehicle caravan took off. He briefly attempted conversation but soon gave up. While she appreciated his effort, she knew it was an awkward situation however you looked at it. What did you say to the daughter of a serial killer? After a few moments of silence he turned on some music and settled in for the drive.

It wasn't long before they left the pavement completely, exchanging it for dirt roads that started out wide and flat but gradually became rutted and narrow and unmaintained. The surface continued to shift until it was corrugated ripples so close together the van rattled her fillings. Along with the corrugation, larger bumps turned the road into rolling hills as they wound around small mountains, gaining altitude while the desert floor grew distant and vast below them. They passed an abandoned jackrabbit cabin, windows boarded up and roof falling in.

The vehicles crept along for another slow and tedious hour, until the lead van containing Daniel and her father came to a stop in an area of smooth boulders so tall they cast shadows in an otherwise-shadeless landscape. On the far side of the boulders, the ground vanished and fell away to a hazy basin stretching to layers of mountains that faded into the sky.

On level ground, where they pulled to a stop, a faint foot trail led away and up. The nearest crest looked like the high point, but it might have been a false peak. Desert topography could be deceptive. Kind of like life. You kept thinking you'd made it, but in reality the place you wanted was always out of reach.

Reni had been in the area long enough to pick up on her body's subtle responses to altitude, and she could feel the change here. It wasn't drastic. She'd guess the elevation to be around five thousand feet. The place felt oddly familiar. Not déjà vu, but more like an echo. She thought about the map on the wall of her house, wondering if this had been one of the locations she'd explored. No, she was pretty sure it wasn't.

She was alone in the van.

At some point, the driver had gotten out. She hadn't even noticed. Given what had happened with her old FBI partner, every slip of her brain was suspect, and every glitch made her doubt herself.

The driver was talking to the other guards. She wanted to put off seeing her father as long as she could, but she also wanted to get it over with. She got out and stood straight, inhaled, looked around. Not at the van with the caged back seat.

High desert, blue sky, wind that pressed her clothes to her body, and sun bright enough to fade eye color. A narrow trail following a ridge that dropped off so quickly it gave her the uneasy sense of being in a plane.

The door to the prisoner van slid open and Daniel, dark glasses in place, stepped out, followed by her father. Benjamin Fisher wore an orange jumpsuit, hands and feet shackled. If not for the wind, she was pretty sure there would have been no sound. Just the silence of collectively held breaths, everyone waiting for her reaction. She maintained her composure and didn't look away, allowing a familiar numbness to descend and protect her.

He was not the man she remembered from childhood. The man standing there could have been a stranger. He'd always been thin. Now he had a belly that hung over the chains around his waist. He was sixty-four but looked older. Thirty years was both long and short. Who was this man? Had her father escaped prison years ago and an impostor taken his place? But his voice hadn't changed. The sound of it cut through the years.

"Little bird?"

The pet name startled her more than his appearance. "Don't call me that."

"You'll always be my sweet little bird." He watched her with pride. His belief that he held claim to any such parental emotion dumped adrenaline into her veins and threatened to shove her out of self-preservation mode. At the same time, she was aware of Daniel standing a few feet away, giving them space, but not too much.

"You look like your mother now," Ben said.

"I don't think so."

"You do."

"You look old, like somebody else."

"I'm glad to see you haven't lost your sense of humor."

"That wasn't meant to be funny. Unlike you, I tell the truth."

"And your hair. I like it long."

Now she really would have to cut it.

Daniel broke in, refocusing the conversation, reminding everyone why they were there. "Where's the body?"

"I have another stipulation," Ben told them. "Since we missed time in the van together, I want to talk to Reni alone. In private."

Her stomach dropped. If it weren't for her years in the FBI, she might have been a mess right now, but thanks to her training she was able to keep herself in check.

Daniel didn't allow Ben's suggestion to linger. "No."

Reni had never gone to prison to see him. She'd never called or written. She'd wanted no contact and hadn't wanted him to have anything of her there. After he'd walked out of the house that night in handcuffs, there had been zero communication. Was this his way of getting back at her? She'd already suspected today would end in no bodies, but that outcome felt more likely now than ever.

She shot a glance at Daniel. Even though sunglasses hid his eyes, she could tell he was wondering the same thing. But they'd known the risk. You couldn't expect a psychopath to play by the rules. Psychopaths *made* the rules, or at least that's what they thought.

"It's okay," she said. "I'll do it." She hadn't put herself through this not to let it play all the way out, no matter the ending.

Daniel motioned for her to join him several steps away, far enough so their conversation couldn't be overheard. "I don't like this."

She kept her eyes on her father. "He's shackled."

"He's up to something."

"I agree. Nothing he does is straightforward. He's a manipulator, that's for sure."

"My suspicion is he's going to try to take you as a hostage."

"I won't let that happen. I won't get that close to him."

"Are you armed?"

"No."

He reached for his handgun. "Take my weapon."

She flinched and said, "I don't touch those anymore. I don't even own one. And anyway, it's better that I don't have a gun. He probably hopes to get it from me." Or maybe he thought he could persuade her to help him. On the surface, the idea was ludicrous. But was it? Could she really trust herself where her father was concerned?

Daniel tucked the weapon away and let his jacket fall closed. He had to be hot as hell.

"I can keep my head." She couldn't be sure of that.

"I still say we abort."

"I think it's worth the risk." They could see for miles. Hundreds of miles, with a sheer drop to the east, the desert floor so far away it was covered in a haze of dust. "There's nowhere for him to run, nowhere for him to hide. What can one old man do?"

Daniel finally relented.

They instructed her father to walk several feet in front of Reni so she could keep an eye on him. Behind them, Daniel and the guards waited, guns drawn as father and daughter followed a faint dirt trail around a giant boulder, stopping when they were no longer visible to the others. But sound carried in the desert, and a call for help would be easily heard.

Ben stared at her for too long while she stood silently, giving him no encouragement, not wanting to make this any easier for him. As the wind whipped what was left of his hair, he spoke in a loud whisper. An old trick of his. Whispers were a way to get someone to lean in.

"I wanted to talk to you," he said with believable sincerity she knew was a lie. "I wanted to tell you I'm sorry I used you."

She didn't respond, but she felt anger building. Was he here because he wanted to make himself feel less awful about what he'd done? Was he looking for forgiveness? She would not allow his apology to lighten whatever burden he might have.

"For my own compulsions," he said. "I can't make excuses for why I did what I did. I'm a psychologist and I don't even understand it myself. I've lived with the guilt of seeing the faces of the women I killed. It's eaten me alive."

Maybe it was true. She hoped so.

"I know you can't forgive me. I'm not asking for forgiveness. I just wanted to see you. But there are a lot of things you still don't know."

She removed her glasses and hung them over the neck of her T-shirt. "Tell me." *Tell me.* It was human nature to want answers even if those answers made no sense.

"It's of no benefit now. I just want you to know I love you."

His words of affection hurt her like no attempted apology could possibly do.

"Do you still like to play Scrabble?" he asked.

Why would she play a game they'd played as a family? "No."

"You should. I wonder if there's still a board at your grandmother's cabin."

"I have no idea, and I don't care."

He shifted, lifting one bound and trapped hand no higher than his waist in an imploring gesture as the chains, reminders of his deviant crimes, rattled. "Come closer."

She did. But not close enough for him to grab her.

"Your mother hasn't visited me in years. I wrote letters that went unanswered. I gave her the divorce she wanted. I imagine that she and

Maurice are enjoying their lives together. Going to art openings and dinner. Without me."

He seemed to know a lot about Rosalind.

"Can I hug you?" he asked.

What a dangerous question. "No."

"Please, little bird."

She reinforced her initial response, maybe more for herself than for him. "No."

He bent in order to extract a folded piece of paper from his breast pocket. Once it was in his hand, he tried to extend his arm, but couldn't. "Take it."

She stared at the paper trapped between two of his fingers. "I don't want to touch anything you've touched." Not really true, because she still had a box of things he'd given her. Cards, drawings, notes he'd written just for her. All things he'd touched and she'd touched.

"I would never hurt you."

"You already have. Can't you understand that? You hurt me then and you've continued to hurt me every single day."

"I mean now, here. But I know. I can see in every fiber of your being that I've hurt you deeply." He stuck the paper back in his pocket. He looked so sad.

At that moment he was the other father, the one she'd loved, the man who truly would never harm her and would always protect her.

She stepped closer. And closer still, while staring into his eyes, knowing that somewhere in there was a very evil man. And somewhere in there was her father.

She'd been a profiler. She knew victims sometimes couldn't help but return to their abusers. It was a behavior that fascinated her. A behavior she feared. That he could turn her so easily. If she'd had a gun, she would have been his hostage by now. She might be dead by now.

He grabbed her hands with both of his, skin against skin. So familiar yet unfamiliar. She should have been alarmed, but she wasn't. Time slipped and memories flooded her brain. Her father tossing her above him in the pool, her father telling her how special she was, her father smiling at her from the front seat of the car. Her father teaching her about different kinds of birds and how she had to protect them.

For a moment, this moment, the killing didn't matter. The man who'd shaped her was here, in front of her, and she suddenly found herself regretting the years she hadn't gone to see him in prison, recalling how her mother had been behind that decision. "He doesn't deserve it," she'd said.

Reni tugged her hands free—and willingly wrapped her arms around him.

He smelled the same. The scent of him washed over her, took her back to another time and place, a time when he hadn't been a bad man, or at least she hadn't known he was.

"This is all I wanted," he whispered. "All I wanted."

She began to cry, knowing her brain was tricking her, confusing her. She didn't have the strength to fight it. Maybe this was all she'd wanted too. "I've missed you, Daddy." She was speaking to the man who'd read to her at night, the man who'd taught her how to ride a bike and how to draw a bird.

"Me too."

And then something very strange happened.

He shoved her. Hard and away. She staggered, trying to make sense of his behavior, while also wondering if her mind was tricking her again.

He smiled and said, "I love you, baby girl." And then he was gone.

CHAPTER 9

One moment he was in her arms and she could feel the heat and life and fragility of him. The next, he was gone.

The world became a swirling combination of fast and slow and beating heart and denial as Reni watched her father fall, her brain marveling at the fabric of his jumpsuit fluttering like orange wings against the blue sky, while it also rejected what she was seeing.

He always did like birds.

The desert floor was far away, hazy, the wind and the roaring in her head so loud she wasn't sure if he made any sound as he plummeted.

She didn't hear him hit.

Standing precariously close to the sheer drop, she saw his body below, legs and arms in unnatural positions, jumpsuit still fluttering in the wind, making it look as if he were writhing in pain.

She must have shouted because Daniel appeared, gun drawn, eyes scanning the terrain as he tried to figure out where her father was. He even checked the sky. And then he was beside her on the flat rock, his jacket gone, shirtsleeves rolled up several turns, glasses poking out of his pocket. He looked from the body to Reni. He was wondering if she'd had a hand in this. He also seemed a little shocked. She felt his eyes on her, trying to read her, gauging her response in hopes of determining what had happened. Was she acting? Was she sincere? Was she relieved? Gloating? Should he offer sympathy, or arrest her?

"He flew away," she said in a flat voice.

Her brain misfired. She was thinking about the next step in their series of plans for the day. This was the place where her father was to lead them to a gravesite. She'd been a detective long enough to understand what was happening to her. It was common for a trauma victim to remain fixated on the day's derailed objective, even if it was something as mundane as driving to the grocery store for some trivial item. Even though there was no next step anymore, the brain couldn't let go. Not yet.

Concern flared in Daniel's face, but, as if he'd caught himself in an unwanted response, that concern was quickly replaced by suspicion.

"I shouldn't have come here," she said.

"I can see that."

"I wonder if this was his plan all along." She was beginning to process what had happened. "Maybe he had no intention of taking us to the bodies. Just like everything else in his life, this was about him. His plan was to tell me goodbye and kill himself."

"What a cruel bastard."

She hadn't reached a suitable response to her father's final act. *This really just happened.* It wasn't her imagination.

Then it hit her that he might still be alive.

"How long have we been standing here?" Minutes?

"Forty-five seconds maybe."

The guards were there now, trying to remain composed while unable to hide their own shock and maybe a little bit of glee. Things probably weren't this exciting at the prison.

"Stay back," Daniel told them. "This is a possible crime scene."

Heads snapped as realization dawned. One of the guards, maybe thinking he was being understanding, muttered something about not blaming her.

Reni didn't care if all of them thought she'd pushed him over the edge. Her father was dead. No matter who he was or what he'd done, *her father was dead.* A part of *her* was gone. She wanted to scream and drop to the ground. Instead, she redirected and scanned the brush, looking for a way to reach Benjamin. She spotted a narrow path to the right that looked to have been created by animals. Feet sliding, small rocks tumbling, she began her descent, Daniel following.

More than once she dug in her boot heels to keep from sliding far and fast, pebbles and rocks skittering away, some cascading through the air. *Why the hurry?* she asked herself. *He's dead.* Nobody could live through that kind of fall. But she hurried anyway, a few times almost falling herself, just managing to catch herself, Daniel warning her to slow down.

She didn't.

It might have taken ten minutes to reach the desert floor and work their way back to where Ben had landed.

Her father's body was facedown, blood pooling under his head. The scene reminded her of another time—a time when he'd slammed a young woman's head against the ground until she stopped screaming. There had been no mercy or sadness from him that day, so why should she feel anything now? She clung to that memory a long minute so she could hate him with one hundred percent of her being and not eighty.

As time held its breath and the unsympathetic wind whipped the hair around her face with the sting of tiny razor blades, she lowered herself in a smooth and slow movement until she was crouched next to him.

Daniel told her not to touch him.

She touched him.

Her father's skin, under her fingertips, was warm. A body imitating life. She lifted one of his arms slightly, just enough to search for a pulse in his wrist. Shattered bones shifted inside his skin like rocks in a bag.

No pulse.

None in his neck either.

A shadow fell across her. She squinted up at Daniel. "He's dead," she said woodenly. And he'd taken his secrets with him. That's what got to her, she tried to tell herself, because her father, the father she thought she'd known, had died a long time ago. In fact, that man had never even lived. And yet she stifled a sob for the bodies they would now never find, and for the loss of the father who'd twisted her into a dark little shadow of himself. Through a blur of tears and emotions, she saw that Daniel was motioning for her to get back. *Crime scene.*

She got to her feet and shivered even though it was so hot the air shimmered. She untied the gray sweatshirt from around her waist and slipped it on, pulling the hood over her head, blocking some of the wind.

She had nowhere to be and nowhere to go. There was just wind and sky and the desert her father had loved. Which was the other thing she didn't mention to Daniel. It made sense that her father had wanted to end his life here. Maybe she would have guessed his plan if she hadn't been so focused on controlling her own emotions.

Daniel reached for her, all cop now. "Let me see your hands."

At first, she didn't understand, then she realized he was doing his job.

She held out her hands, palms down. He took them in his and examined her fingers, doing his due diligence as a detective, looking for broken nails with embedded skin that would indicate a struggle had taken place.

He turned them over, examining her palms. They were bloody. He said nothing as he continued to bank information that made her look guilty.

"From his head," she said. She was surprised to see the blood even though she'd touched the body. Her brain was misbehaving again, and for some reason she thought about her dog's ashes above the fireplace at her cabin. Just a few days back she'd been a different person. She'd had a mission and she'd had focus and she'd been healing.

What would happen to her father's body? Would it be cremated? Who would want the ashes? Should she bury them? Scatter them here? Should they just leave him and let wild animals eat him? It would give his life at least some good and it would seem fitting. A killer providing life for desert creatures.

Daniel pulled out his phone and took photos of the body. He created a video that included a view of the drop and the cliff they'd been standing on.

Once he tucked his phone away, she said, "I didn't push him."

Could she be sure of that? Especially given her recent history? Even under the best of conditions, memory was one of the most unreliable aspects of any case and the reason hard evidence was so important and why Reni wasn't a fan of lineups where victims identified possible perpetrators. False memories made her question eyewitness testimonies, and even accurate memories changed over time. False memories could also be scars that protected a person when reality was too painful.

"I didn't say you did. Hopefully forensics will be able to sort it out. Dust his skin and clothing for your prints. A more involved process, but we need to do it."

"I hugged him."

He locked eyes with her, and she could see things were going from bad to worse. "What?"

"I gave him a hug."

"You know how this is looking, right?"

It wouldn't be enough to arrest her, but it could be enough to distract them from what they should be doing. Looking for the women Ben Fisher had killed.

She remembered the paper her father had wanted her to take. "Check his breast pocket. He tried to give something to me. Maybe it's a suicide note." For her, but more likely for her mother.

Daniel walked over to the body and rolled it enough to access the pocket. He pulled out the piece of paper, unfolding it as he straightened, read it, then turned it around for her to see, an expression of cautious satisfaction on his face.

In his hand was a map of the surrounding desert, and several locations were marked with a red *X*. Maybe Ben Fisher hadn't taken all his secrets to the grave.

CHAPTER 10

Back up on the plateau, Reni beside him, Daniel used a satellite phone to communicate with Homicide, sending their location and a list of people to contact. The search-and-rescue team, the deputy coroner investigator, and their crime-scene specialist. Search-and-rescue because he'd decided it would take their skill and equipment to get the body up the sheer drop.

Once the calls were done, he visually examined the area where Ben Fisher had stood before jumping. Or before being pushed. Mostly rock, but there was a bit of loose sand. He crouched closer and could see no sign of a struggle. No gouges in the ground, and the few plants like creosote bush had no broken branches. He photographed the area, wishing he had his SUV with the crime-scene supplies he kept in the back.

He took everyone's informal statements, including Reni's. Formal and more thorough on-camera accounts would be recorded at the San Bernardino County Sheriff's Department tomorrow morning. Memory was unreliable and could change rapidly, so it was best to grab witness reports on-site even if it meant interviewing traumatized people. He'd learned to never put off questioning. Along with the informal statements, he documented the time and drew a layout of the setting.

When he was done, the guards left in a prison van. No need for them to remain. Daniel would drive the second vehicle back to San Bernardino, where it would be collected later, dropping Reni off at her truck. He would meet her again in the morning to take her formal statement. Better yet, he would pass the job to another detective.

He'd tried to talk her into returning with the guards, but she hadn't wanted to leave. He should have pressed harder, if only for the selfish reason of his wanting to be alone. He was grappling with his own disappointment at the turn of events.

"I'm going back down," Reni announced once the dust from the departing van had settled. "Someone needs to watch over the body. To keep animals away."

He looked at the sky. A few turkey vultures were circling high above, checking them out. All the dead were food. He couldn't leave her alone with the body due to the risk of evidence tampering, so he followed her down.

Hours later, still waiting for the rescue team and deputy coroner, Daniel and Reni sat in the shade with their backs to a boulder, Ben Fisher's body several yards away but out of their line of sight. It was oddly like a wake, almost spiritual due to the location.

Even though the temperature was close to ninety, Reni, her face drained of color, kept putting on her sweatshirt and taking it off. Every once in a while, a shiver ran through her and she'd make a small sound of acknowledgment, maybe at her inability to control her own body.

Whatever had happened on the plateau above, her father was dead, and she was dealing with a lot; her silence and shaking evidence of that. Daniel had to keep his own emotions in check as he tried to tell himself all wasn't lost. They had the map, with ten locations marked. Yet the map might be nothing more than a way for Fisher to mess with them from beyond the grave. Giving them busywork that would lead nowhere. And the trip to the desert just a way for Fisher to see his daughter before committing suicide. Prison was an unappealing place. Daniel couldn't dispute that, and maybe Ben Fisher had simply formulated a plan to never go back. A psychopath's brain didn't fire like the average human's, so there was really no telling what his intent had been.

If she hadn't pushed him, and he hoped to God she hadn't, it meant Ben Fisher had jumped right in front of his own daughter. That was some seriously cruel shit right there, but certainly not the worst thing the man had ever done. And if she had pushed him, could he really blame her? Wouldn't he have done the same if he'd been in her situation?

He didn't think so.

He was a facts man, and was cautious when it came to gut instinct. Gut instinct could blow up in your face when confronted with pure evil. People like Ben Fisher hid their true nature because—and this was the crux of it—some psychopaths were empathetic. That gave them a distinct advantage because they *understood* their victims and the people they manipulated. That was how it worked.

Still, Daniel took full responsibility for what had happened, and he'd make that clear when he wrote up his report tonight. This might or might not result in a short forced leave of absence. He wasn't making excuses, but the captain of Homicide and his own father had been right: he was too close to this case.

"You didn't have to stay," he told Reni, breaking the silence that had descended after he'd made a few failed attempts to engage her. He wasn't used to so much sky and land and emptiness and silence. That alone could make a guy jumpy.

"I know," she said. "But a lot of my life is unfinished stories and things I don't remember and things I have misremembered. I need to see this through so it will be clear in my head. For my own sanity."

Her admission took him by surprise. In his experience, most people didn't like to talk about their own mental health. But after a traumatic event, people could temporarily lose the desire to hold their stories and emotions close. And yesterday Reni's mother had called to chew him out, letting him know just how fragile her daughter was. No real surprise there. People didn't quit an FBI job like hers and move to the desert for no reason, especially at such a young age. But maybe he hadn't understood the extent of the damage. He'd been focused on himself and his need for resolution, not how deeply this could impact her. Now he weighed the situation, trying to decide between digging for more answers and leaving her alone.

"You're sitting there wondering what to say to me," she said. "Do you offer sympathy? He was my father, after all. But then you wonder, did I push him? Was that *my* plan all along? You're thinking about checking with the prison when you get back to see if we've had any contact with each other. Letters, phone calls, visits. Either of us might have lied about that."

All true. And there was nothing psychic about her reaction. She'd been a detective and she still thought like one. And he was pretty sure she was more skilled than he was.

"We didn't," she said. "Have any contact. But I'm sure you're good at your job and will confirm that."

"You could have formulated the plan later, after I first reached out to you," he suggested.

"Or it could have been spontaneous, with no forethought. Just a victim reacting to years of abuse. Just a push." She got to her feet and moved to the shade of another boulder, a little farther from Daniel but facing him.

"Or he jumped," she said as she sat back down. "Are you the kind of detective who speculates? If so, what's the theory at the top of your list? Do you have any sense of the truth here?"

He was glad they were having this conversation. It was good for both of them to question everything and think like cops. And the very act of talking about what had happened seemed to bring her out of her stupor. "If you were in my position, what would you think?" he asked.

"I'd maintain suspicion."

Her color was better.

"And to be honest, I wondered the same thing. Did I push him? I'll admit that was my first thought after I realized he was no longer beside me. Because I question things that have happened and continue to happen to me. Memory is delicate. So yeah, I wondered, and I wonder. But I think if I'd planned this, I would be high-fiving myself right now. And I would have no reason to not admit it. After all the things he did to me, it would have been a fitting end, and I have no fear of prison. My life as I know it has *become* a prison. I don't think it would be much worse inside than out. For me anyway. And if we find the map isn't real, I wouldn't feel the compulsion to keep looking for the women he killed, to spend my days digging holes in the desert, if I were locked up."

Daniel didn't like hearing that she had the same suspicion about the map. "So you don't think it's real?"

"I'm not sure." From a backpack, she pulled out a container of water, unscrewed the cap, took a long drink. "Unless the burial spot involved a recognizable landmark, I don't know who could possibly remember the exact location in the vastness of the ever-shifting Mojave Desert. Not after a year or two, let alone thirty. My father was highly intelligent, but as far as I know his memory wasn't anything unusual."

Daniel looked at the unfolded paper again, trying but failing to orient himself. It was a drawing, more like a crude treasure map than anything else. He would have expected Ben Fisher to be more precise, but this was probably part of his game. That's what it looked like. Something from a scavenger hunt.

He moved next to Reni in the shade and handed her the scrap of paper. "You recognize anything?"

She offered him her water. As he drank, she examined the drawing and pointed to a crude landmark. "I think these might be the boulders above us."

"So that *X* is near here, right?"

"Close."

He passed the water back.

"If you return with the search crew, I hope you're more prepared." She pulled a ziplock bag of trail mix from her magic backpack and scooped out a handful of fruit and nuts, then offered him the bag. She'd probably put it together herself.

"Thanks."

Elbow to knee, appearing a part of the alien landscape, she bit into a piece of dried pineapple. "It's weird. Even now, even though I know what we all know, it's still hard for me to accept that this man killed people," she said. "And I saw it with my own eyes, though I didn't know that's what was happening. He's never fit the profiles we like to use."

His response was cautious. He didn't want to spook her by coming across as an interrogator. "Like how?"

"For one thing, we used to work at the food bank on Thanksgiving. My dad's idea, but my mother was supportive. And he always gave money to the homeless. He'd park his car and get out to hand money to someone he'd spotted while driving. I remember once we were coming out of a deli and he gave a man on the corner everything we'd just purchased. His dying leaves so many questions unanswered. I didn't think that would bother me."

It wasn't that odd for a killer to have someone or something they showered with affection, but the kind of broad kindness she was talking about was unusual. "Maybe he was working on his public persona," Daniel suggested. "Or maybe he actually felt some sort of remorse and he was trying to atone in his own way."

"Or maybe he got off on it in the same way he got off on killing. It might have stimulated the same area of the brain, providing a similar satisfaction."

"That's a good theory."

They'd been waiting for so long, but Daniel felt disappointed when he heard the sound of approaching vehicles. He wanted the conversation to continue now that she was loosening up and confiding in him.

From the plateau above, they heard doors slam. Daniel jumped to his feet and shouted. Seconds later faces peered over the edge and within a few minutes a team with a stretcher was inching and sliding their way down the steep slope.

Once they arrived, things moved quickly.

All suicides or suspected suicides were processed like a crime scene. The coroner, a man who looked to be in his fifties, pronounced Ben Fisher dead. The crime-scene team, a group of two men and one woman, smelling of sunblock and wearing dark sunglasses and beige caps, took notes and photos. Someone asked if the body had been moved, and another person bagged the hands, which would be examined for skin and evidence of a struggle. The body was zipped into a black bag and a chain-of-custody label was attached. Now that others were on-site, Reni watched in silence, her face unreadable.

"I'd like to be there for the autopsy," Daniel said as they strapped the body into the orange stretcher and prepared to file away.

The coroner nodded. "I'll make note of that."

An hour after arriving, the vehicles left, and Daniel and Reni slipped into the prison van as the sun sank behind the mountains, bats swooping against a red sky.

"I'm not a fan of the desert," Daniel confessed, putting the van in gear, attempting to resurrect the conversation, any conversation, because talk, even indirect talk, often led to unexpected places. "I've always been more of a forest and ocean kind of guy."

"It grows on you," Reni told him. "Not everybody, but it's been a big part of my life. My grandparents moved to the desert in the fifties. Built a little cabin on five acres they acquired through the Homestead Act. Hard to believe anybody tried to grow crops there. They had to actually dig up creosote bush and Joshua trees in order to keep their land and prove they were trying to farm it. Most people didn't stay, but my grandparents did. Some of my earliest memories are of my grand-mother's cabin. Hauled water, no electricity. I loved it."

"Your father's mother?" he asked even though he knew the answer.

"Yes."

"What was she like?"

"Meaning did she have dark, psychopathic tendencies?"

"Yes."

"I don't remember anything dark about her, although she wasn't fond of men in general. But then I didn't see my father for the monster he was. Believe me, I've wondered and searched my brain, but she seemed perfect to me. She was the person who made everything okay."

Fathers were important, but sometimes Daniel thought a strong female influence and role model—mother, aunt, grandmother—could be more important in childhood development.

When they were back on the highway leading into Joshua Tree, Daniel's phone rang. Surprised to have cell service once again, he slowed the van and checked the screen. His father. Not his biological father, but the man who'd adopted and raised him. "I have to get this." Forgoing the van's Bluetooth connection in order to keep the conversation semiprivate, he answered.

"Hadn't heard from you," his dad said. "Just checking to see how things went today."

"Not great," Daniel said, acutely aware that Reni could hear his side of the conversation.

"Any success?"

"No."

"I'm sorry, kid."

The compassion was almost too much. "Me too." He glanced at Reni's silhouette. She probably thought he was talking to a significant other. "I'll tell you all about it when I get home."

"Is she with you?"

"Yep."

"Okay. Be careful."

"Always." He disconnected and tucked his phone back in his pocket, his fingers coming in contact with the scrap of fabric he carried with him, the fabric he'd hoped to match today if Ben Fisher had been telling them the truth.

CHAPTER 11

Thirty-five years earlier

He didn't like fabric stores. They made him sleepy, and they were boring. Nothing to do. Right now his legs couldn't hold him up any longer and he collapsed on the floor, weak from exhaustion.

His mother bent over him, a smile on her face. "We've only been here twenty minutes, Danny. Tell you what—why don't you help me pick out the material for my dress? I'm trying to decide on a color." She motioned to a section of bolts, as she called them. He didn't know why they were called that. He thought bolts were metal things, but these bolts were pieces of cardboard with fabric wrapped around them.

"Choose from this area," she said, "because it's the cheapest. I can't afford the nicer material. We're so broke I shouldn't even be buying this."

He knew all about the word *afford* and how he couldn't always have the toys or clothes his friends had. She sewed for a living and made a lot of his stuff. His clothes were one of the reasons people thought he was weird, but he didn't understand why clothes made people tease him.

No longer tired now that he had a job to do, he jumped to his feet. So many colors, so many rows of fabric. "I like this one." He touched a bright yellow with white dots. She shook her head a little and lifted her eyebrows, hinting that it wasn't right for her.

He looked some more. "The blue one?"

She smiled again but said nothing. She was the best. She was never mean and never yelled at him like other moms yelled at their kids.

He moved down the aisle. Green, more blue, red. A lot of red. She liked the color red. "This one. I like this one." He pointed to a red fabric with tiny pink flowers. She smiled again, and he could see she was happy with his choice.

All the bolts were shoved together like books on a shelf, and she had to tug hard to free the one he'd chosen. Once she had it out, she unrolled the material a little and bent close so he could get a better look, stroking her hand across the fabric. "I think this is perfect, don't you? There's nothing wrong with a cotton blend."

He touched it. It felt weird to him, but he remembered what she'd said about money, and nodded. "It's pretty."

"Okay, so now we need to find thread and a zipper to match."

He helped her with those too, and the store didn't seem as boring anymore.

At home in their tiny Pasadena apartment, she spread the fabric on the floor and showed him how to arrange the thin brown paper pattern so there was enough material for the whole dress. It was hard, but they were able to make it fit by turning some of the pattern pieces upside down and putting other pieces against the fold. He even helped her pin everything, something they'd never done together before.

After dinner they cut out the dress with big, heavy scissors. The sound of the metal against the cloth and paper made his ears happy. The next day, after he got home from school, they removed the pattern and pinned the cut fabric, bright sides together. Then he helped sew it.

She had him sit on a chair with a pillow under him so he could reach the sewing machine. "Seams are always five-eighths of an inch," she told him. His feet dangled in the air, so she pressed her bare foot with its red nail polish against the pedal on the floor to control the speed of the needle and helped him sew a straight line while she marveled at his skill.

"Why, you've been holding out on me, young man." She pulled the sewn piece from the machine, cut the thread, and opened and pressed the fabric to her stomach, over her jeans and sweatshirt. It didn't look like a dress yet, but it looked like more than just fabric.

It didn't matter. What mattered was that she was happy. She hadn't been happy for a long time, not since her last boyfriend left "for someone else." He'd liked that boyfriend. That boyfriend had taken him to the beach and had told him he wanted to be his dad. Daniel didn't understand how someone could want to be your dad one minute and be gone the next. Not dead, like the husband of the lady who lived upstairs. Just gone.

He tried to imagine the old boyfriend living somewhere else, with other people, laughing at the dinner table, maybe tossing another kid, not him, into the air, calling him his little buddy.

But his mom was happy now. Maybe for a little while. Maybe longer.

She stayed up late working on the dress, and in the morning while he ate his breakfast at the kitchen counter, she modeled it for him.

"What do you think about the material you picked out?" she asked. "Do you like it?"

He loved it.

"I still need to hem it, but that won't take long. I'll have it ready by tonight, for my date."

Date was a weird word. Something high school girls said too, like the girl who babysat him sometimes. She talked about dates and going out with boys. And her cheeks would flush, and her eyes would shine, just like his mother's eyes were doing right now.

That night, he watched her while she put on makeup and brushed her hair.

"Go get your camera," she told him with a happy grin. "So you'll have a picture of me with the dress we made together."

He'd gotten a little Instamatic for Christmas. He ran to his room and returned with it. The camera was blue and had a flashcube on the top that would take four pictures. She stood in front of the living room door in her dress, and she looked so pretty. Different, like someone on TV.

He held the camera to his face and pressed the button. The flash went off.

"Let's take one more. Both of us this time, the two of us, mother and son. Give the camera to Janine."

He handed the camera to the babysitter. His mother stood with her back to the door, Daniel in front of her, her hands on his shoulders. "Smile."

The camera flashed and the sitter gave it back to him. "I think that's the last one on the roll."

"We'll take the film to the grocery store and get it developed," his mother said. "You're the best boy." She crouched down and gave him a hug, squeezing him so hard he thought he might break. Then she kissed his cheek and left in a flurry of red material, closing the door behind her.

He knelt on the couch and watched through the window as she drove away.

Janine sat down beside him. "My mom says a date should always pick you up."

"Why?"

She shrugged. "It's polite. It shows the guy cares."

"Maybe it's different when you're older."

"Maybe, but I think it's bad manners not to come to the door."

His mother called Janine a know-it-all, so maybe she was right about the manners.

He'd already eaten, fish sticks and macaroni and cheese. *A rich man's dinner,* his mother had said earlier with a laugh as she'd eaten one of his greasy fish sticks.

Janine had brought some movies. They made popcorn and sat on the couch in front of the television.

He tried to stay awake. He wanted to be awake when his mother got back home, but he couldn't keep his eyes open. That always happened, and he would usually wake up the next morning in bed, with no memory of Janine putting him there.

That happened this time too. He suddenly heard someone crying and was surprised to see it was morning. He didn't remember his mother coming home. He needed to get to school.

He got out of bed and shuffled into the living room. Janine was still in their house, and there were two policemen standing near the door where he and his mother had stood last night.

He didn't know why they were there. He ran down the hall to tell his mother. She wasn't in her room, and her bed was made. He didn't understand. He hurried to the bathroom, shouting her name, then to the kitchen. Not there either.

One of the policemen, hands on his belt, was talking to Janine. "She probably just slept somewhere else last night." He glanced at Daniel and acted a little uncomfortable. "You said she went on a date, right?"

"She wouldn't do that," Janine said. "Sleep somewhere else."

"How well do you know her?"

"I've babysat for her for two years. She always comes home when she says she's going to." She looked at the clock on the wall. "I have to go to school."

"What about the kid?" the policeman asked.

"My mom's coming over to watch him."

Both of the officers seemed relieved. "We'll follow up later."

Janine's mother came and took Daniel to her house. She helped him pack up some of his things. Before leaving, he added his camera and scraps of fabric from the red dress to his little suitcase that said *Going on Vacation*.

They waited days. He didn't go to school.

Janine's mother got his film developed, and he spent a lot of time looking at the photo of his mother in front of the door. One day she was there, and the next she was gone, just like the boyfriend. Policemen questioned him, asking if he knew where she'd gone that night.

"She met a man."

"Where?"

"Don't know."

He heard them whispering, saying things about her running away. She would never run away. People were always talking about earthquakes. Maybe an earthquake got her.

CHAPTER 12

Present day

Daniel sat at his desk, watching the video interview with Reni Fisher that had taken place in one of the interrogation rooms a few hours earlier. The camera was mounted high on the wall, giving him an odd perspective as he looked down on both people in the small room. Across from Reni, her back to the camera, sat a female detective.

Reni's hand, when she reached for a glass of water, appeared steady. No sign of the shaking he'd noted yesterday. She was calm, her story didn't change, and she added no new information to what he already knew. That, combined with her exemplary professional record and no evidence hinting of a push or a struggle, moved the needle closer to suicide. The autopsy would help confirm it.

When the video ended, he sat back and thought about Reni's history, personal and professional. She could be an asset. He'd been searching for his mother for far too long to ignore any avenue or opportunity, especially one that had pretty much fallen into his lap. Decision made, he walked across the busy room and knocked on the door of the only private office in Homicide Detail, and was told to come in.

The division commander, Captain Edda Morris, had worked in Homicide thirty years, most of that time spent in the San Bernardino County Sheriff's Department, the law enforcement agency overseeing the largest geographical county in the nation. One office wall was covered with framed photos of grandkids in various stages of their lives.

Edda was sort of an earth mother who made everyone feel at ease and important. Feathered lines around her eyes, gray hair in a bun at the back. He'd seen it down a few times and it almost reached her waist. But pity the person who overlooked or disregarded her. She knew her stuff, and Daniel had learned a lot in the three years he'd worked under her.

She rolled her chair closer to her desk and sat down. "Have you scheduled a press conference?"

"For later this afternoon." So far, news of the incident in the desert hadn't been leaked, but they needed to stay ahead of gossip. "I have an idea I wanted to run past you." He settled into a seat across from her. "What do you think about bringing Reni Fisher on board?"

She recoiled, then made a quick recovery. "Isn't she currently a suspect in her father's death?"

"I'm convinced she's innocent and I expect the autopsy to confirm it. She could be beneficial in helping to find the bodies. I'd hate to have her slip away now that we have her attention." Not the best way to phrase it—she'd lost her father—but it was true she was now engaged, and that could change quickly.

"I'm not even sure I want *you* on this case," Edda said. "And yet you're without a doubt the most qualified detective I have. You probably know more about Ben Fisher than anybody in the building. But I don't know if being involved is healthy for you. And Ben Fisher is dead, which means we no longer need her."

"She knows the desert. She's a profiler. She was a good agent back in the day." Someone he'd admired and respected. "And she might have untapped, inside information about her father. I'm not talking about bringing her in as a partner, but as a consultant. The way we sometimes do with private investigators. Someone to focus completely on her father's case and the missing women."

"What you're talking about is an expense we really can't justify for more than a short time. You understand that?"

"Yes."

"Does she know about your mother?"

"No."

"What about Ben Fisher? Did he know?"

"I didn't think so at first, but now I wonder." Some of the questions Fisher had asked at their meeting now seemed either a little too relevant or deliberately misleading.

She leaned back in her chair, a contemplative look on her face. "It's strange how lives intersect, isn't it? It seems nothing is linear and we're really moving in converging circles. Your mother, you getting this job, Ben Fisher requesting you, now Reni."

Daniel didn't mention that the job hadn't been a complete coincidence. He'd been watching for an opening in the department that had worked to catch and convict Ben Fisher.

"It would be a shame not to see where this goes when the universe has worked so hard to create this intersection," Edda continued. "But I want a report every few days, at a minimum. And remember, this is going to be short-lived, so get as much out of her as you can."

He received a text alert and pulled his phone from his pocket. The message was from the deputy coroner investigator, letting him know he planned to start Ben Fisher's autopsy in an hour.

And I have some peripheral information you might find interesting, the text said.

Coroners. They liked to go for the hook.

He got to his feet. "I'll keep you updated."

"I'll be ready to pull the plug at any given moment."

"Me too."

On his way to the coroner's, he called Reni to pitch his idea and let her know that with the aid of Ben Fisher's map he planned to start searching soon. He realized his offer was a little premature, but he was enthused about the idea of working with her. "This request hinges on autopsy findings, but I want to give you a little time to think about it and let you know I'm not talking about bringing you on for one day. I'm talking about as this unfolds." He'd seen how she lived. He guessed she could use the money. She'd get the rate they paid most freelance investigators. Not great income, but not bad. He hoped that would be enough to entice her.

"Not interested. I'm already in my truck heading home, but I'd appreciate being kept in the loop."

He appealed to her compassion. "You know the desert. You know how to survive out there. You already pointed out my ignorance more than once."

"I'm sure you can find another desert rat."

The coroner's office was located two miles from the county sheriff's department. In the time he'd been talking to Reni he was almost there. "Listen, you've been searching for these women for years." He turned off Lena Road and pulled into the parking lot. "If anybody has the right to be in on this, it's you. At least think about it."

The silence that followed was telling. She finally cursed under her breath, and he smiled to himself.

"I gotta go." He cut the engine. "I'm attending the autopsy."

"Where? The county coroner's office?"

"Yeees," he said with reluctance.

"Have them hold off. I want to be there."

This wasn't the kind of involvement he had in mind. "That's not happening. You aren't attending your father's autopsy." It wasn't just that he never allowed a close relative to witness such an event no matter how much that person thought they could handle it, but he also might have some sensitive questions for the coroner he wouldn't want her to hear. And there was the cryptic text he'd received from Gus.

"I'll be there as soon as I can," she said.

"You won't be allowed in." He'd make sure she didn't get past the front desk.

"Then I'll wait outside. Oh, and Daniel? You're right about the women. If I wasn't looking for them physically, I was searching for them in my dreams. I'll work with you."

CHAPTER 13

Deputy Coroner Investigator Gus Waters was one of the most trusted and busy coroners in the county, so Daniel had been surprised to get his text, and even more surprised to find he was the one actually doing the autopsy. A jump or fall like Fisher had taken shouldn't hold any big surprises, and Gus Waters was known for taking the trickier cases. Daniel was under the impression he rarely did autopsies at all anymore, and instead focused on overseeing other coroners or forensics. But this was a well-known case, which might have explained his interest. The Inland Empire Killer was one of the most famous criminals in the area, ranking up there with the Black Dahlia in terms of public curiosity and obsession. And Benjamin Fisher had managed to maintain his place in the mind of California crime culture for decades. The killer who looked normal, acted normal, and moved in charmed circles would always fascinate and horrify.

Getting out of his unmarked car, Daniel scanned the parking lot and street. No sign of Reni's truck. He ducked inside and told the woman at the desk not to allow Reni past the security door.

"Should I call the police if she shows up?"

"No." He was reluctant to disclose any information, since news of Fisher's death wasn't out. "Just a grieving daughter who doesn't have any business inside." They dealt with that kind of thing a lot.

The woman nodded. "Got it. Dr. Waters is in suite two."

This would be a fresh body, so Daniel suited up, noting the new gowns, the pale blue ones having been replaced with yellow. Yellow was such a bright and happy color. But also the color of danger. The gloves were purple. He felt like a team mascot.

In the autopsy suite, Gus Waters, a man with a distinguishing gray Afro, welcomed him with a smile as he turned to a small wheeled table and laptop. They had the place to themselves, not even any other bodies in the room. That was unusual too. Daniel had never been in a suite that didn't have at least a few people either assisting or working at another autopsy station.

At the laptop, Gus opened X-ray images and clucked over them. "So many shattered bones."

Out of respect for the deceased, some coroners kept the body covered until it was ready for the scalpel. Gus appeared to feel no such need, or possibly he simply felt this man didn't deserve that extra measure of respect. Either way, Ben Fisher was uncovered, nude, positioned on a stainless-steel gurney two feet from Gus, a body block employed to extend the chest area for the Y incision that hadn't yet been made. The temperature in the room was chilly, and a gauge on the wall read sixty degrees.

Finger on the trackpad, eyes on the monitor, Gus circled an image of a forearm. "I can't even count the breaks. The bones are like dust." He pulled up another set, these of the head. The skull was shattered too. "Death would have been near immediate due to the severity of trauma."

"What about how he landed?" Daniel was looking for anything to reinforce Reni's innocence. "Is there any way to tell what hit first?"

"Arms and head took a lot of the initial impact. You'd expect legs first if someone jumped. This is more like he dove. Or flew. Or tried to fly."

Which fit Reni's description of what had happened. When she told him he'd almost flown, Daniel had wondered if she'd been using imagery, given the situation. She'd wanted to think her father had experienced something positive. But it sounded as if he'd really spread his arms. Welcoming death, embracing it. In other words, deliberate.

"None of this is really unexpected," Gus said. "But this is not what I wanted to share with you." He closed the image files, brought up more files, talking as he worked. "You're most likely unaware of the university medical center study Benjamin Fisher signed up for when he was a student studying psychology."

It must have been a deep secret, because Daniel thought he knew everything about Fisher that could be known. "I've never heard of it." But he *was* familiar with the multitude of studies financially strapped students could participate in to make a little extra cash; it was just hard for him to imagine Benjamin Fisher signing up to be a lab rat. Then again, maybe Fisher had been curious about himself and his own dark nature. Probably the same reason he went into psychology.

Gus sat down on a stool and pointed to another one across the room. "Like most of these things, the participants' identities were protected and the results never made public."

Daniel grabbed the stool, rolled it across the floor, and sat down near Gus.

Adjusting his heavy black glasses, the coroner opened a file. "How much do you know about the research that was done here in California by the serial killer brain expert?"

"The neuroscientist who died a few years ago?" Daniel had read about him. His studies focused on genetics and brain structures, not the typical animal-abuse and bed-wetting scenarios everyone and their uncle were familiar with. "I know the basics." He theorized three things were necessary for a subject to become a serial killer. One, an aggressive gene he called the warrior gene. Two, inactivity or damage or malfunctioning of the temporal and frontal lobes, which could be determined in a functional MRI. And three, early abuse that took place right after birth.

"I worked under him," Gus said, "and I was part of his research team way back when. Fisher applied for the study and was accepted. I have to admit we were giddy when he presented with results a person might expect to find in a serial killer."

"I thought research like that was anonymized."

"It's supposed to be, but when you have results as stunning as ours, things get leaked, at least within the team. Fisher had it all. The warrior gene, a prefrontal cortex that didn't respond to stimuli . . ." He clicked keys and pulled up several colorful brain images. "No activity in the area that controls morality."

"It's blank."

"One of the most severe cases we'd ever seen. For reference, here's a normal brain." He dragged an image over. "During the study, we researched serial killer genealogy going back to the 1800s. The other thing we now know—or think we know, because more research needs to be done—is that this behavior clusters in families."

"Inherited." The very thing Daniel had danced around yesterday when talking about Reni's grandmother. Psychopathy could carry through generations. The more severe the psychopathy, the more likely it was to be inherited. And a recent study had suggested mothers were the stronger carrier of the gene, though Daniel wasn't yet convinced of that.

"I'd like a copy of this information," Daniel said. He wanted his own study of Benjamin Fisher to be as complete as possible.

"I'll see what I can do, but it can be extremely difficult to get research like this released. Otherwise nobody would sign up."

Ah, the reason they were the only people in the suite.

Daniel went through the next couple of hours trying to keep his head in the autopsy, thinking about what Gus had told him and wondering if Reni was outside. At one point, Gus opened Fisher's skull and removed the brain. Cradling the slippery organ with both hands, he placed it carefully on the scale.

"This is the part of the autopsy I'm most interested in," he said, eyes on the digital readout. "Weight is normal." Returning it to an exam table, he did a full probe, appearing fascinated and then disappointed. "I'm not seeing anything obvious like a tumor or lesions that could cause malfunctioning."

The exam wasn't over, but Daniel told Gus to contact him if he found anything suspicious or of interest. After tossing his disposable gown and gloves in the biohazard bin and downing some Tylenol at the drinking fountain, he left the building to step outside into the bright sunlight.

Reni was sitting on the sidewalk in the shade, her back against the stucco building, wearing canvas sneakers, jeans, and a white T-shirt, eyes closed as she waited to hear what he'd learned inside. He would not mention what Gus had shared about the brain research.

CHAPTER 14

When Reni spotted Daniel exiting the coroner's office, she got to her feet, heart pounding. It hadn't been easy sitting outside, knowing her father's body was in there being cut up. She really thought it might have helped for her to be able to observe rather than imagine.

"His injuries fit your description of a deliberate dive," he told her.

She let out a relieved breath. Deep down, she felt she hadn't pushed him, but she also knew she couldn't completely trust herself. "And yet you look like you got bad news," she said.

He slipped on his glasses. "Just tired."

"What will happen to the body?"

"If you or your mother don't claim it within ten days, it'll be donated to science. I'm going to assume that's what you'll choose to do."

Part of her wanted to make sure there was nothing left of him. She'd claim him and get him cremated. Not because he was family no matter what, but because she wanted to be sure he was gone. Not floating in a vat somewhere, not sliced and diced, no pieces of him on a shelf in a jar. She certainly didn't want the ashes, but she'd have to take them so nobody began selling tiny vials of the Inland Empire Killer on eBay. A lot of people wanted a connection to a serial killer.

A white utility van with a local TV logo on the side pulled into the lot.

Daniel tensed, and Reni controlled the urge to duck and run.

After her father's arrest, crews had begun parking outside their home. She and her mother became prisoners, unable to even go to the grocery store. At some point in the string of days that all seemed the same, Maurice had hatched a plan to sneak them both to his cabin in Idyllwild. Under cover of darkness, they'd crept from their house to his. As the sun rose—Maurice at the wheel of his Cadillac, Reni and her mother on the floor in the back, blankets over them—they rode to freedom. Maurice was charming, and on the way down his driveway, he boldly lowered his car window and said hello to the die-hard paparazzi camped on the street.

But they should have known there was no escape. Nothing short of plastic surgery. Eventually someone recognized Reni and her mother. The press descended again, this time on the little mountain town where they were hiding. So they adopted a new strategy of no eye contact, no matter how insulting the questions hurled at them. It took about a year for things to die down, and when Reni hit puberty people stopped recognizing her. And yet she never doubted that she'd done something very wrong by simply not doing enough. If she'd told someone other than her mother and Maurice, the killing might have stopped. But maybe not. It was so unbelievable.

"They must have caught wind of something." Daniel began walking.

Even though her truck was in the other direction, she fell into step beside him, hoping he might share a little more of what had gone on inside the morgue.

Van doors opened and the crew flowed out, setting up a camera in front of the doors to the coroner's office. One of the bunch shouted Daniel's name and jogged over. He had a lanyard around his neck with a badge and photo attached. *Josh Perkins.*

Daniel glanced at the van. "What have you heard?"

"Not much." Josh looked over at Reni and dismissed her as unimportant.

Funny.

"Rumor says it's something about the Inland Empire Killer. Can you confirm or deny that?"

"I can't tell you anything. We'll be holding a press conference in two hours."

"So it *is* the Inland Empire Killer. Has he finally revealed the location of the missing women?"

"You know I can't go into this. Don't use our wives' friendship to get around that."

Wives?

"I was just hoping to break a story for once," Josh said. "It's tough out here."

"I'd like to help you, but I can't. Not this time."

He accepted the rejection. "No worries. See you in two hours." He turned and walked away, shaking his head to the crew as he approached.

"Wife?" Reni asked once he was out of earshot.

"Ex, actually."

Divorced. That didn't surprise her. Marriages took a hit in this business.

"Go home," he said. "Sleep. I'm guessing you didn't get much more than I did last night, which was zero."

"None." She'd spent most of the night sitting in a chair outdoors, wrapped in a heavy blanket, drinking too much coffee, looking at the stars. Once the sun rose, she went inside the cabin, tried to eat, but just the thought of oatmeal made her queasy. But at least what had happened out there with her father was starting to seem more real. She was processing it, beginning to accept it.

Still, the thought of joining Daniel on his investigative journey was mentally risky. She'd kept it together yesterday, but the protective fog that fell over someone when dealing with death was lifting. She needed to return to her home in the desert and hide. Maybe even take something that would knock her out for a while.

"Will I see you tomorrow?" he asked.

"I'm having second thoughts."

93

"If it makes any difference, it'll just be the two of us until we find something. I got the okay to bring you on board, but I was unable to get approval for a search crew. Funding isn't there. I'll be at your place tomorrow morning at six a.m. If you decide you don't want in on this, leave a note on your door and I'll drive to the desert alone."

"You shouldn't go by yourself." The thought of him in the desert alone would have been laughable if it weren't so dangerous. She could imagine him bringing one bottle of water and nothing else. She, on the other hand, would spend hours prepping. There would be packaged food to purchase, gallon water jugs to fill, batteries, flashlights, sunblock. Realizing that her mental supply list confirmed her plans to join him, she turned and walked to her truck, passing the media crew on the way. Again, nobody noticed her. That would likely change once the press conference aired.

CHAPTER 15

Lying on the couch, laptop on her stomach, Gabby Sutton scrolled through Facebook. The activity was her own form of self-medication. Her husband sat nearby in his overstuffed chair, feet up, remote in his hand, trying to find something for them to watch. This was their evening ritual.

She laughed to herself at a cute dog video, shared it with her Facebook friends, liked a post of her son's, scrolled, then paused on a local station's live feed.

She didn't know how she felt about news feeds on Facebook. Facebook was a way for her to get away from the bad things in the world. She didn't want her buzz killed by the news. She wanted puppies and kitties and birds. Maybe an occasional llama. Anything fun and distracting. But something made her fingers pause.

Just seconds into the online newscast and without conscious thought, she let out a faint whimper and pressed her hand hard against her mouth to catch and trap the sound.

"We could watch another episode of the show from last night," her husband said. "That sci-fi thing. It was a little slow, but it might pick up."

Gabby continued to stare at her laptop screen.

"I hate slow-moving sci-fi," he said.

A detective stood in front of the San Bernardino Sheriff's Department, microphones in front of him. Press conference. His name popped into the ticker at the bottom of the screen. *Detective Daniel*

Ellis. Her brain stopped and started, only catching some of what he was saying. But one thing jumped out. Benjamin Fisher, the Inland Empire Killer, was dead.

Was this real? It must be real.

"What's going on?"

She dragged her gaze from the screen. Her husband was waiting for her reply, sitting there with a half-annoyed, half-worried expression on his face.

"He's dead," she said in disbelief.

He straightened, fully worried now. "Who?"

Years ago, before they were married, she'd told him about Benjamin Fisher. About the attack and how she'd gotten away. She'd thought it was something he should know. It was the only time they'd talked about it. Not really talked, because he hadn't responded. Just stared at her from across the restaurant table for maybe a full minute, then went back to methodically eating his fish and acting as if she'd never said a word.

Thirty years later and she was still waiting for his response.

Most of the time she wished she hadn't shared her pain that day. His cold reaction had made her feel ashamed, like a victim all over again. After that, she swore to keep the attack to herself.

But she'd always hoped this day would come. For years she'd waited to hear Fisher was dead. She'd given up on lethal injection and had started hoping for a report of death by natural causes. Anything so she could know they were no longer living on the same planet. Dead was dead, no matter how it happened. She'd just wanted him gone. Now, in her shock and need to share, she blurted out the news.

"Benjamin Wayne Fisher."

Her husband's shoulders relaxed, and she realized he must have thought someone in the family had died.

She returned to the feed. "He killed himself," she said. "In the desert."

"What do you think?" her husband asked.

Finally. He wanted to talk about it. "I don't know." She couldn't process it. Suicide. In the desert. How did something like that even happen?

"I vote for sci-fi." He was still talking about whatever damn show they were going to watch. Years ago she'd made excuses for his behavior. He was young and overwhelmed. Awkward, not knowing how to respond to such a personal, intimate story. So he'd said nothing. But he was a grown man now. She needed him and he was sitting there staring at the television, remote in his hand, going through the menu on the screen. While her pain filled the room and she fell apart only feet away from him. His indifference cut to the bone.

First the monsters come, then the indifference.

Maybe it was her fault. She'd buried it so deep. And had certainly never pushed a conversation.

Don't blame yourself.

But she did.

Their marriage had been years of loneliness, a life imitating life, she herself guilty of not sharing her feelings and making more attempts to speak of what had happened. Instead she'd carried it inside her, never allowing it to escape again, lest it be trivialized once more. Even her grown children didn't know the extent of the attack that night, or how close she'd come to being killed. The horror of such a violation. They just thought it was cool that their mother was the person behind the arrest of the Inland Empire Killer. They didn't know his face continued to haunt her. Through all the events of her life. Her wedding, pregnancies, childbirth. Now both her son and daughter were grown and out of college, and she was here, needing someone to understand what she was going through, lying on the couch, shattering, while her husband, her life partner, sat a few feet away, deliberately, yes, deliberately, oblivious to her pain.

Slowly, she closed her laptop, set it aside, and stood up. She had to get away from him. As she left the living room, she said, without looking at him because she couldn't, "Watch it without me."

In the bedroom, in the bathroom, she locked the door, turned on the shower, lowered the toilet lid, and sat down.

Dead. He was dead.

And she didn't feel any better.

Because he wasn't gone. He would never be gone. Maybe when she grew old and dementia took over her brain. But even then, the old memories were the last to fade. She'd seen that in her own mother. What a horrible thought that was. To have nothing remaining but Benjamin Fisher.

With her throat so tight and raw it felt like it might explode, she let out a loud sob, the sound hopefully covered by the shower and the television. His stupid sci-fi show. She'd never felt so alone, not even directly after the attack. Right now it was almost like Benjamin Fisher, a dead killer, was her only companion on this journey.

CHAPTER 16

Reni waited outside for Daniel to arrive. The sun was just rising, temperature in the high forties. Later it would be close to ninety. The joke in California was that you could experience every season in a single day. People dressed in layers to be removed as the hours progressed, the clothing put back on once the sun dropped below the horizon and the air took on a chill. Reni was starting the day in jeans, leather boots, and a denim jacket over a gray hoodie. Near her front door and in the back of her truck, supplies were stacked. At the last minute, she'd decided to grab her tent in case their vehicle broke down or their quest turned into a several-day search.

She was relieved to see he'd left his suit at home and was more appropriately dressed in jeans and a flannel shirt. Trying maybe a little too hard, but trying. People who were used to wearing suits never looked comfortable in everyday clothing.

"Tent?" he asked.

"Something I learned from my father and he learned from his mother. Don't go into the desert unless you can sustain yourself for a few days."

While he grabbed the tent, she pulled a spade, a long iron bar for probing the ground, and a metal detector from the back of her truck. "I had car trouble once and had to hike forty miles. It's not that hard if you're equipped."

"I thought you were supposed to remain with your vehicle."

"That's typically the best idea. I waited twenty-four hours before starting out. If I hadn't had supplies, I wouldn't have done it even then."

They loaded her gear into the back of his SUV, adding to the few things he'd brought, like a shovel and water. She slammed the tailgate of her truck and went back inside the cabin for one final thing. The map from her wall. Outside, thankful for the lack of wind, she spread the map on the hood of her truck.

"Do you have my father's drawing?" she asked. "Let's see if we can match any locations."

Daniel placed Ben's sketch over one corner of the map from the wall.

To someone unfamiliar with the area, it might have been hard to make sense of the drawing, but she was able to recognize landmarks and point them out on the map. She noted that her father's work was actually quite detailed now that she was no longer shocked by its very existence and the circumstances by which they'd come to have it at all.

"This is where we are, outside Joshua Tree. And this," she pointed to a red *X*, "is pretty close. It shouldn't take us more than three hours to get there."

"What about this place?" He indicated a small square.

"That's my grandmother's. Probably included for orientation, just like the mountain ranges and other landmarks. I've searched that area more than anywhere else and have had no luck." Not that her failures proved anything; the desert had a way of erasing things, sometimes even overnight. Still, her father might not have wanted to hide bodies so close to home turf.

With Daniel behind the wheel, they headed east out of Joshua Tree on Highway 62 through Twentynine Palms. Then it was a series of turns on narrow paved roads that eventually gave way to dirt and a rolling landscape of burrobush, mesquite, blackbrush, a brilliant sky, and mountains in the far distance, some hundreds of miles away.

"Back in the fifties, when people homesteaded this area, all the roads were like this," Reni said, clinging to the handle above the passenger door, bracing herself for the next bump while wondering how long to wait before telling Daniel he needed to slow down. City drivers had a tendency to drive too fast on desert roads. Their brains couldn't adjust to the need for a much slower speed. "I hope you brought your satellite phone because you might need to call someone when you break an axle."

He pulled to a quick and dusty stop. "You want to drive?" No annoyance or irritation in his tone. Just someone recognizing his own limitations.

"Seems the practical thing to do."

While she drove, he navigated with the use of her map. Sometimes she'd pull to a stop and they'd lean over, heads together, orienting themselves before continuing on. As they rode, they ate snacks, stayed hydrated, and listened to music. Their taste was slightly compatible. Reni imagined a Venn diagram with a thirty percent overlap. It didn't matter; right now it was hard for her to care about anything but the goal. Unlike him, she had little interest in what went in her mouth or ears.

"Care to talk about why you left the FBI?" he asked at one point in their journey.

She'd been prepared for the question, yet she didn't know how much she wanted to share with someone she barely knew. "I was becoming paranoid about some of the people I worked with," she said, giving him a watered-down version of things. "I think what happened with my father set me up to distrust people." She hesitated, then added, "Especially my partner."

"Are you sure you were misreading him?"

"I think he was a decent guy. Here's the deal, and this is something nobody but my doctors and mother know." Full confession. And once she thought about it, something he should be aware of. "There was a time when he looked like somebody else. And I'm not talking about similar features. One night when things got intense, guns drawn, extreme danger, his face morphed into my dad's and I almost fired at him."

He went still. "Wow."

His one-syllable word held sympathy that made her blink hard to bring the desert back into clear focus. "That very night I checked myself into a mental-health clinic. I was there a week before I called my mother. She flew out to get me and drove me home to California. That was three years ago. So now you know what you're dealing with. If you want to withdraw your request for my help, I get it."

"Have you misread anybody else?"

Good question. Logical question. "Never to that degree. I never hallucinated before or since."

"It sounds like pretty classic PTSD." The sympathy was there again. The understanding. So many cops dealt with PTSD that went untreated. He could be one of them himself. Show her a cop who didn't have any baggage and she'd flag him as someone who was either new to the job or shouldn't be a cop.

"It's being classified as chronic trauma." She turned up the AC and aimed a vent at her face. "I've been working on keeping my paranoia tamped down, channeling calm, taking people at face value, or just plain avoiding them. Trying not to look or dig beyond the skin. Focus more on facts. Facts give us what we need without the color and confusion."

"I'm trying to remain more fact-based myself," Daniel said. "At Homicide, we're transitioning away from the old model of FBI profiling that's been so sensationalized."

"Even though I taught it, I'll be the first to admit it was extreme," Reni said. The turn to a familiar topic calmed her. "Too much emphasis was put on gut feelings. They have a place, but the dangerous take-away was that logic should be ignored in favor of instinct. Logic should never be ignored, and gut instinct can turn on a person. Say you have a perpetrator who's handsome and glib. Maybe posing as a repairman, standing in your doorway, one hundred percent charm, while scanning your home for signs that you're alone. You see the scan, but you ignore it because of his charming smile. *Oh, he's just curious.* If you ask for ID, he'll smile sweetly, maybe even tell you to call his company if you're worried. He might even give you the number. You don't call because he's so smooth and seems so genuine. It's human nature to want to trust people. But logic, *logic* is going to be your friend in that scenario. Look at the bait tactic my father used. Logic would tell the victim that something was off. But he played on the victims' emotions. He used emotions and empathy to his advantage."

"You really should consider teaching again," Daniel said. "Freelance, I mean. Nothing that's attached to the FBI or a government agency. I think police departments around the country would be interested and could benefit from your experience. Not your experience with your father, but just general knowledge."

"I like my clay."

He laughed at her choice of words, then sobered. "Maybe someday. Just something to keep in mind." With a rustle of paper, he turned his attention back to the map. "We're supposed to look for a giant rock. In parentheses, it says 'not *the* giant rock.' Does that mean anything to you?"

"*The* Giant Rock is located northwest of Joshua Tree. It's a George Van Tassel thing."

"Van Tassel?"

"You really don't know your California history, do you? Van Tassel lived underneath a seven-story rock and communicated with aliens there. Doesn't ring a bell?" She fed him more information. "They told him to build something called the Integratron that was supposed to make a person young again. Does any of this sound familiar?"

"They don't teach outsider history in school."

"He spent twenty-four years creating this wooden dome that has no nails in it, but he died before he finished so he was never able to rejuvenate himself."

"Unfortunate."

"And now we'll never know if it would have worked." Her words were spoken with the implied wink of a local.

"California is weird."

Odd thing for him to say. People from California tended to love and defend and embrace their state, earthquakes and fires and all. "Didn't you grow up here?"

"I did, but I know weird when I see it."

"It's still history, regardless of how out-there it might be. History is history."

"You're not going to start talking about vortexes, are you?"

"Scoff all you want, but I've felt some things in the desert that I can't explain."

"Those things are often substance-related."

"Not always. As you take in a surreal and unwelcoming landscape, you have to learn to feel in a different way. You have to change your focus from near to far, like opening a camera's depth of field. You have to look at the sky and not at the ground. And once your brain finally makes the change, you'll see it, really see it, and understand that the world is made up of all kinds of beauty, even in places that at first seem harsh. Places where the absence of trees and shade and things that are physically close allows the mind to expand, to see in a new and different way."

"You are *so* California."

"I'm not talking about anything abstract."

"Yes, you are."

"Okay. Never mind."

"You just basically told me to embrace the desert."

"I did not."

"Okay, sorry. I'll take what you've said and try to be more under-standing. I'll try a little harder. I might have some reasons for my dislike."

Here it was. His dark secret. "Like something abusive?"

"No, more like falling on a cactus and getting needles embedded in me. I mean hundreds. I was especially freaked out because at the time I believed cactus needles could travel through your bloodstream to your heart."

"Interesting how kids can profoundly misunderstand what adults tell them. You probably heard someone say—and accurately—that cacti can cause serious infections that have led to heart issues and even death."

"Look." He pointed, their light conversation interrupted by the reason they were actually there. A cluster of boulders, one much bigger than the others, stood tall and alien against the terrain.

She aimed the vehicle up a steep incline. Once the ground leveled out, she pulled to a full halt and cut the engine, squinting through the dusty windshield. She didn't realize she was holding her breath until he spoke.

"What?" he asked.

Keeping her eyes focused on the landscape, she said, "This looks familiar."

"Maybe you transported here once." He laughed. "Sorry. Couldn't help it."

She concentrated, trying to grasp any faint memory. "I might have been here when I was little." She got out of the car and walked toward the giant rock, stopping a few feet away, hands on her hips.

Behind her, a door slammed and she heard the soles of Daniel's shoes scuffing pebbles and stirring up loose sand. He stopped beside her while she kept her eyes on the boulder.

He finally said, "I think you *have* been here."

There was a drawing on the rock. Of a bird. And not just any bird. It looked exactly like the bird she used on her pottery.

CHAPTER 17

Thirty-three years earlier

Desert.

They'd been driving a long time, Reni in the back seat of their Ford Granada, her father behind the wheel. Along the way to wherever they were going, they'd passed a lot of Joshua trees. Joshua trees looked like people, and the only time she saw them was when they went to her grandmother's cabin or on one of these rare desert drives with her dad.

"Are we going to Grandma Beryl's?" she asked, looking at the back of her father's head. He was wearing a floppy hat that protected him from the sun.

"Not today, little bird," he said, glancing at her in the rearview mirror. "We're just taking a drive."

"Please? Can we go to Grandma's?" she begged.

"No." His voice went stern. "I said not today."

She crossed her arms and hugged her elbows, chin down. She didn't know why they couldn't go to her grandma's house. Her grandma was her favorite person in the world, maybe secretly even more favorite than her daddy and certainly more favorite than her mommy. She was too little to remember, but she'd been told her grandmother had taken care of her after she was born. Her mother got sick and couldn't take care of a baby, so Reni's father packed her up and took her to the desert to stay with her grandma Beryl until Reni's mother felt better. Once Reni was back home, she still visited her grandmother a lot. People called her grandmother tough, a pioneer. Her house didn't have electricity, and a big truck with a tank on it brought water. Reni liked hearing that she'd spent her first months of life there, with a tough pioneer who later taught her a lot of what she knew about the desert.

"Joshua trees don't grow anywhere else in the whole world, sweet little bird," her grandmother had told her. She always added the *sweet* when she called her little bird. "That's how special they are. You should never climb on one or pull their branches. You can sit in their shade, but don't hurt them. They only grow a fraction of an inch a year, so they're very old and very wise. And the only way *more* Joshua trees can grow is with the help of the yucca moth."

She'd imagined the moths clapping dusty wings as they encouraged baby trees to pop out of the ground. "Do they like books?"

Her grandmother had been a librarian before moving from some mysterious place called "out east." In the desert, she didn't have a television, but she had stacks of books and she read to Reni all the time, even big grown-up books with no pictures.

"Joshua trees love books," her grandmother said. "And they love to be read to."

Sitting cross-legged in the desert sand as lizards skittered past, making the dry shrubs rustle, Reni had read her own books to the Joshua trees, telling them stories about dogs and cats and families, sometimes making up stories herself to match the pictures. She liked to believe the trees enjoyed the sound of her voice even if they just stood there silent and watchful with their big arms reaching to the clouds.

Her dad stopped the car at a place where there were a lot of giant, smooth rocks, some taller than houses. There were no trees where they parked, just big rocks and big sky.

"Come on." He opened the back door. "Too hot for you to wait in the car." Together, her father holding her hand, they walked to a shady spot next to one of the boulders. "Wait here and watch for wildlife, especially the birds." He gave her a small book.

She could read now, not everything, but enough to know the book said *Birds of the Desert*. She knew the word *desert* because it was on a lot of things. Even towns like Desert Hot Springs. And gas stations and places to eat, and places where you could buy a giant cactus if you wanted.

She'd seen the book before, at their house. It was boring the way a lot of adult books were boring, but at least this one had pictures.

"When you see a bird, look it up in the book. If you can't read some of the words, I'll tell you what it says when I get back. Can you do that?"

"I can, Daddy."

"Stay here. Don't leave or you'll get lost. People who get lost in the desert are never found until they're a pile of bleached bones."

She imagined somebody pouring a bottle of bleach over bones.

It was true about dying. She'd seen it on the news. A lady fell and broke herself and died in the desert. And hikers died all the time.

Being dead was mysterious. Someone was there and then they weren't. It seemed like something that shouldn't happen to anybody, not even bugs. It wasn't fair. She never hurt bugs and she never hurt trees, because she didn't want them to go away and never come back.

He left her standing by the rock, telling her to stay in the shade, then he drove off in a puff of dirt, the tailpipe of the car rattling until it faded and she couldn't hear it anymore.

At first she wasn't scared because she knew her father would come back. He always came back and he always did what he said he'd do. This trip was connected to the game they played in the park. She didn't know how, only that the visits to the desert sometimes came after the park game.

She sat in the sand and watched the sky like she'd been told to do.

There were a lot of birds in the desert. And animals. Her grandmother had told her coyotes could pick up cats and dogs and run away with them.

"Can a coyote carry me away?" she'd asked one day when they were sitting on the porch eating breakfast, which had been cooked over a stove that burned wood.

Her grandmother's intense blue eyes squinted at the valley that glowed pink in the distance. "It might. They've carried babies away before. I know somebody who lost a baby that way. She was hanging up clothes and left the child outside for just a minute. Came back out to crying and a coyote scurrying away with the baby in its mouth."

Reni hoped the story of the coyote and baby was like the story of Hansel and Gretel—something that wasn't true, but scary fun to hear. Kind of like the games she played with her dad.

Her grandmother didn't seem to like men very much even though she dressed and acted more like a man than a woman. Her clothes were usually jeans and work shirts. Not a single dress. Unlike Reni's mother, Grandma Beryl didn't own any makeup, and she wore her hair short like a man's. But Reni had seen a picture of her with long hair, a dress, and a sweet face.

On one of their magical mornings together, her grandmother told her that men were behind all the problems in the world, and that women had to take care of each other.

"But Daddy's good, isn't he?" Reni had asked.

"Better than most, but he and your mother are both a piece of work. Ben isn't like your grandfather, who was a mean son of a bitch."

"He beat you up."

"He did."

"And he broke your arm." Her grandmother had told her so.

"Did that too. More than once. And what do men think with?"

"The worm between their legs."

Her grandmother laughed. "That's right." She looked off into the distance and said, almost to herself, "Sometimes you just have to make the bad people go away."

"Did you make Grandpa go away?"

Grandma Beryl chuckled. "That's my little secret. And your father's."

At the rock, as Reni settled in and waited for her father's return, she spotted a bird with a fluffy white chest. She dug through the pages of the book until she found the right picture, along with a word she sounded out: *fal-con*. Later, she saw a smaller bird, black this time, with shiny wings. It was yelling at her from the top of a tree.

But most of the time nothing happened.

She got hot and thirsty and so bored her eyes kept closing. After looking at the bird pictures for a long time, she dropped the book and crouched on her heels, knees to her chest, and searched for pretty rocks. She found some and used a sharp one to draw in the dirt. Later, when the spot of shade became a sliver, she used the rock to scratch a drawing on one of the big round boulders.

It was fun for a while, but she got tired of that too and began to wonder if her daddy was really coming back. Maybe something had happened. Maybe the car stopped running. Maybe a coyote carried him away. That didn't seem possible because he was big.

Maybe he forgot about her.

She tried not to worry.

The sky turned red and the air was cold by the time he finally returned. He had the ugly look on his face she didn't like, and his plaid shirt was untucked and dirty, his hair sweaty, and he smelled funny, like when you drive past a dead animal on the road.

"What's this?" He walked up to the boulder and stared at her artwork, hands on his hips. "Was this here before?"

"I did it. It's a bird." She waited for him to praise her and tell her what a good job she'd done.

"I can see it's a bird, but this isn't cool. It's defacing nature. You can't do that, Reni. We have to protect nature."

She didn't know what *defacing* meant, but the anger in his voice and the strange look on his face told her it was bad. "Like we protect the trees?" she asked.

"That's right."

"I can erase it."

"You can't erase it. It's scratched into the stone. It's there for good."

She clutched the bird book to her stomach, her heart pounding. "Can we paint over it?"

"No, we can't paint a rock. That would be even worse."

She didn't want to be a baby, but she couldn't help it. She started crying.

"Hey, hey, hey."

He picked her up and she tried to ignore the way he smelled.

"Don't cry. Just don't do anything like that again, okay?" He was using the voice she liked. Carrying her, he walked to the car and settled her into the passenger seat instead of the back seat. She hardly ever rode in front.

"Let's head home. Your mother's going to wonder what happened to us."

"Can we stop for ice cream?"

"I think we can do that."

On the way out, he drove slowly past her artwork. It seemed like he was silently punishing her, wanting her to see what she'd done. She looked through the window at the bird drawing, watching it grow smaller as they bounced down the dirt road.

CHAPTER 18

With Daniel standing beside her, Reni stared at the crude bird draw-ing on the rock. Yes, it was exactly like her logo. And it was unsettling to find herself transported back to a day she'd completely forgotten until moments ago. She could feel the sharpness of the small rock she'd clutched in her hand when she drew the bird, and she remembered the intense heat of the sun, along with how she'd tried to control her fear after her father drove off. The book of desert birds. What had happened to it?

"He left me here and drove away," she told Daniel. "Far enough that I could no longer see or hear the car." She concentrated, trying to pull up more memory, but even though some things were vivid, others remained obscure and hazy.

"He left you alone? In the desert?"

"Yes."

"How old were you?"

"I don't know. Maybe five? Six?"

"Was it just the two of you, or was someone else with him? With you?"

"I don't remember anybody else." She felt light-headed. "I've got to sit down." She dropped heavily to the ground in a strip of shade, maybe the same spot she'd sat that day years ago.

Daniel left and returned a few moments later with water for both of them. He handed her a bottle and sat down next to her. "Did he bring you out to the desert often? And why leave you alone? I don't get it."

"He was probably babysitting me. He did that a lot. My mother wasn't good with kids, and being around me was stressful for her." She took a long drink. "Specific memories of that day are clear now. The birds I saw, how hot it was, the small rocks I collected." She screwed the cap back onto the bottle, running her recollections through her head again, trying to follow the logic of her father's behavior. "I'm pretty sure he was disposing of a body."

Daniel choked on his water, then recovered. "That's sick." His voice sounded incredulous, but he needed to consider who they were talking about.

"Even now, I swear I can smell the rotten body on him when he came back to get me. Like roadkill."

"I can smell it too."

They looked at each other in surprise, then jumped to their feet and began searching the area. Highest on Reni's list of possibilities was finding a dead animal, but she also searched for ground that might have been disturbed recently.

"Careful of snakes," she warned.

His eyes widened, but he didn't say anything.

"They sleep in the shade this time of day. I once found one inside my truck, under the dash."

"Oh, hell no."

A suspicious and disturbed spot wasn't hard to find now that they knew what they were looking for. Reni called it—an indentation behind the giant rock where the soil was especially loose.

They retrieved shovels from the SUV and began digging, careful in case they were dealing with a crime scene, both of them stepping back from time to time in order to take deep breaths before diving in again, no possibility of conversation.

Two feet down, they uncovered clothing.

Their eyes locked. Wordlessly, they tossed the shovels and began digging gently with their hands until they removed enough soil to reveal long dark hair and a female body dressed in jeans and a black T-shirt lying facedown, hands behind her back.

Definitely not a body from thirty years ago.

They both gagged from the intense odor and scrambled far enough away to pull in huge gulps of air and hold a conversation.

"How long do you think she's been here?" Reni asked while trying to figure out how her father had known about this person. He'd drawn a map of the location. Were there more bodies, older bodies? Was this a killing field?

With an arm pressed to his nose, Daniel said, "Couple of weeks, maybe? Hard to say in this heat, but not more than a month."

Her father had been in prison when the crime had taken place. Was it just a coincidence that they'd found the spot where someone had recently been buried? That seemed unlikely. Did her father have an accomplice outside? Had he led them here on purpose, so they'd find this body? And what about the body he'd disposed of that day, the day of her memory, if that was what he'd been doing?

"The crime could have been committed by someone who helped him in the past," she said. "Or it could have been someone he shared his history with in prison." That happened sometimes. People became close in such an insular environment. They shared stories about themselves. Her father might have created a disciple who, when he got out of prison, took up where her father had left off.

That idea, the idea of someone carrying on her father's work, was something Reni couldn't think about right now. She had to shove the thought away, push it down deep, because the homage, if that was what this was, breathed life back into Benjamin Fisher. But her father was dead, and someone was still killing young women.

CHAPTER 19

Amazing how finding a body lit a fire under people. Two days ago Daniel hadn't been able to get approval for a crew to perform a simple grid search—which was understandable. Homicides were up over forty percent in San Bernardino County, and law enforcement agencies were spread thin due to the increase in violent crime and the vastness of the area they covered. The distance alone made being a cop in San Bernardino a challenge. If you called for backup, it could take hours for someone to arrive. Most cops knew they were on their own. It fell on park rangers to take up some of the slack, but they could only do so much. They were all fighting heat and size and remoteness. So of course Daniel's request had been turned down. The Inland Empire Killer was only one story in a large number of cold cases, and the Mojave Desert was the biggest killing field in the United States. Captain Edda Morris liked to say it was more crowded than most cemeteries. But today, after they'd spent the night in the desert, Daniel in the SUV, Reni in her tent, the area was swarming with people. This was no longer a cold case.

Early that morning, crews had arrived and trail canopies had been erected to supply much-needed shade. Generators were going, and a couple of portable toilets were on-site. Perimeters had been established and a crime-scene crew was in the process of digging up the body. A grid had been set up with string, and several people were meticulously going over it, looking for anything that might possibly be attached to the scene. The searchers wore backpacks with yellow flags protruding, but as of yet no evidence numbers were in place and nothing had been found.

They were still waiting on the arrival of a guy who had something called the body finder. It looked a little like a baby stroller. The device rolled across the ground and used ground-penetrating radar to find the bones.

They were busy back at Headquarters in San Bernardino, too, going through missing persons reports. Almost two hundred adults a month were reported missing in the county alone, over forty thousand a year for the entire state. Even after limiting it to adults only, it would take time to come up with a list of possible victims.

Daniel and Reni stood not far from the dig site, wearing caps and sunglasses, his with the department logo, hers faded and shredded, advertising a saloon. She seemed to be unaffected by a night spent in the desert. He, on the other hand, had a raging headache and hurt all over. And then there was the smell of the body. Right now it was the star of the day because there was no escaping the stench.

When he thought it couldn't get any worse, it did, each movement of dirt and each degree in temperature rise lifting the odor a few notches. Some of the crew wore carbon masks, but it was almost too hot for that, and a distance of twenty yards wasn't enough. Hell, he suspected a person would still catch a whiff a mile downwind. Reni seemed to have gotten used to it because she was watching the dig while drinking iced coffee she'd grabbed from the food and drink table, her mask pulled down around her neck. Or maybe she was so shut off she didn't notice.

It was hard to gauge her reaction to it all. So far, he was getting the old FBI poker face. He'd seen the light on in her tent last night, and a few times he'd been tempted to leave his SUV and try to engage her in conversation, but he'd also gotten the sense she needed to be alone. Locations had ways of really messing with a person's head, and this had to be bordering on inhumane, returning her to a place she'd mentally buried long ago. He took responsibility for that, and was wondering if it had been wise to pressure her to join him on his blind quest to find his mother, a person Reni didn't even know about. He'd been so focused on his own agenda that he hadn't considered the depth of what this could mean to her, what it could do to her. Yes, she was holding up just fine. That alone worried him.

And yet they'd both known they couldn't leave the body for fear of wild animals destroying evidence. At several points during the night, he'd even heard packs of coyotes howling and had been glad to be in his SUV no matter how uncomfortable. While Reni had truly come prepared with an inflatable mattress, sleeping bag, pillow, and that damn tent that had seemed so ridiculous yesterday morning.

Now, as she and Daniel looked on, four geared-up people wearing layers of latex gloves positioned themselves to lift the corpse to the white body bag spread open on the ground beside the shallow grave. They'd already discussed the heat, how much rain the area had received over the past month, the typical decomposition time of bodies on body farms in arid locales. All things that would have to be considered to determine approximate date of death. Current guess was less time than Daniel had initially predicted.

Two people in white paper Tyvek suits worked a sheet of heavy plastic under the body. Once it was in place, the team lifted the decomposing remains from the grave and positioned them on the open bag, then rolled the body so it was faceup. The woman still wore two gold hoop earrings that might help ID her.

A bullet fell from the skull, dropping to the plastic.

Everybody froze. An investigator carefully picked up the projectile and dropped it into a paper evidence bag. "No bullet hole through the front," he said.

"Execution style," Reni noted.

What a cruel way to go. Driven all the way to the inhospitable desert, probably begging for her life. She had to decide to fight or do what she was told. Always a hard choice, and it varied with each situation and the mental state of the assailant. Daniel usually recommended fighting. It wasn't the most popular advice because fighting could escalate the situation, but it was the advice he always gave, maybe because he too often saw the consequences of not fighting.

With the peripheral evidence secured within the confines of the bag, Daniel snapped on a pair of exam gloves, crouched next to the body, and slipped his fingers into the pockets of the jeans, feeling for anything like a billfold. Nothing.

As they were easing the body into the coroner's van, Daniel told Reni he planned to head back to San Bernardino. "I don't want to miss the autopsy." He didn't mention he wanted to avoid another night spent in his vehicle and that he also needed time alone.

Things were under control, and most of the existing crew planned to camp there and continue searching. By tomorrow, the FBI would probably be involved. They might even want to take charge. "If anybody finds anything, they'll give me a call. You can stay and ride back with someone if you want to stick around."

"Drop me at my place on the way. I'd like to get in on the autopsy."

No backing down from her. No, she was charging right into the fire. He might have looked at her a little too long, and he hoped she didn't pick up on the guilt he felt for not sharing his own history with her, which some might consider a lie of omission. If she stuck around, his personal story would have to come out eventually. But not now. He wasn't ready.

CHAPTER 20

The day after the body was recovered from the desert, Reni tossed her jacket in her truck and strode across the parking lot toward the San Bernardino medical examiner's office, where the autopsy of Jane Doe was scheduled to take place. It was early morning and she could hear rush-hour traffic in the distance. The air had a bite to it, but temperatures were rising rapidly.

Phone pressed to her ear as she walked, she continued a conversation with her mother, updating her on the latest. News about Jane Doe was already out, and stations were bouncing between Benjamin Fisher's death and the mystery woman discovered in the desert.

Reni still had mixed feelings about becoming involved in the case, but she didn't think she could sit home wondering what was going on and whether her father had or hadn't played a part in it. She needed answers. Answers probably wouldn't relieve her guilt and suffering, but being instrumental in giving victims' families closure would get her some points, at least in her own mind. Still, she was sure she would go to her grave feeling complicit. And that was okay. She *was* complicit.

Yesterday had been tough. No lie about that. She'd almost lost it a few times out there in the desert, but she'd made it through the night without breaking, which had led to fresh resolve. It was interesting, but there had been times when Daniel had seemed more upset by yesterday's discovery than she was.

"I can't leave my house," her mother said. "And whatever you do, don't attempt to come here."

As expected, reporters were in swarm mode with vans already on the street in front of Rosalind's home.

"I can't give you any information right now," she told her mother. "We don't know much. I've gotta go. Call Maurice if things get too crazy there. I'll talk to you later." She disconnected.

Press were in front of the medical examiner's office too. Local affiliates, teams from LA, even a few national outlets were trying to find an angle on a story that was still unfolding. Crews were set up in front of the main entrance, hoping to grab a sound bite.

Rather than walk past them or through them, Reni ducked behind vehicles, hoping to slip by unnoticed. A movement caught her eye, and she spotted Daniel standing near the back of the building, waving her over. She changed direction and the two of them slipped inside, the metal door locking with a firm click behind them. She hadn't told her mother, because she knew Rosalind would insist they not contact the morgue about the remains, but Reni planned to claim and make cremation arrangements for her father's body while she was there.

The medical examiner performing the autopsy met them in the prep room. She was young, with straight mahogany hair pulled back in a ponytail, and a dark complexion that didn't look like it had ever seen a blemish. Her eyes, behind stylish frames, were green.

Reni recognized her. Evangeline Fry. She'd been in the news lately. A little bit famous in California and beyond. Reni had been glad to see a young female doing so well in what used to be a predominantly male field. Evangeline was ranked as one of the best medical examiners in the country, mainly due to her involvement in solving a mass murder case that had stumped detectives. Maybe Daniel had requested her. Reni would have done the same if she'd been in charge.

"I heard you're going to have a show on the Discovery Channel," Daniel said as he and Reni slipped into yellow paper gowns.

Evangeline laughed. "Crazy, isn't it? We're still in discussions, and I'll believe it when it actually happens. You're going to need these."

She passed out charcoal masks—reminders of yesterday's stench. "The exhaust system is on high, but it's not handling the odor a hundred percent. Hey, you two should be on an episode. The producers would love that."

Reni grimace-smiled while thinking, *That won't be happening.* Daniel, on the other hand, seemed to like the idea.

They followed Evangeline into an autopsy suite, the three of them rustling as they walked. Evangeline's casual demeanor changed as soon as they gathered around the sheet-covered body on the stainless-steel autopsy table. She was professional, sure of herself, intense, and passionate.

"Honestly, I was hoping this would be a little tougher," she confessed. "We took X-rays before you arrived, and cause of death is looking to be pretty straightforward. Bullet to the head, as you know, but I'm still hoping the autopsy turns up something helpful." She pulled the sheet from the body. The face had been wiped free of sand, and it looked even more mummified than it had in the desert.

Evangeline began with the Y incision, cutting with scissors, the sound loud even with the exhaust fans going as she sliced through the tough layer of hardened skin.

"How long do you think she was out there?" Daniel asked.

"Taking into account our dry spring, I'd say she died about three weeks ago. I emailed an image to a body-farm specialist and he concurred. I'll also run it past our forensic anthropologist when he comes back from vacation. A month in the desert is like a year on the East Coast."

They always followed the same protocol when doing an autopsy. Reni had seen so many that the process was commonplace now, but this one had deeper meaning due to the connection to her father. The weighing of organs, the dictation that documented everything—it all felt more personal.

There was never any telling when something from the autopsy would end up being crucial during a trial, and things got a little more interesting when Evangeline examined the stomach contents.

"Pomegranate seeds."

"I could never understand how or why people eat those," Daniel said.

Evangeline dropped a few seeds into a solution. "I like them in salad dressing."

"But do you actually swallow the seeds?" he asked.

"Sometimes."

"Even if you do, what a pain. It's like eating food meant for a Barbie doll."

Both women laughed, and Reni's tense muscles relaxed a little at the brief but welcome bit of humor.

"There is little sign of insect activity," Evangeline said, getting back to the exam. "Another result of a desert death."

"Are those breast implants?" Reni leaned over the body, pointing but not touching. Not all implants had serial numbers, but many did. A serial number would give them a name.

"Yes." Evangeline lifted an implant from the body and placed it in a stainless-steel tray, where she examined it more closely. "Looks like it has a serial number. We shouldn't have any trouble tracking her down."

"That can sometimes take time," Daniel said. "We'll need a court order. I'll get that rolling."

"Before you run off, let me pause the exam to tell you the good stuff I've been saving." Evangeline covered the body with the sheet, snapped off her gloves, and stepped to a computer. With a few key clicks, she opened and enlarged a series of numbered and dated X-rays. "I know you found a bullet on-site. Here we see the entry at the back of the head, no exit." She circled with the mouse.

"Not the MO of the Inland Empire Killer," Daniel said.

Reni agreed. Was this not connected to her father?

"I'll show you something else." Evangeline brought up more images. Using the mouse, she highlighted an area of another X-ray.

"Broken nose," Daniel said.

"Yep."

"As we suspected, an execution killing," Reni added. She put the puzzle together in her head and visualized the woman standing at the foot of her own grave.

The scenario didn't really need a play-by-play, but Daniel laid out what they were all thinking. "Shot from behind. She falls forward into the pit, breaks her nose."

There were people like Reni's father who fetishized killing. There were people who murdered in the heat of passion and then covered it up. But this kind of thing was harder to understand because it was so calculated. "It's a cruel way to kill someone, so it might have been done for pleasure," she said. And yet the dissimilar MO made a connection to her father less likely.

"Or practicality," Daniel said. "No need to transfer a dead body. No blood in the car, no blood on clothing."

"Prints don't match anything in the database," Evangeline said. "But this is what I wanted to show you. I sent images to a colleague who specializes in facial reconstruction. He's testing some new software and was looking for a challenge." She clicked a few keys. "Here's what he came up with. Please keep in mind that this software isn't for public use yet and could still be fairly unreliable."

The face on the monitor looked like a combination of an actual human and something created digitally. But it was recognizable as a person. She was Latina, with shoulder-length hair, high cheekbones, narrow jaw. About thirty.

Reni grew tense again. The woman looked familiar.

"Send that to me and I'll run it through our missing persons data-bases," Daniel said.

Hundreds of adults vanished under suspicious circumstances from San Bernardino County every year. Expand that to include all of Southern

California and the numbers were staggering. Add unknown circumstances, and that figure increased to three thousand. Voluntary disappearances? Those people could fill a small city. But despite those staggering numbers, this person was not going to be hard for them to identify.

"I don't think you need to run it," Reni said quietly.

The media hadn't bothered her much over the past ten years, but as soon as she let her guard down, it seemed some reporter would show up at the most inopportune time and place. Once she'd had a woman follow her into a restroom and make demands from the opposite side of the door while Reni sat on the toilet. But no one had come to her desert sanctuary until a month ago, when she'd answered a knock to find a journalist standing there. A young woman with long shiny dark hair, brown eyes, and gold earrings.

She'd introduced herself and handed Reni her card. "I'm working on a piece about your father."

"I'm not interested," Reni had told her. "And don't come back here again."

"You might want to hear what I have to say."

It was a familiar line many of them opened with. Reni had fallen for it a couple of times, but not any longer.

Standing in the morgue, she recalled the name on the card and pulled out her phone. A quick Google search, and she had the person she was looking for. She turned the screen around so Daniel and Evangeline could see the headshot, surprised that her hand wasn't shaking now that they had confirmation of a connection to her father, no matter how tenuous at the moment. "Her name is Carmel Cortez."

Daniel and Evangeline leaned close. "That does look like her," Evangeline said.

"She's an investigative journalist from Rancho Cucamonga," Reni explained, tucking her phone away. "She showed up at my place about a month ago, asking if she could interview me."

"And?" Daniel asked.

"I told her to leave."

He didn't break eye contact. "And now she's dead."

Exactly.

No sound but the fans. Then finally Daniel said, "If she tried to contact you, it would also make sense that she might have reached out to your mother or even your father."

Reni agreed. "My mother recently mentioned someone harassing her. I'll follow up with her."

Daniel pulled out his own phone. "I'm contacting Jan in Records and Research." He made the call. Paused while someone answered. "Did you get a chance to look up Benjamin Fisher's prison visitors?" he asked. "You did? Sorry, I was out of town and off-grid. Check the file for me and see if there's a Carmel Cortez on it. No?" He glanced at Evangeline and Reni and communicated with a shake of his head. "Any other visitors over the past two months?"

Daniel was good at self-control, but Reni saw dismay and puzzlement in his face. Evangeline noticed too, because she shot Reni a concerned glance.

"Thanks." Daniel put his phone away. "Your father told me he hadn't had a visitor in a long time, but he actually had two in the month before his death. One was someone named Maurice Albert Aston."

Maurice? That was a surprise. Reni hadn't realized he'd kept in touch with her father. "He's my mother's neighbor and a close family friend," she explained.

"Interestingly enough, Aston visited just a few days before your father reached out to me."

"The other person?" Reni asked, wondering if it could have been Carmel.

He paused, looked uncomfortable, then said, "You."

CHAPTER 21

The next several minutes were a blur. Reni excused herself to remove her mask and gown, tossing them in the biohazard container, distantly aware of a door closing behind her as Daniel entered the prep room. Without glancing in his direction, she made her way outside, where she stood shivering and rubbing her arms in the hot sun. Somebody shoved a microphone in her face.

She'd forgotten about the press.

Daniel appeared and pushed the mic away. "Let's go to Headquarters."

Reporters shouted questions at him, most wanting to know about Ben Fisher, but some asked about the body found in the desert. "Have you identified it? Is it a woman?"

"We plan to hold a press conference soon, and we'll let you know all the details at that time." Daniel grasped Reni lightly by the elbow and steered her toward his vehicle.

"I drove here," she mumbled.

"I'll bring you back."

Everything was bright sun and voices and faces and lights and the sound of traffic. Passenger seat. Door slam.

They pulled out of the lot, a sea of people moving away. "I don't remember visiting my father," she said. "I don't think I did, but I also know I can't trust myself and my own memories." She watched as a red light turned green. "You shouldn't either. Trust me. *Don't ever trust me.*"

"We'll figure it out easily by requesting video footage from the prison."

"And the journalist. What about her? And the bird on the rock. I'm connected to all those things. It might not mean anything, but if I were investigating this, and I guess I am, I'd be a suspect."

"Don't worry. I'm not letting you drop off my radar."

At the San Bernardino Sheriff's Department he escorted her through security. They picked up their belongings on the other side of the X-ray machine and took the stairs instead of the elevator to the second floor and Homicide. As they walked through the sunny room, people glanced up from their work, but no one seemed overly curious.

Daniel's phone rang. He answered and thanked the person on the other end. Jan again. At his desk, he gestured for Reni to take a seat while he settled into a padded office chair, rolling closer to the monitor so he could begin typing, concentrating, all business.

His desk was sloppy, with stacks of papers, an overflowing in-box, Post-it notes everywhere. Time passed. Maybe fifteen minutes when neither of them said anything and he sat there clicking away, sending and receiving emails, Reni chewing nails she never chewed. At one point, she got a drink from the watercooler and sat back down. Daniel finally turned the monitor around so she could see a paused video.

"Using time stamps, the prison was able to pull up footage of the two visits." He hit the play button. As they watched, her father was led into a small room. Shortly afterward, as Reni waited to see herself on the screen, a young woman appeared and sat down across from Ben Fisher.

Carmel Cortez.

What the absolute hell? Bafflement warred with Reni's overwhelming relief at finding she wasn't losing her mind. She'd never visited Ben. No audio, but her father appeared surprised and upset. Of course he was. He'd been expecting his daughter. Carmel had been looking for something. Had she gotten too close?

"There you go," Daniel said. "She probably attempted to see him under her own name. He refused, so she forged an ID and pretended to be you. He took the bait."

"Did she visit before Maurice?"

"Yes."

"Interesting. Not sure if that means anything, but it might." Had Carmel's trick visit triggered Ben's desire to really see Reni, or was there more to it than that? She'd bet it was just a small piece of the story.

"Agree." Daniel opened a second file. Same setting and camera angle. This guest was Maurice.

Again no audio, but this one appeared to be an amicable visit. There was nodding and smiling, Maurice looking sympathetic. Seeing the two of them together was surreal. They'd been such good friends for so many years. Her throat tightened at the memories that surged forward of the good days, the days she'd thought were good until they weren't. It had almost been like having two fathers. And once Ben was gone, Maurice had stepped in, quickly replacing him.

Reni swallowed hard. "I didn't realize Maurice ever visited him," she managed to say. Why had he lied? So her mother wouldn't be upset?

Daniel glanced at her, concern in his eyes. He'd noticed her response. "The main thing is that we cleared you," he said.

It was oddly comforting to realize Daniel hadn't believed she'd been there when she herself hadn't been sure.

"While we're waiting on solid confirmation on the body," he said, "let's surprise Maurice with a visit."

Her thoughts exactly.

CHAPTER 22

"This was my life for so many years," Reni said as they turned onto her mother's palm-tree-lined street. She was talking about the carnival atmosphere. Media vans were parked in front of the house, even on the sidewalk. Yards were packed with reporters, some live broadcasting, others waiting for her mother to emerge from her home. Neighbors stood on front lawns, drinking coffee, talking to one another as they tried to figure out what was going on.

The area had changed over the years. Some residents had taken the opportunity to sell when housing prices exploded; others had simply died off, because Palm Springs was a popular retirement community. The changes meant many current inhabitants didn't even know about the events of thirty years ago. That was how it was in fluctuating towns. People came and went, ignorant of and uninterested in what was going on next door until the cops showed up. And Rosalind had been happy to have the story fade so she could reclaim her life. Now the nightmare and intrusion were starting all over again. Reni felt bad about that.

They were going in cold. Although the visit was to a family friend and they were just fishing for information, Daniel had favored no phone call or text beforehand. Reni agreed that an element of surprise could work in their favor. Not that she suspected Maurice of murder. He was too much of a gentle soul for that. But he might be able to shed light on some of the mystery. Or not. Just someone to check off their list.

Because of the crowd, they parked a block away and walked. As they closed in on their goal, the sidewalk became more crowded and a few people began to recognize Reni. Most were press who'd done their research before invading. A few of them recognized Daniel, too, and put it together.

A young man cut in front of them. No press badge, walking backward, holding his smartphone high. Maybe a YouTuber. It seemed everybody had a YouTube channel today. "Is there a connection between Benjamin Fisher's death and the body found in the desert?" he asked.

That hadn't taken long.

His heel caught on the uneven sidewalk.

"Careful!" Reni grabbed his arm, steadying him while Daniel told him to shut off his phone and gave him the regular spiel about waiting for the press conference.

Hardly missing a beat, the guy shifted his attention to Reni. "You're the daughter, right?"

She let go, smiled, and said nothing.

They reached the walk that led to Maurice's. "Don't follow us," Daniel told the young man.

The pretend reporter dropped back, then turned his phone around and began talking. "I just spoke with Detective Ellis and the Inland Empire Killer's daughter, Reni Fisher. They can't confirm anything at this point, but . . ."

His dialogue with his phone faded as Reni and Daniel put distance between them. "You're too nice to people," Daniel said.

"Not always." She thought about Carmel Cortez as she pressed the button next to the ornately carved door. Hopefully Maurice would look through the peephole and see it was them and not the press. If he was home. "I can be hard if I have to be, but I've learned it's better not to piss off the media. I've had some unflattering things written about me over the years. About how I was the one behind my father's behavior."

"I've seen that stuff. There will always be people who defend killers and psychopaths."

"I've never cared what the press said about me, but I know it bothered my mother."

"You were a child."

"Evil starts somewhere."

He made a sound of surprise, then said, "So you think an infant can be born evil?" He was looking at her a little too closely.

"I think an infant has the potential with the right guidance. Or wrong, I should say."

"What about genetically?"

"We don't have enough data. More studies need to be done, and of course that's almost impossible because studies need large numbers of participants. What are behavioral scientists going to do? Run an ad for serial killers and wait for the phone to start ringing?"

"I'm imagining the hook for the ad: 'Only serial killers need apply.'"

She rang the bell again. "Thanks."

"For what?"

"For not immediately thinking I was in on my father's recent plans."

The door opened a crack. When Maurice saw who it was, he widened the gap and told them to come in, locking the deadbolt behind them. Reni introduced Daniel.

"This is kind of déjà vu," Maurice said, gesturing to the people on the other side of the door. He was wearing cargo pants, a white V-neck T-shirt, and leather loafers. She was used to seeing him clean-shaven, but he had a little shadow today.

"They were there when I woke up this morning, and the crowd just keeps getting thicker. I told your mother to come over because I didn't want her dealing with this by herself. It brings back a lot of bad memories." He gave Reni a look of sympathy. "She should be here soon. Come on. I'll get you some coffee. Got great bread from the local bakery if you'd like toast." He checked his watch. "Oh hell. I thought it was still morning. Too much drama."

They followed Maurice through a living room of white walls, dark furniture, and artwork. His house had always felt safe to her. A refuge. She didn't know what she thought of it now that she knew he'd visited her father shortly before his death.

"I wouldn't mind a little something to eat and drink no matter what time it is," she said. He liked to take care of people, and feeding them made him happy.

In the kitchen, they sat down with coffee and freshly toasted bread. The table was vintage farmhouse, the chairs mid-century modern. Tile floor, a teal retro stove, and more art, along with plants. He loved his plants.

"You might have heard about the body found in the desert," Daniel said. "We have reason to believe the victim met with Ben not long before she went missing."

"Wow." He looked surprised. "But I don't understand what that has to do with me."

"We happen to know that you visited Ben a few days after this person."

Busted.

Maurice gave Reni an uncomfortable glance. "It's true. I did visit him sometimes. Your mother didn't know about it. I didn't want to upset her." He grew agitated, probably at the thought of letting her down. "She doesn't need to know, does she?"

Without answering his question, Daniel asked, "Did he say anything to you about his plans? About the bodies? About the woman who'd visited him?"

"No."

"What did you talk about?" Reni asked.

"He asked about you and your mother. He always did. Wanted to know how you were both doing. If you were married, if you were happy. He never asked much about me."

Poor Maurice. He was almost an active bystander in their lives.

"There's not a lot of common ground when you're talking to some-
one who's been in prison for so long," he continued, making excuses for
Ben's thoughtlessness. "So much has changed in the past thirty years.
I never stayed very long, but I don't know. I'm not sure why I went."
Maurice's lips trembled and his eyes glistened.

Unable to keep from comforting him the way he'd comforted her so
many times over the years, Reni gave his arm a squeeze. She understood
the pull her father had. And she'd never been sure who Maurice was the
most smitten with: her mother or Ben. Regardless, she didn't like that
Maurice had been sharing information with her father. They'd never
talked about her not wanting Ben to know anything about her life, but
discovering Maurice had been filling him in all these years made her
feel a little betrayed.

Daniel pulled out his phone and showed Maurice the headshot of
Carmel Cortez. "Have you ever seen this woman?"

Maurice leaned close, considered the image, and shook his head.
"No. I'm sorry."

A moment later they heard a sound at the kitchen door and
Rosalind stepped in.

Reni caught her up on what had happened. Daniel showed her the
photo of Carmel Cortez. Her response was different from Maurice's.

"Yes." She nodded. "I'm pretty sure she's the woman who showed
up at my house about a month ago. The one I told you about, Reni."

The timeline fit.

"She said she was working on a story. You know, like they always
do. I told her to leave. And I even spotted her following me a couple of
times. Once she showed up at the café when I was having coffee with
friends. I don't think it was a coincidence. But that's awful. I'm sorry
if the body ends up being her." She looked near tears. "I help young
women. If I'd had any idea she might be in danger . . . But you know
how it is, Reni. We have a knee-jerk reaction when somebody is sniffing
around for a story."

"Try not to let it get to you," Reni said. "I did the same thing. I slammed the door in her face." She was more forgiving of her mother's reaction to Carmel than her own.

Moving on, Daniel asked, "Any idea why Benjamin told me he'd had no visitors in months?"

"It could be he just wanted you to feel sorry for him," Reni said. "Which is pretty ridiculous for a cold-blooded killer."

Daniel received a text and pulled out his phone to read the message. "Excuse me." He typed a response, waited, read the reply, and his face drained of color. "We've got to go." No explanation.

They left through the front door. Outside, Daniel explained. "They found another body. I told them to hold the dig until we get there."

As Maurice locked the door behind them, Rosalind stood at the large living room window, to the side and in shadow, so reporters couldn't see her. She watched her daughter and the detective who looked too young to be a detective walk down the sidewalk. Reni, dressed in jeans and a white T-shirt, was tall and slender, with long legs she'd gotten from Rosalind's side of the family. Her stride was confident, and she held her head high with no ducking or attempting to hide her face. Her hair was in one thick braid down her back. Rosalind wished she'd let her cut it the other day.

Without taking her eyes off the two, watching them smoothly maneuver through the press, Rosalind spoke to Maurice, who was somewhere behind her in the room. "I don't like that she's working with a detective," she said. "And now here we are. Everything is happening again. I'm worried about Reni being thrown back into this. She's so fragile."

He came closer, looking outside along with her. "She's not that fragile."

"I always just wanted to keep her safe."

"I know. We both did. But Ben is dead now. I hope she can move forward."

"He's alive. In here." She tapped her head. "Ben is here with us whether we want him or not. We'll never be free."

She turned to look at him. Maurice. Sweet Maurice.

"Everything I've done has been for you and Reni," he said.

"I know."

"Do you ever think about what our lives would be like if we'd never met him?" Maurice asked.

"I do." She shook her head.

She and Maurice had been a couple in college when they met Ben. They both found him charming and hard to resist. He had a way of making a person feel like the only one who mattered to him, the only person in the room. And she discovered that she and Ben had many similarities. She thought she'd found her soul mate.

Maurice put a hand on her shoulder, and she reached for it, saying, "But then Reni wouldn't exist, so that's impossible to even consider."

He was quiet, too quiet, and finally said, "That might have been for the best, Rosalind. The two of them together were a toxic mix that should never have existed. You know that."

She was already struggling to keep her relationship with Reni stable. She didn't need his words undermining her work. "Don't ever, ever say that to me."

It was hard when your child wasn't like you. She'd confessed that to Maurice years ago and he'd been so sympathetic. When the child seemed like a stranger in your home. Reni had just been different. Rosalind had tried to be a good mother, but it had been hard. So the fact that Maurice had always loved Reni unconditionally was impressive and said a lot about his character. He was one of the people who didn't believe Reni was innocent, though he blamed Ben for everything that had happened. He felt Ben had warped and controlled her and turned her into a mirror image of himself. And yet Maurice protected her and lied for her and loved her just the same. Rosalind adored him for that.

"All those young girls might still be alive today if not for Reni," Maurice reminded her gently.

Maurice's take on the events that had unfolded years ago might have been skewed, but what he said about Reni was true. She'd been Ben's muse. And they'd both had dark tendencies.

CHAPTER 23

San Bernardino County was the largest county in the contiguous United States, which meant policing was a challenge and getting from point A to point B was time-consuming. Daniel employed lights but no siren in the unmarked black sedan. Driving over the speed limit, taking dirt roads too fast, they were able to make it to the site in a little over two hours. Reni had never come close to covering that expanse so quickly.

As they crested the plateau where Bird Rock, as she'd begun calling it in her head, was located, she noted the scene looked even more like an archaeological dig today. Additional tents had been erected, and generators were humming obnoxiously. More vehicles. More of the area had been marked with small yellow flags that fluttered in the strong wind. She'd been so fixated on the giant rocks last time that she'd missed the high population of Joshua trees. They were scattered everywhere. And this new body? Did it have anything to do with her father? Would it be another fairly fresh kill?

Daniel was out of the vehicle first, practically diving. Without a glance in her direction, he moved rapidly toward a group of people clustered in the distance under the shade of a brown tarp.

The crime-scene specialist from yesterday spotted them, caught up, and walked them the rest of the way to the gravesite. "We've been waiting to transport." He sounded annoyed. "I don't know why you detectives have to be here for every little thing."

Daniel didn't respond. He was focused on the ground and the rectangular grave. On the opposite side of the hole was a zipped bag. It was easy to see a body was already inside.

"You've bagged her," Daniel said. "I told you to wait."

"I saw no reason to," the specialist said. "Sun's going down. Everybody's hot and tired, and we're trying to get done before dark." He crouched and unzipped the bag.

People stepped closer. Some pulled out cameras. Someone else was writing in a tablet, probably noting time of day and position and what had been done and not done on-site.

"It's like a mummy," someone whispered.

Yes. Mummified flesh over bones.

Human. Female. Just skin over a skull, dark teeth that seemed too big, hair long and brown. Nude. This victim had been in the ground a lot longer than a few weeks. Reni's legs threatened to buckle. Was it out of relief after all the years of searching? Or fear that she might recognize the person?

Someone was crying. A woman who had a crime podcast. Probably unused to seeing the real thing. Maybe she'd volunteered to help with the search. No, it wasn't all fun and games. Reni had to look away.

The sky was pink, the smooth, giant boulders casting long shadows the way they did in the evening, the Joshua trees silhouetted like people standing guard over the dead woman. Above them, a bird circled and screeched, wings black against the sky.

The beauty of the moment brought calm, and Reni immediately wondered how she could possibly capture it. On canvas, in clay, in her heart that was swelling right now. Why did people do that? Want to replicate the beauty that was in front of them? It made no sense. *Enjoy it for what it is; don't try to re-create it.* Had her father said that?

Along with her awareness of the contrast of the corpse against the surreal and breathtaking landscape came an unexpected and unwelcome rush of feelings for her father as she remembered his love of the desert and nature.

He hadn't brought the bodies here to hide them. He'd brought them here to share the magic, to leave them in a special place. At least in his own twisted mind. Because, as law enforcement had pointed out over the years and Daniel just recently, it would have been easier to dispose of them closer to home.

"What about the dress?" Daniel asked, his voice tight. "You mentioned a dress."

"It's already in an evidence bag."

"I want to see it."

"It's sealed."

"I want to see it."

"You'll have to break and re-sign the chain-of-custody label."

"Fine."

Someone handed him a pair of gloves and a paper bag. He slipped on the gloves, tore the bag's label open, and pulled out a dress. Red with a small floral print. Faded and dirty, darker stains that were most likely blood. Daniel held it high and the dress fluttered against the setting sun, the fabric itself almost seeming a part of the landscape.

As the dress moved in the wind, dirt fell. "You could be losing evidence," Reni said quietly. Hair. Fibers. Odd and sloppy behavior for a detective.

With a jolt of awareness, Daniel put the dress back in the bag, closed the seal, signed his name, and passed it to the person in charge of evidence. Woodenly he turned away, but not before Reni heard him let out a sound not unlike a sob.

She glanced at the others, unsure of what she'd just witnessed. A few of them seemed perplexed as well, but most didn't appear to have noticed. They looked exhausted; they probably just wanted to get a meal and take a shower and go to bed.

Daniel was a cop. He was used to dead bodies, and this body didn't even really look like anything that disturbing. No putrefaction. More like paper and leather. Maybe he too felt the power of the moment, the kiss of the desert and the hushed magic. And yet . . .

She watched him stumble away to vanish behind a tent.

CHAPTER 24

Daniel stood behind a tent, bent over, hands on his knees, breathing shallowly, trying not to faint. *Don't have a meltdown,* he told himself. It might not even be her.

But the hair. The dress.

It was impossible to know if the fabric was a match. He'd have to present his scrap to Forensics to get their conclusion. He'd been flying under the radar thus far, and the idea of sharing information about his past with people he worked with made him feel a different kind of ill. Too much coming at him at once.

When he was little, he'd imagined finding her living in a basement somewhere, or locked in an attic. But alive. Always alive. He'd storm the stairs and break down the door and rescue her. But as he got older, and once he became a detective, he knew enough about missing people to know the odds weren't good. Not good at all. His expectations changed and redirected. As the years passed, he gradually went from hoping to find her alive to hoping to find her body.

Like all the families of the Inland Empire Killer's victims, he wanted closure, but after thirty years he'd begun to accept that it would never happen. Then Fisher reached out to him, and Daniel started to hope again. For at least a body.

But in his mind, this new hope had involved digging and finding his mother in her red dress and the makeup he'd watched her apply. And in his fantasy, she'd look peaceful. And he'd finally have his closure. Even though he of all people knew better and knew what a person dead for decades would look like, his mind had never allowed him to go there. In his dreams, waking and sleeping, she'd always been beautiful. Not shrunken and dehydrated, every drop of moisture sucked from her body by the arid surroundings and the sand that had covered her. He'd also never imagined all the people at the scene. And her nudity. Something about her being buried naked, the dress included as a hasty and insulting afterthought, had knocked the wind out of him because it told a tale he didn't want to hear.

He understood that a lot of what he was thinking didn't come from the brain of an adult. It was residual, and he was plugged right into young Danny. Which would always be the foundation of the emotions he felt when he thought of his mother and what had possibly happened to her. It made no difference that he was a cop now. An adult now. He thought of her with the heart of a child.

He heard soft footsteps, then Reni's voice, quiet, concerned. "You okay? Can I get you something?"

Without trying to straighten or look at her because he still felt light-headed, he lied and said, "I just had a little too much sun. That can creep up on you." He didn't feel comfortable telling her what was going on, especially here, with twenty people not far away. Very few knew his past. That was one of the good things about being adopted. When his name changed, he'd shed that outward identity even though he'd remained the same person inside.

Reni ducked into the tent and returned to his side, uncapped a water bottle, and handed it to him. "Certain cases can really get to a person."

His hand shook as he accepted the bottle. After drinking half of it, he decided to move farther from the dig site. He needed to sit down. He needed physical distance. Off the road a short way, he scaled a cluster of boulders and stared at the place where the sun had vanished. Reni joined him. Without speaking, he offered her the bottled water. She took a drink and passed it back.

They sat in silence for a time, conversation drifting from the dig site, enough for him to understand they wanted to wrap up for the night.

"I've had a hard time forgiving myself," she said.

"For what?"

"For helping my father."

"You were just as much a victim as the girls he killed."

"Thank you. Logically I know that's true, but it doesn't matter. I was there. If that's one of his victims, she might still be alive today if I hadn't helped trap her, trick her. And I think the method is what weighs so heavy on my conscience. These women, who might normally have been resistant to a stranger, responded to me. Responded to a child in need. And I don't think I'll ever be able to accept that or put it in the place it needs to be. It defines me. It's my identity. And the only way I have of making the pain stop even for a while is to keep looking for the young women in order to bring them back home." She paused. "I guess I'm saying I understand some of your emotions. You've been researching this case for so long that it feels a part of you. And when you actually find a body, it's overwhelming."

She'd filled in the blanks as best she could, and he appreciated her attempt to try to understand what was going on with him even though she didn't know the story.

It had gotten darker while they were talking. They climbed down the rock and headed back to the dig site, where the bag had been zipped and tagged and was being carried to a waiting van which would take it to the San Bernardino County medical examiner's office. They had a forensic anthropologist on staff who was an expert on remains that had been in the desert for months or even years.

"I appreciate your sharing," Daniel said. It couldn't have been easy. She was either honestly responding to his unspoken pain, or she was the sociopath some thought her to be.

CHAPTER 25

"I don't know about you," Reni said as they headed back to San Bernardino, "but I need something to eat."

She didn't really. She could go without food for a long time when engaged in a case, and she often forgot to eat. But what had happened out there in the desert with Daniel still hung heavy in the air. Riding together in the dark, the twin headlight beams cutting down the barren highway, hadn't opened him up. She was hoping some food and maybe a drink would help. He was in pain, and she responded to that. It broke through walls today and it had broken through walls when she was a child, going all the way back to the first person she remembered trying to save even when she thought they were playing the game, a woman named Cathy Baker. And though she was her father's daughter, she knew that deep empathetic response separated her from him. She found that a comfort in a sea of things that felt too bleak to shine a light on.

They stopped at a popular roadside bar in Joshua Tree. It was late and they had the place mostly to themselves. They took a booth in a dark corner and ordered tacos, coffee, and beer.

The food came, and Daniel took a few bites before going pale, grabbing his glass of beer, and drinking deeply. Then he sat there at the table, forearms framing the plate, hands clenched.

"Have you ever heard the name Alice Vargas?" he finally asked.

She thought a moment. "I don't think so. Should I have?"

"She went missing over thirty years ago."

"And you think the woman in the desert might be her?"

"Maybe." He leaned to the side, pulled out his billfold, retrieved an old photo, and handed it to her.

It was of a dark-haired young woman standing in front of a door. She wore a red dress, the fabric very similar to the dress from earlier today.

"The missing woman," she said.

"Yes."

As she suspected early on, he had more skin in this game than he'd been willing to share. And here we had it. Someone he'd known. But she didn't have the full story. "I still don't get it."

"I thought you might remember her."

"Alice Vargas." She spoke the name aloud, trying to recall.

Like a magician, he produced something else, a small scrap of fabric. He placed it between them on the table. Red with pink flowers. Brighter than the fabric they'd seen at the crime scene, but similar.

She could feel a dark cloud creeping over her brain, closing things off, protecting her. "Where did you get this?" she managed to ask while at the same time wanting to get up and run away, cover her ears, not hear his words.

"It belonged to Alice. We've never been sure if she was abducted by your father. He wasn't the only person working that area of California at the time. We know other serial killers were abducting women. And she could also have been one of the people who voluntarily vanish every year in California." He swallowed. The mask was gone from his face, and he suddenly looked as vulnerable as a child.

The fabric, the dress, and the woman's face seemed slightly familiar. He was watching her closely, waiting for a reaction, his eyes glistening, begging her to put it together so he didn't have to explain more.

Had Reni seen this woman before? The women her father abducted all blurred together, many sweet faces in similar settings.

How does this dress look on me?

"You shouldn't carry evidence with you," she said.

"It's not evidence." He repositioned it on the table, next to the photo. "Look at it again. Look at the woman in the picture."

What was his connection to her? They didn't have the same last name. A family friend? A relative? "I don't know . . ."

"The reason I have this photo, and this fabric, is because I helped make the dress the woman is wearing."

His words were a punch to the stomach.

Yes, a woman, hurrying down a park path, looking upset. She was crying. So pretty though, with dark hair. Did she crouch in front of Reni and ask if she was okay? The fabric of the dress, the hand on her arm, the lamplight, the darkness Reni pointed to, a darkness where her father was lurking. *Come find me.* The woman took Reni's tiny hand and together they walked into the woods.

How does this dress look on me?

"The woman in the photo is my mother," Daniel said.

She could hear the pain behind his words, words she'd forced him to speak because she'd needed the story to go a different direction. Now it was Reni's turn to feel sick. "Not the same last name," Reni insisted, not wanting to believe any of it.

"I was adopted after her disappearance." His voice sounded far away.

With a roar in her ears, her vision narrowing, Reni tossed bills on the table and left the bar. Outside, she leaned against the side of the building, inhaling the night sky as she braced her hands against her knees. She finally straightened to look up at the blurry stars.

A door slammed and Daniel was there, silent, hands in his pockets, probably holding that scrap of fabric, waiting for her to say something.

What if the body from the desert *was* his mother?

This was too close, too real. Until moments ago, the missing women had been almost mythical. Hazy, tragic beauties who had no families. In her head, when she'd pictured them, she'd never given any of them children. Now one of the children stood next to her, increasing the level of sin she must atone for. Instead of knocking her back, she felt a stronger sense of resolve, and her need to find all the bodies increased.

Yet under that was a nagging memory that vanished whenever she tried to examine it too closely.

How does this dress look on me?

CHAPTER 26

Thirty-one years earlier

"You have to stop this. Right now," Daniel's foster mother said. "No more talk of someone harming us. That's not going to happen. We know your mother was going through a rough time, and we also know she was prone to irrational behavior."

She was upset because he sometimes asked if his mother's date would come and take his foster family away. Or maybe their dog. Or his foster sister. It scared her. "Who said that about my mother?" he asked.

"I don't remember." She shrugged. "It's just something I heard or read."

"Was it a neighbor? A cop?"

"Drop it. You're frightening the other children. We've even had complaints from the school. You're scaring your sister. And you're making the whole house uneasy. I want a peaceful environment here, and you're disrupting it. You were very young, and you've imagined a lot of things that didn't happen the way they really happened. It's very possible that someday your mother will show up and apologize for leaving you. It was an awful thing for her to do, but right now you have a home and people who care about you. So no more talk about your past or solving your mother's case. There is no case. I'm sorry, honey."

His foster family cared about him, and they wanted the best for him. They were good people, as the caseworker liked to say, but they didn't love him like his mother had loved him.

Daniel made a zipping motion with his hand in front of his mouth. This was what she needed from him. A promise to shut up.

As time passed, he replayed her words in his head and wondered if she was right. He *had* been little, and memories from that period were confusing and getting fuzzier all the time. But one day he was home by himself, lying on the floor in the living room doing homework in front of the TV, when someone on the news said something about the arrest of a guy called the Inland Empire Killer.

"This is a person who has preyed upon young women and eluded law enforcement for years until one of his victims escaped and reported the attack," the person on television said. "He claims to have killed close to twenty women over a period of years. But at this point, only two bodies have been found."

Daniel stared at the black-and-white photo of a man who didn't look like a killer. He was thin, with glasses and short hair. And a tie. He was wearing a bow tie. Daniel didn't know killers wore bow ties.

The news shifted to another story, and Daniel abandoned his homework to search the stacks of old newspapers his foster parents used to start fires in the fireplace. In the papers he found more about the killer. He had a name. Benjamin Wayne Fisher. The police believed his killings went back several years.

Why hadn't anybody told him about this?

He got out the phone book and called the local police station. He told them he might have solved a case, but the woman who answered wouldn't let him talk to a detective. He hung up and went back to the phone book and looked up *private investigator*. He chose a business that said it specialized in missing persons cases. He bundled the newspapers, stuck them in a big envelope, and caught a bus to the address he'd found in the listing.

The receptionist was an older woman with a lot of big jewelry. She wasn't mean like the person on the phone. "Sure, come on." She led him down a hall. Without knocking, she opened a door and pushed Daniel into the room, announcing, "Bo, this boy thinks he's solved a cold case."

Unlike guys on TV, the detective wasn't young or handsome. He said goodbye into a clunky beige phone, hung up, and leaned back in his chair, hands behind his head. He was older than Daniel's foster father, closer to grandpa age, balding on the top, and with a belly that stretched his white dress shirt tight.

"That right?" he asked. "You wanna be a detective? Because I've got a lot of cold cases that need to be solved."

They were making fun of him.

"I said I *might* have solved it. And I don't want to be a detective. I want *you* to be the detective."

"My fee is one hundred and fifty dollars an hour, plus expenses. How does that sound to you?"

"I'm looking for someone to take my case *pro bono*." He'd seen that in a movie.

The man laughed.

"You've been talking about hiring an intern," the receptionist said. They were still making fun of him.

"How old are you, kid?"

"Eleven."

"I'd call that babysitting. I never had such a young assistant, I can tell you that. Have I, Mirna?"

"Nope. Never."

The detective motioned to the manila envelope under Daniel's arm. "Let's see what you got."

Daniel pulled the newspaper clippings out and placed them on the desk. Mirna indicated he should take a seat in a thick wooden chair. He did. After a moment, he dug into the back pocket of his jeans for the photo of his mother he'd taken the night she vanished. He placed it on top of the clippings. From another pocket, he produced a scrap of red fabric with pink flowers. "I think my mother was kidnapped by the Inland Empire Killer, and I want you to find her."

CHAPTER 27

The night of Daniel's shocking revelation about his mother, Reni slept in her truck. She could have gone to her mother's, but so many things went along with that. The house. The press camped outside. Her mother's need to mother. Reni could have driven from San Bernardino to the desert, but her cabin was an hour away. Too tired. She probably could have stayed at Daniel's if she'd brought it up. Didn't like to ask for favors. She could have gotten a room somewhere, but she was exhausted and broke and every one of those things seemed harder than doing nothing. So she'd ended up grabbing snacks and toiletries from a gas station and parking in a discount store lot to spend the night in her truck.

It wasn't that bad. The truck was old, with a wide and flat bench seat. With her knees bent and a coat under her head, she was able to get in a few restless hours of sleep, though what little sleep she managed to get was often interrupted by chirping birds. Interesting fact: Living in the city changed the biological clocks of birds. City birds got less sleep than rural birds.

When she wasn't asleep, she used her phone to dig up more about Daniel's mother. She was unable to find much due to lack of press coverage and how long ago the events had taken place. When day broke, Reni drove to the nearest library, waited for it to open, and began searching their archives, loading plastic reels into a microfilm machine.

Still very little information. An article about Alice Vargas's disappearance. A murky copy of the photo Daniel had shown her, plus another that could have been taken at the same time, this one of Daniel standing in front of his mother, her hands on his small shoulders.

How does this dress look on me?

In the photo, they both appeared happy. Daniel, with his deep dark eyes, had the face of a child wise beyond his years. Not a lot of investigating seemed to have gone into the case. That was a typical problem when people went missing, especially adults, especially single women. Neighbors helped search for Alice for a while, then the household belongings were auctioned off, and the house, a rental, was re-rented. Daniel went into foster care.

Reni fed quarters into the machine, and a nearby copier spit out copies of the articles, along with an image of Alice Vargas. If Reni had anything to do with her disappearance that night, maybe the photo would eventually spark a memory.

While at the library, she took the opportunity to use the restroom, brushing her teeth with the toothbrush and toothpaste she'd picked up from the gas station. She examined herself in the mirror, noting the circles under her eyes and a few wrinkles she swore hadn't been there a week ago. Her mother might have been right about her hair. She looked like someone who didn't give a shit. Still, she made an effort to not look as if she'd slept in her truck. She finger-combed and re-braided her hair, then washed her face, drying it with a brown paper towel that was as rough as a grocery bag.

Outside, the sky was deep blue and the morning air had that California crispness. The touch of it made her aware of how tight and crawly her skin was from two nights of little sleep. It also served as a reminder to drink more of the water she'd picked up at the station. California could suck the juice right out of you before you knew it even happened.

Despite everything going on, the coolness of the morning still managed to foreshadow change around the corner. *This is not what the world will be like in two hours. This day will turn into something else that will feel completely different.*

It was still early, and she hadn't yet heard from Daniel, so she found a coffee shop that looked like something from the sixties, a retro style that was popular in the area right now. It had a vintage sign outside that promised and lived up to the turquoise padded booths inside. Gold light fixtures emulating stars dangled from the ceiling. It almost felt decadent to be there so early in the day. The throwback ended with the healthy menu. No greasy heart attacks on a platter here. Everything was organic and locally sourced. Even the coffee, when it arrived, tasted healthy.

Health.

It *definitely* wasn't something she thought about.

As she sipped freshly squeezed orange juice and ate a warmed slice of banana avocado bread, she went over the articles she'd printed at the library, looking for similarities or differences that might indicate errors.

Seeing the photo of Daniel and his mother combined with scents of coffee and breakfast must have triggered some brain cells. A sleeping neuron awoke and fired. The elusive memory came creeping back . . .

"How does this dress look on me?" her mother asked as Reni and her father sat at the breakfast table, Reni so small her legs dangled and her feet didn't touch the floor.

"Pretty," Reni said, cereal spoon in her hand.

Her father's face turned white. "Take that off."

"Why?" Reni's mother spun around in front of the refrigerator, then posed like a magazine model, head back, hand on her hip.

"Where did you get that?" he asked.

"I found it in your office. I thought maybe you left it there for me."

"Take it off right now!"

"You can be such a drag."

Sitting in the coffee shop, Reni tried to keep the memory from slipping away. She replayed it in her head. Had it really happened? Had her father left a victim's dress in the house? Was that why later, once he'd been arrested, they'd never found any trophies? Had the occurrence with the dress driven him to be more careful? None of it made sense. The dress had been found *with the body*.

She was lost in thought when she received the anticipated text from Daniel.

I'm heading to the coroner's office to observe the autopsy of the body from the desert.

She stared at her screen a moment in disbelief, recalling how adamant he'd been when she'd thought to observe her father's autopsy.

She replied: *No you aren't.*

He answered with a question mark.

Wait for me. I'm just a few minutes away. Clarifying her stance, she added: *You aren't going to the autopsy of someone who might be your mother.*

She left a tip and tucked the articles into her bag. She was almost out the door when she retraced her steps and wrapped the remaining bread in a napkin, then headed for her truck.

On the way to the coroner's office, she called her mother to ask about the dress.

"I have a vague memory of that morning and your father getting upset."

Thinking about her grandfather and his violent behavior, Reni had to ask: "Did he ever hit you?"

"Your father? No! Never! Why are you asking about the dress?" Her voice was full of confused concern.

"Don't share this with Maurice, because we haven't released the information to the public." And Maurice could be a gossip sometimes. "We might have found the dress you were wearing that morning in the kitchen. It was buried with a body you'll be hearing more about soon."

Her mother let out a gasp. "You mean I might have been wearing the dress of one of Ben's victims? That is truly horrifying. Just when we thought he couldn't get more evil."

CHAPTER 28

If a person were to look up the word *mummy* in the dictionary, the first definition would be about the Egyptian process of mummification. It might even go into detail about the removal of organs, the use of cedar oil and beeswax resin and spices and sawdust, and later cloth wrappings. But the word *mummy* also meant a body that had been preserved and dried naturally, like the one on the stainless-steel table, the light above so bright it exposed everything and created a scene of very few shadows.

Minutes earlier, Reni had managed to talk Daniel into staying away from the autopsy suite. It hadn't been as hard as she'd expected. He'd agreed to let her stand in for him and report back while he spent time in another area of the building, trying to track down someone named Fritz who specialized in fabric.

In the suite, the first thing Reni noticed as she approached the table was the missing hand.

"Did the body arrive this way?" she asked.

Evangeline seemed happy to explain. "The hand was too dried out to extract prints in its current condition, but there are several techniques we can use to revive flesh. My favorite, and the one I've had the most success with, is soaking the fingers in embalming fluid. If you know anything about embalming fluid, you'll also know there are many kinds. I've tested enough different brands and formulas to have a favorite. Anyway, this morning I cut off the hand and it's now soaking in the solution." She pointed to a labeled jar on a nearby shelf. A dark shriveled hand floated inside a creamy solution.

Reni was glad Daniel wasn't in the room. "How long before you can get a print?"

"*Maybe* get a print. And time can vary. It typically takes one to three days. If we wait any longer, the skin expands too much and we won't be able to lift anything. That can happen no matter what," she warned. "But we have another hand to work with if we fail the first time."

Yay? "What about age of the victim and how long the body was in the ground?"

"X-rays put her between twenty and forty. Hopefully I can narrow that down more, but I think it's best to see if we get a print match and go from there."

"I agree."

"We also have some new and amazing ways to extract DNA from many things: skin, even fabric. One is called the wet-vacuum method. As far as time in the ground, I'll be bringing in our specialist to help determine that. And again, if we get a print match, I'm not sure we'll even need to pursue it further."

"Cause of death?"

"That, I can answer. Blunt-force trauma to the head. I'd guess it was caused by a strike against a hard surface. Like a rock or even cement. We sometimes see this kind of injury with falls of a great distance."

Reni flashed on her childhood and a scene she preferred to keep locked up tight. Her father holding a young woman by the front of her shirt and slamming her head against the ground. *None of it's real, little bird. She's an actor. The blood is fake.*

"I'll pass the information to Daniel," Reni said tonelessly as she moved toward the door.

"One more thing."

Reni paused in her escape.

"I'm sorry about your dad and what happened to you."

The comment came from a good place, yet Reni inwardly flinched. "Thank you."

"I have to tell you one of the reasons I went into this field was because of your father and all the press about him when I was a kid. My parents were glued to the television, and I became a little obsessed myself. I feel weird sharing since we're talking about your life, but I wanted you to know."

"Thanks for telling me." Interesting what a reach Ben Fisher had and continued to have. Did Evangeline know about Daniel? It didn't seem like it. Did anybody in the department know?

Reni and Daniel were adults now, both carrying deep wounds, his just as deep as hers. Some might argue she'd also lost someone, her father, but it wasn't the same. Regardless of what they discovered about this woman on the table, if she was or wasn't his mother, he'd still lived with the daily thought that she might have been killed by a monster.

"We all have our ways of dealing with evil," Reni said before quietly leaving the suite.

In another brightly lit room with white walls and white counters and white lab coats, she caught up with Daniel. He'd found Fritz, who was at that moment comparing a small piece of the dress found in the desert to the piece Daniel had pulled from his pocket last night. Maybe it was because she knew the story now, but she sensed a quiet desperation in him.

"We don't see this kind of material anymore," Fritz said. "It's a cotton and polyester blend. The print carries through to both sides, which makes it hard to tell which was intended as the outside of the garment. But when you examine it under the microscope, it's easy. Want to have a look?" Remaining in his chair, he rolled away from the counter.

Reni stepped forward, tucked a stray strand of hair behind her ear, put an eye against the microscope, and blinked the sample into focus. The fibers went bright, and the difference in the threads within one single piece was noticeable. The two scraps didn't look identical to her untrained eye, but they were similar.

She straightened. "They don't look exactly the same to me."

Fritz nodded. "That's because they aren't."

She noticed Daniel relax beside her. If the fabric didn't match, he wouldn't have to deal with his emotions today.

"They don't look the same because they haven't lived the same life," Fritz continued. "One has been buried underground for decades. The other, oddly enough, shows more wear, yet the color is brighter."

Last night Reni had assumed Daniel brought the cloth to the desert because of the investigation. Now she wondered if he'd carried it in his pocket for years.

"So, same fabric?" Daniel asked. "Or not the same?"

"You know how fabric is printed in runs? No? Well, it is. Not only is it the same, but I'm going to guess it's from the same run."

Beside her, Daniel stiffened, and beads of perspiration popped out on his upper lip. His face went so pale she could see freckles on the bridge of his nose.

She turned him toward the door and gave him a gentle shove. "Go get a drink of water."

With no argument, he stumbled from the room. Unwilling to share information that wasn't hers to share, she made light of his behavior and sudden departure. "He's not feeling well today," she told Fritz.

"I trust the visual match," he said, still caught up in the fabric. "But I'm going to run an XPS to pull up the chemical signature of both pieces." He was talking about an X-ray technique that could reveal the chemical makeup of fibers. "I'll contact Daniel when I have the results."

She said something about good work and caught up with Daniel in the hallway. He looked a little better already.

"So that's it," he said.

"Not really." Understandably, he wasn't thinking straight. They'd need more than a fabric match. "Not a hundred percent." Without going into detail about the hand in the embalming fluid, she said, "Let's wait to see what Evangeline finds out. We need prints or DNA to make a definitive call."

His phone rang. He checked the screen and answered, his side of the conversation giving no hint as to what it was about. When he disconnected, he said, "Confirmation on the first body. It *is* Carmel Cortez."

No surprise, but it highlighted the big question: How was this connected to her father? "We'd better contact next of kin." She realized she was talking as if she were in charge. She corrected. "Or whatever you think our next step should be."

He nodded. Right now, after the semi-confirmation he'd just gotten, he looked shaken. One or two mental-health days would have been advisable, but a detective didn't always have that luxury.

"And another press conference," he said, doing a good job of pulling himself together and staying on track. "Once we're done with that, I want to visit Cortez's place of employment and see what she was working on at the time of her disappearance. It could give us clues about her death. And I'd like to get there as quickly as possible. Once the story breaks it'll be hard to get interviews. The press will be all over this."

"I'd suggest her home too," Reni said. Know the victim, know the killer.

CHAPTER 29

Back at Headquarters, Daniel and Reni learned that Carmel was single and didn't have family in the area. Her parents lived in El Paso, Texas. Daniel always tried to break the news of a loss face-to-face. Hearing of a loved one's death was never easy, but he felt delivering that news in person allowed for supportive interaction if needed. But in a case like this, when distance was an issue, Daniel was left with no option but to cold-call.

He was straightforward in his sharing of information with Carmel's mother. She wailed and her voice became faint. From his end, it sounded as if she'd abandoned the phone. He remained connected. A man finally picked up and began speaking, asking if this was a joke. Daniel assured him it wasn't and relayed the circumstances as sympathetically as possible.

"We haven't heard from her in a few weeks," the man said. "But she disappears sometimes. We've even reported her missing in the past, and boy did she get mad about that. So we learned not to say anything. She always shows back up." A sob escaped him before he could clamp down on it.

Daniel gave him a moment to compose himself, then said, "I'd like to ask you some questions, but I can call back if you need some time."

"No. Let's talk. Because I want to find out who did this to my little girl."

Daniel asked about Carmel's friends, relationships, any people who might have wanted to harm her, anybody she was afraid of, but the father didn't supply any obvious red flags. He'd already portrayed a somewhat-estranged relationship, and his lack of knowledge supported that. But her place of employment and her address were confirmed.

"Did she ever say anything to you about Benjamin Fisher?"

"The Inland Empire Killer? No, why would she?"

"She visited him in prison."

"She was a journalist and was into true crime stories. Podcasts, TV, all of it. I think she really hoped to write a book one day, and she wanted to break a case. My daughter had her problems, but she was a good girl. And she was good at whatever she set her mind to."

Daniel thanked him for the information. "And again, I'm sorry for your loss."

"Find who did this."

Carmel had worked for a small newspaper called *Inland Empire Free Press*. It was located in the town of Rancho Cucamonga, thirty minutes from Homicide and still within San Bernardino County. Outside the sheriff's department, he and Reni got in his SUV and took 210 west to Highway 66.

Rancho Cucamonga was one of those small cities that sometimes made the list of best places to live. Earthquakes aside, the weather was favorable and the setting beautiful, nestled as it was in the foothills of the San Gabriel Mountains.

Inside the two-story brick newspaper building, through security and a metal detector, Daniel flashed his badge and asked to talk to Carmel's supervisor. The girl at the desk went pale. The homicide report must have reached them already. News outlets had some serious channels, and it wasn't unusual for them to get stories before the cops.

They were shown down a hall into a private office, where they sat in sturdy chairs with black leather seats.

"I'm sorry to hear about Carmel," the editor in chief said from the other side of her desk. "That's why you're here, right?"

"What can you tell us about her?" Daniel asked.

"She was a good reporter, but she wasn't happy here. She quit about six weeks ago."

Daniel and Reni looked at each other in surprise. "Can you go into more detail?" Daniel asked.

The woman's take on Carmel corroborated what the girl's father had said. "She came here from LA. We were a real step down for her. She wanted to be big-time," the woman said. "What she really wanted was to be an investigative reporter. We talked about it, but we don't even do that anymore. I told her we're a small paper and we don't have the budget for that kind of thing. We installed security after someone got shot here a year ago, and that wiped out our funds. She knew it, so I don't know why she was so insistent. Like I said, she was an excellent reporter, and I did understand her frustration over being sent to cover local campaigns and school fundraisers. And I'm sorry she's dead."

"Do you know if she had an interest in a specific subject? Did she want to investigate anything in particular?" Reni asked.

"I can't even remember the idea she pitched," the editor said. "I was in a hurry that day, preparing for a conference call. I think I stopped her before she got very far." She wrote down phone numbers of coworkers for them, and then they were back outside in Daniel's vehicle. With the AC running, he made a call, arranging to be met by the building manager at the apartment where Carmel had lived. "We should be there in about thirty minutes," Daniel told him.

Upon arrival, Reni noted that the building was typical of California, with two rows of one-story apartments, front doors facing each other, a sidewalk down the center, and a low stucco wall surrounding the grounds. Something that would have rented for very little in another state, but was probably more than most single people could afford even in a town forty miles from LA. It seemed like everybody had to have a side hustle just to survive anymore. Carmel's side hustle might have been a story about the Inland Empire Killer.

The apartment manager met them in his office located at one corner of the complex. It was a little like an old motel lobby, leaving Reni to wonder if the place had actually been a motel at one time. It had an unintentional retro look about it, with a pegboard on the wall that held keys.

The manager was a small wiry man with a dark mustache and so much energy it was possible he was getting some "medicinal" help.

"Why didn't you report her missing?" Daniel asked.

"You kidding? If I reported everybody who skipped out on rent, that would be almost half the people here. She was two months behind, and I'd already issued an eviction notice. Then she just took off and never came back." He shrugged. "That's what they do."

"Did you ever know her to have trouble with anyone?" Reni asked. Dropping back into the role of investigator felt natural to her. "Fights? Anybody suspicious hanging around?"

"I don't pay attention to what the tenants do. I mind my own business. But I will tell you, she never caused problems. Nobody ever called the cops on her. Nothing like that. I'm sorry she's dead." He shook his head. "I've been here twenty years. People die. We had one person killed, but nothing of this level. And like I said, she seemed like a sweet kid. Just having a hard time, like most of us."

"Can we see her apartment?" Daniel asked.

"It's rented to someone else now. The current resident isn't home, and I would need her permission to get inside. Anyway, there's nothing to see. All of Carmel's stuff is gone and the apartment was scheduled for painting and new carpet, so I had that done before the new tenant moved in. I'm not sure what you'd find."

"What happened to her belongings?" Daniel asked.

"They went where they always go—to a storage facility a few blocks from here. I store it for a year, and if the person doesn't come back, I sell it. I've only had one person return, and the sale of the junk I drag out is never enough to make up what I'm owed."

"We aren't concerned about that," Daniel assured him. "But we'd like to see her things."

"No problem." The manager grabbed a set of keys and gave them the location. "Lock up and bring these back when you're done."

Reni asked for the apartment number. "I'd like to look around the grounds before leaving," she said.

Outside, she and Daniel walked down the sidewalk. Apartment 6 was located at one end of the complex. Some kind of flowers climbed a trellis. A faded turquoise door. Reni took a couple of photos, then walked around the building to the parking lot. They both took pictures of the back entrance. Nothing jumped out at her. No gouges in the wood around the door or windows.

"The fresh paint and new carpet are suspicious," Daniel said.

"I agree, but it's also something done with rentals."

The storage facility was easy to find. Another sad place, rows upon rows of low metal structures, each with its own garage-style door. A city lot of metal and concrete, along with the requisite broken glass that caught the sunlight. They found the unit they were looking for and unlocked it, pushing the door to the ceiling. A blast of heat hit them in the face.

The usual household belongings. Stacked furniture, lamps, framed art, and boxes, all labeled with the occupant's name and apartment number. Because of the heat, they arranged a couple of chairs in a patch of shade just inside the unit and began going through boxes.

"Nothing like digging through someone's dark life," Reni said.

She opened her fourth box. This one looked promising. A couple of minutes in, she had what they were looking for. Worn files dated thirty years ago and labeled "Inland Empire Killer." She passed a file to Daniel, and together they went through the stack. "These can't have been hers," Reni said. "She was too young."

Daniel found a name on a file and Googled it. "The reporter worked at *Inland Empire Free Press*. Died a few years ago. Carmel must have found his research files."

"And maybe decided to do some investigating of her own?"

"That's my guess. Tried to present the idea to her boss and was turned down."

"And explored it anyway."

"Maybe. If so, she might have found something. But what?"

"And did it have anything to do with her death?"

"This should be logged in as evidence," he said. "I suggest we both go back to Headquarters and go through the rest there."

They loaded the four boxes, each one weighing about twenty pounds, each one given a chain-of-custody form that Daniel attached and signed from the evidence-gathering supplies in his SUV. Reni locked the padlock on the storage unit, and they returned the key to the manager, along with their contact information.

"I thought of something while you were gone," the manager said. "When I told her she was going to be evicted, she said not to worry. That she'd be able to pay me back and even pay for several months in advance."

Reni and Daniel exchanged looks. Money was often a big motivator. "Did she give you any clue where this money was coming from?" Reni asked. If she was on the trail of some new evidence related to Ben Fisher, she might have been hoping to sell an Inland Empire Killer piece to a major news outlet, or even get a book deal.

"Maybe an inheritance." He shrugged. "Drug money. I dunno. Again, I don't ask. Not my business." He thought a moment and it seemed he might be trying to decide if he should share something else. "Another thing. You aren't the first to come here looking for her. There was a man who showed up a few weeks ago. Said he was an FBI agent. Like you, he wanted inside. But he didn't have any ID, seemed shady, so I didn't tell him anything."

Daniel settled his sunglasses on top of his head, and Reni could see he was as surprised by this new information as she was. "Name?"

"Don't remember. I'm not sure he even gave me a name."

"Description?"

"White dude in a suit." He looked at Daniel. "Kinda dressed like you, but older."

"What about security cameras?" Reni asked. "Do you use cloud storage or an SD card?"

"I don't know about any of that stuff. I'm just the manager here. You're going to have to talk to my boss."

Daniel got the boss's phone number. Outside, he called Jan in Research and passed the information to her. "Even if he still has access to footage that old, he might not just hand it over," he said. "We might need a subpoena."

Back at Headquarters, the building strangely quiet due to the late hour, Reni and Daniel carried the boxes inside and unloaded them on a table in a meeting room. Sitting across from each other, they began going through Carmel's files. Daniel ordered food and coffee to be delivered to the building. As they worked into the night, they fell into a rhythm that was often silent, with occasional theories tossed back and forth as they continued their archaeological dig.

Newspaper clippings of missing women. Articles about a body found in a park. And then stuff about Reni herself, along with grade-school photos and an ancient picture of her taken on the sidewalk in front of her house, clinging to her mother's hand as they hurried to the car, trying to avoid the press. So strange to see herself as a child, in the aftermath Ben Fisher had condemned them to. She was surprised to find that her heart wasn't pounding and she wasn't shaking. In many ways, it was like looking at someone else's life. That seemed like a good sign. Or was she in denial just like Rosalind?

At one point, Daniel asked, "How you holding up? Should we call it a night?"

She checked the clock. Three a.m. She wasn't driving home now and would probably spend the remainder of the night in her truck again. She might as well stay where she was.

"I'd rather finish," she told him. "We have one box to go." But he looked wiped out, hollow-eyed and needing a shave. Tie and suit jacket abandoned long ago. It had been a rough twenty-four hours for him. "Go home," she said with sympathy. "I'll finish."

"I'll just grab thirty minutes in the break room."

He probably didn't want to leave her with the evidence. She didn't blame him.

Maybe it was being alone, or maybe it was that point when the night began to feel a little more like the next day, but Reni began having trouble staying awake herself. She settled down on the carpeted floor, back to the wall, and closed her eyes. A little later she awoke with a jerk, disoriented, wondering where she was. Seeking caffeine, she drank what was left of her coffee, not caring that it was cold, and tackled the last box.

It proved to be more informative and personal than the previous ones, and she wished Daniel hadn't left so she could share the eureka moment with him.

The files, with their soft, worn edges, were composed of the deceased male journalist's personal notes and interviews. Also inside was a small case filled with mini-cassette tapes, the kind reporters once used for interviews, all labeled and dated. The typed notes were transcripts of the audio recordings. She was impressed by the thoroughness of the research. This kind of in-depth investigating wasn't seen that often today, not in this new world of short attention spans.

Had Carmel stolen the interviews in hopes of breaking a story of her own? More likely she felt she was salvaging them, because from what they'd learned at the newspaper, no one at *Inland Empire Free Press* cared about the old research.

The interviews were with the families of missing persons, and with people who might or might not have seen something on the nights various women disappeared. When Reni reached the bottom and spotted a name written in black Sharpie on a file tab, her hand froze.

Gabby Sutton.

The only person to survive one of Ben Fisher's attacks. And she not only survived, she escaped and identified him.

Reni sat there a moment, took a deep breath, and opened the file.

There were a lot of handwritten notes on the transcripts, many pointing to a theory that had been tossed around before. A theory that now, with the discovery of Carmel Cortez's body, seemed worth considering.

The possibility of a second killer.

Highlighted in the interview with Gabby Sutton was actual mention of another person at the scene. Not a child, not Reni, but an adult.

Why hadn't that information been pursued or made public?

Reni opened the browser on her phone, searched for Gabby's address, and found she still lived in California. She called Daniel and woke him up.

"We're going to need to talk to Gabby Sutton," she told him.

CHAPTER 30

Gabby pulled the curtain aside a crack, enough to watch for Reni Fisher to arrive, uneasy at the thought of finally meeting the person who'd saved her life that night in the park. So many times she'd replayed the attack in her head, revising it as the years passed. Her own scream of terror, the killer's hands at her throat, the moment she thought she recognized him as a past instructor, the surprise on his face when he recognized her too. Those were the things she could never forget. His hesitation, enough for her to struggle and kick him. She remembered fading and coming back. A child screaming.

"Daddy, stop! You're hurting her!"

That same child jumping on her father's back in her cute pajamas as she struggled valiantly to pull him off Gabby. She was like a bug that couldn't be shaken.

Even today, Gabby sometimes heard the child's scream. Usually in her dreams, but occasionally the sound would return full-blown when she was awake, emerging from something familiar. Like a flock of seabirds lifting and settling on a grocery store parking lot, their call turning into a high-pitched scream. Those kinds of unnerving occurrences almost always ended Gabby's plans for the day. She'd have to return home, take a sleeping pill, and crawl into bed.

The night of her attack, Ben Fisher had tried to shake the child off, but the little girl had clung to him, her tiny arms around his throat as she sobbed, begging him to stop.

Gabby had heard stories about how Reni Fisher had been complicit, how none of her father's attacks would have happened if not for her. Gabby didn't believe that. The child had saved her life. And she'd never seen her again. Not in person anyway. She knew about her becoming an FBI agent and a fairly famous profiler. And even about her more recent shift from police work to artist. She'd almost bought one of her clay bowls through her website but had been afraid Reni would recognize the customer name.

She'd never thanked her for saving her life.

Today would be her opportunity.

Gabby's memory was murkier when it came to what happened after Ben Fisher let go. Maybe due to the lack of oxygen. She went from the near-death of being choked to having his weight gone, his hands no longer squeezing her throat, father and daughter absent. Then faces appeared, asking if she needed help. The child's screaming had attracted others. Someone in a car wanted to know if she needed a ride to the hospital, but Gabby had scrambled away, running blindly down the jogging path toward her dorm room, trying to yell as she went. Her mouth was open, but barely a sound squeaked out. Her vocal cords were injured.

Even at the time, she knew she'd just escaped the Inland Empire Killer. And she knew his face and name. It was a lot to take in.

Now, as she watched from her house, two people got out of an SUV. A tall man in a dark suit and a woman with straight dark hair dressed in jeans and a black jacket. The smooth shine of her hair had caught Gabby's attention that night in the park too. She remembered it falling forward over the child's face as she tugged at her father's arms.

It felt like somebody else's memory, which was why she'd initially said she couldn't talk to them. She'd been trying to put it away for decades. Years of therapy had made no difference. Facing it . . . no. It hadn't worked for her. Living her life had helped as much as anything.

This reminder didn't belong here, and they certainly didn't belong in her house. But to meet them out in public would have been awful too.

The doorbell rang.

She hadn't told anybody they were coming. She didn't plan to tell her husband or kids. Now that they were here, she thought about not answering, thought about dropping to her knees and crawling past the window to the back of the house. Maybe run all the way to the ocean, which was thirty miles away. Salt water was healing.

Instead she took a deep breath, and opened the door wide.

The two visitors stood there in the California sunlight, the scent of orange blossoms in the air, flowers from the house across the street becoming extremely important, invading Gabby's field of vision, calming her as long as she stared at them.

She might have smiled. She did invite them in. All the way to the kitchen, where more sunshine poured through the skylight and bounced off the white tile floors and white cabinets. So brilliant, so unlike the darkness of that night.

It took her a moment to realize the man had said something, she didn't know what. He pulled out a small digital recorder and placed it on the table.

The woman's hair was so long and dark and shiny. Not black, not *that* dark, but it still reminded Gabby of a blackbird's wing. She was pretty in an unexpected and almost accidental way. Tan, a real tan, the kind outdoor people had. Joggers and hikers and surfers. She didn't look like a surfer. Gabby swam in the ocean, but she didn't hike or jog anymore. No trails or parks for her.

The woman's eyes were really blue. Surprising. Gabby would have expected brown with that hair color. Maybe she wore contacts. No, that didn't seem likely. She gave off the aura of being unaware of how she looked. Gabby understood how a person reached that point.

"Do you mind if I record our conversation?" the man asked. Had he said his name was Daniel? That seemed right.

171

"That's fine," she told him with a strained smile. "Did I ask if you wanted anything to drink?" Her voice was steady but her heart was slamming, and she was still thinking about the ocean. It was roaring right now in her ears. She imagined running into it, the water splashing to her waist. Then she'd make a shallow dive and start swimming.

"We're okay," the man said.

Had the woman spoken at all? Reni Fisher. Gabby had this idea that when she opened her mouth, she'd shriek, *"Daddy, stop! You're hurting her!"*

Instead, the woman turned to her partner and said, in a low and very normal voice, "Could you leave us alone for a few moments?" Then she looked through the patio doors—a green hummingbird was visiting a feeder. "Maybe you could take your recorder and go outside for just a bit."

He didn't like her suggestion. Gabby could tell. But the woman nodded and gave him a look, a silent communication that he responded to by picking up the recorder and slipping out the door. Frightened, the hummingbird darted away.

Gabby and the woman watched Daniel move away too, rolling his shoulders and taking a little stroll as if to demonstrate his removal from the situation. Gabby almost wished he hadn't left because now she was alone with the woman with the bird-wing hair. Now she was forced to look at her and converse with her.

"Would you like some tea, maybe?" Gabby asked. Had she asked that already? "Or coffee?"

"Water would be great."

"Oh. Yes. I can do that." Water was easy.

The woman actually helped her get the glasses and pour from a pitcher. They both took long drinks.

"I got these glasses in Palm Springs at a vintage shop," Gabby said. She liked bright things, and they had bright, happy flowers on them.

"They're lovely."

They put the glasses down.

"I've thought about you a lot over the years," Gabby finally said. They were both standing awkwardly near the sink. Maybe Reni was waiting to be invited to sit down.

"Can I give you a hug?" Gabby asked.

The words were unexpected, and they both seemed surprised by them. One minute Gabby had wanted to run. The next, weird words were coming out of her mouth. But she could see Reni understood. They were connected in a way two people should never be connected.

Reni opened her arms wide, and Gabby walked into them. And those arms felt strong and sure, no longer the arms of a small child. The bird-wing hair was just as silky as Gabby had imagined. With her own arms wrapped around the woman, her new friend, they clung to each other for maybe a full minute before breaking apart. And when Gabby looked into Reni's eyes this time, those blue eyes were shiny with tears.

Gabby finally spoke the words. "Thank you." She could see this was as hard for Reni as it was for her. Maybe harder. If she hadn't been so consumed by her own fears, she might have noticed that immediately. Reni wanted to run too. Maybe not to the ocean, but maybe somewhere else where the sun burned hot and turned her skin a deep brown.

"Not for saving my life," Gabby said. "Well, yes, that, but thank you for being so brave and strong, thank you for doing what was right even when you were afraid yourself."

"I feel like I know you." Reni put a hand over her own heart. "Right here. Like you've been living here most of my life. Since that night."

"I think I have."

The detective, Daniel, had found a lounge chair and was sitting quietly, so quietly that the hummingbird had returned and was putting on a show at the feeder. These were good people.

She almost hated to break the spell, but her husband would be coming home in another couple of hours, and they needed to get down to business.

"You wanted to talk to me," she said. Ten minutes ago, she hadn't been ready, thought she'd never be ready, but she was ready now and anxious to begin.

Daniel returned and all of them sat down at the table. It was still blindingly bright in the kitchen, but now the brilliance of it felt more like a promise than a warning.

"I heard about your father," Gabby said. "About what happened to him. And I'm sorry." Not sorry he was dead. Oh, hell no.

"Thanks," Reni said. She seemed to understand what Gabby meant.

Why, she loved him, Gabby thought. After all this. And the strange thing was, Gabby kind of did too. He'd been her psychology professor. All the girls had liked him, all the girls had crushes on him. Just the way it was. Just the way things were back then.

After the attack, when she'd run back to her dorm, nobody believed her. Some even accused her of provoking the encounter. Some said she was lying to get him in trouble. But then she showed them the bruises on her throat, and fear went screaming through the building. They all knew about the Inland Empire Killer.

The professor was arrested at his home a few hours later.

Gabby had always wondered about Reni. What had happened to her after Gabby ran away? Had she gotten in trouble? What kind of punishment did a man like that inflict upon his child? Had she been home when the police came to get him?

Reni and Daniel asked her a lot of questions, all of them ones she'd been asked in the past. But then the conversation turned, and they brought up the topic of the presence of another person.

"In all my research," Daniel said, "I've never heard this theory. But we've come across some old files belonging to an investigative reporter.

In his notes, he claims to have talked to you, and you mentioned a second adult. Do you remember anything about that?"

There were things about that night that were as clear today as they'd been hours after the attack. But there were other things that were fuzzy. And some memories were no longer there at all. Just gaps. Like getting from the park to her dorm. No memory of that. She suspected her brain had built a scar around that night, and she might never have access to those memories again. "I don't remember."

"It's unusual," Reni said. "Especially since nobody else has mentioned it. It didn't come up in any other reports we've read."

"What about you?" Gabby asked. "Do you remember anybody?"

"I don't. But I wasn't there the entire time." She seemed uncomfortable again. Gabby reached across the table and gave Reni's hand a reassuring squeeze. So strange to be touching when an hour ago she hadn't even wanted to be in the same room with her.

"My job was to stop you and leave," Reni said in a strained voice. "I always went back to the car, where I was supposed to put my head down and cover my ears. But I heard you scream."

"And you got out of the car and ran to help."

"I'm not sure if I ran. And I've never said this before, but there were other times when I heard screams and didn't help."

Poor thing. She was suffering too.

"It's okay," Daniel said. Gabby could see he was worried about Reni.

They talked a little more, but Gabby didn't have anything new to tell them. She wanted to help, wished she could help. That would give her purpose. She understood the urge eyewitnesses had to make things up. She wouldn't do that.

"I think we've bothered you enough." Daniel pulled out a business card and put it on the table. "Call if you happen to think of anything. Sometimes a conversation like this will trigger old memories."

That was what she'd been afraid of. She didn't tell him she remembered Reni's yellow pajamas with ducks on them. She'd never forgotten those, but that wasn't anything they needed to know. Back when she'd contemplated having children of her own, she'd thought about those pajamas and almost decided not to have kids. But she had them, a boy and a girl, and they were grown now, living elsewhere, mostly untouched by what had happened to their mother before they were born.

Reni found a pen, turned the card over, and jotted down a number. "My cell," she said. "Call me about anything. Doesn't have to be about this at all. Maybe a movie you just saw. A book you read. We could even meet for coffee or lunch."

They were in a sisterhood. "You mean like friends?" Gabby didn't really have any friends. That was one of the things the attack had changed about her life. At one time, she'd been popular and fun and one of those girls everybody wanted to hang out with. But after . . . no.

"Yes."

Daniel was watching in silence, and Gabby got the idea he was surprised by the exchange. She picked up the card. She didn't want her husband to see Reni. She didn't know if she wanted to see or talk to either Reni or Daniel again. She suspected once they were gone and some time had passed, she would re-bury everything in that very shallow grave.

"I've found creating has helped me a lot," Reni said. "I make pottery now."

"I almost bought something from your online shop," Gabby confessed. "But then I imagined you filling out the address label and seeing my name, so I didn't complete the order."

"I'll make you something. A design just for you. What colors do you like?"

"Blue. Teal. Like the ocean and the sky. And that would be wonderful." She could already imagine it sitting on a shelf in the living room.

What would she say if her husband asked about it? That she'd gotten it from a gallery. No need to mention Reni. After the way he'd acted the other night when she'd found out about Benjamin Fisher's death, he didn't deserve to know.

Gabby told them goodbye and stood at the front door as they got in the car and pulled away. Thirty minutes later, her husband came home from work. He poured two glasses of wine and they sat on the patio. The hummingbird came. He told her about his day, but she didn't tell him about hers.

CHAPTER 31

In Daniel's vehicle, heading back to San Bernardino, Reni replayed their visit with Gabby in her head. She was shocked and a little horrified at her reaction to the woman her father had almost killed. She'd dreaded the meeting and had expected to feel deep shame. Instead, she'd been overwhelmingly drawn to her. The kinship she'd felt had been overpowering. Horrifying, because it was a moment when she'd felt her tenuous control beginning to slip.

"I didn't expect to be able to relate to her," Reni said. Seeing Gabby had also triggered her own memories of that night.

Her father hadn't been mad at her. In fact, she couldn't recall a time when he'd ever been mad at her, really mad. There was the rock drawing, but even his reaction that day had been mild, his chill attitude possibly due to an inability to feel strong emotions of any kind. When they returned home, he'd put her to bed the way he always did, kissed her goodnight, and told her he loved her.

"Relating to her makes sense to me," Daniel said. They were caught in stop-and-go traffic, a string of red taillights in front of them, yet he appeared unruffled. Under normal conditions, the drive should have taken less than an hour. Not tonight.

"You both suffered at the hand of the same person," he said. "Just in different ways."

"I used to think my inability to recall events and details was because I was a kid, and kids get things confused and have trouble with memories," she said. "But I think Gabby and I have both blocked a lot of our past."

"How do you feel now about the second-adult scenario since she has no memory of someone? Do you think there was another person involved?"

"We've got a murdered journalist. Even if there wasn't another person that night, somebody might be trying to cover something up. I will say, I think it's important to keep Gabby's name from the media even though it's been thirty years. I doubt she's in danger, but someone might begin to worry that she has information."

"Agree." His phone rang. The caller's ringtone was a familiar melody she couldn't quite place. Some old song. Leonard Cohen, maybe.

He answered. Only hearing one side of the conversation, she could still easily tell the caller wanted to know when he'd be home for dinner. She was impressed with the way Daniel had been able to compartmentalize the discovery of his mother's body, but she also knew how something like that could hit hard once a person put the day aside. She was glad he wouldn't be alone tonight.

"Pizza, right?" he asked. After a pause, he told the caller he'd be home as quickly as he could, then hung up. "When'd you last eat?" he asked Reni.

It took time to remember. Had it been the food Daniel had ordered when they were going through Carmel's boxes?

"Come to my house to eat."

"I'm fine." She just wanted to go to her cabin.

"It'll take another thirty minutes to get back to the department and your vehicle. Let's just stop at my place on the way. Traffic will be better later. Seems logical."

She didn't like the idea of dropping into someone's home and having to make small talk over a meal. It was unsettling. Twice now his partner had called him about dinner. She was picturing a conventional family. People she could in no way relate to. The idea of enduring that kind of situation, with not even a car as an escape, gave her a stomachache.

"Just drop me off somewhere. I can catch a cab or Uber."

"Come on. We're trying this new diet that's supposed to be super healthy. I'll bet you could use a healthy meal. Do you like homemade pizza?"

"Yes."

"Well, then I guarantee you won't like this. Because the crust will be undercooked and the toppings will be things like Brussels sprouts and tofu."

"That sounds horrible."

"It is."

"And you want me to come and help you eat this horrible concoction?"

"That's right. Suffer together."

Now she was picturing a young wife, no kids in the house, maybe a boisterous dog.

She *was* hungry. Even soggy crust and soft tofu sounded good.

His house ended up being a modest one-story stucco located south of the 210 on a cozy street not far from the airport. A couple of palm trees out front, along with various kinds of cacti she spotted in the headlights as they turned into a breezeway carport that allowed them to enter the home through a side door, dumping them right into the kitchen, no foyer where a person could take a breath to ready themselves. Standing there, spatula in hand and white apron around his waist, was a gray-haired older gentleman, no young wife in sight, the table set for two.

"You didn't tell me you were bringing a guest." The man's voice was rough, maybe a smoker, although she didn't smell evidence of that. Previous smoker, then. And the lack of welcome had her congratulating her initial reaction to the dinner invitation. She didn't belong here, and it wasn't good to mix life with work. But was that her excuse and not the real problem? The feel of this space—the coziness, the warmth, the welcoming and safe vibe—hit her in the gut like nothing else she'd dealt with in the past few days. She could brace herself, prepare herself for familiar locations and familiar scents and crime-scene photos of her father's victims and snapshots of herself as a child enduring the aftermath of Ben's destruction. Those had been surprisingly easy for her to come face-to-face with. But there were moments like this that should have been easy and straightforward, moments that took her breath away and almost kicked her legs out from under her.

"I'm not staying," Reni assured the man, ready to turn and head right back out the door. "I'm going to call an Uber."

"Stay." Daniel slid his laptop case down on the counter and tossed his jacket over a chair. "This is Reni Fisher," he told the grumpy guy. To Reni, he said, "This is my father, ex–private investigator Bo Ellis."

CHAPTER 32

It turned out Bo was actually a softly packaged grump. He talked Reni into staying while Daniel set another place, scooped salad from the two bowls into a third, and got out another wine glass.

The pizza wasn't nearly as bad as Daniel had predicted. Maybe because she had such a poor diet and anything healthy seemed gourmet. It had goat cheese and basil. Fresh tomatoes. She was impressed. And thankfully the conversation was fairly neutral even though Bo had to know who she was. No questions about her father; nothing was said about Daniel's mother. And oddly enough, after her initial panic, she relaxed and found herself lulled by the space and the company. And she wondered if she'd ever had anything like this in her life, even before Ben Fisher's arrest. Hadn't there always been an undercurrent of something when the three of them sat at the table together? Her desire to please, her father's desire to be entertaining, her mother's boredom with them both.

When they were done eating, Daniel excused himself. "I'm going to check the department database for any updates."

With everything that had happened, she'd almost forgotten he was waiting on lab results that could prove the body in the desert belonged to his mother.

Reni helped Bo clear the table.

"I've been trying to get Daniel to eat better, so he doesn't end up like me," he said. "Most detectives have poor diets."

"You look pretty healthy."

"I'm fine now, but I had a heart attack a while back. Daniel insisted I move in with him. Packed me and my things up and brought me here. He's a good guy. A little strange, a little intense. I was a private investigator with a pretty decent business when he came walking in one day and told me he needed my help to find his mother. He was eleven."

"Gutsy."

"Right. I took him under my wing, and later adopted him. Me, a bachelor who'd never wanted kids. It was the best decision I ever made. He's mellowed a little over the years, but he's tough, loyal. And once he gets something in his head, he doesn't let it go. Which can be good or bad."

"His mother?"

"Yeah. I hate that finding her has become a life obsession. I really think it's why his marriage fell apart. He was never totally plugged in."

She was looking for some indication that her father might not have killed Daniel's mother. She didn't know if she could handle that much reality. "Do you think the Inland Empire Killer did it?" Even though Bo knew who she was, it was much easier to talk about her father as if he were a myth and not someone she'd known personally.

"I'm not at all sure, and that's the shame of it. Daniel has put so much of his focus on your father's case that it honestly might have distracted him from more likely suspects. Which is what I meant when I said he can't let something go."

Bo must not have known about the newest body. It wasn't for her to tell him.

"So he spent years looking for her?" she asked.

"Her disappearance informed his life. He became a detective because of her. So he could search and keep searching."

When they were done cleaning up the kitchen, Bo announced he was going to bed. "Not to sleep," he clarified. "I like to watch comfort TV in comfort."

"What's your favorite?"

"Baking shows."

Delightful.

Bo left and Reni began to wonder if Daniel was ever returning. He'd been gone quite a while. Maybe he'd fallen asleep. After the last few days, she could forgive him for that. She was about to call an Uber when he appeared in the kitchen doorway, his face ashen, his hair wet with perspiration. Without speaking, he motioned for her to follow him.

In a dark office down a short hall off the kitchen, he pointed to a chair positioned in front of a desk and glowing monitor. She sat down and recognized the sheriff's department logo in the corner of the screen. Daniel had logged into their database to view the most recent autopsy report on Jane Doe. Standing to one side, his hand on the back of her chair, he pointed to a specific area of the screen.

Print match.

Apparently Evangeline's technique for recovering prints from a mummified body had worked. The file contained several fingerprint images, new and old. Near the bottom of the second page was a head-shot of a woman. Below it, her name.

The astounding result? Jane Doe wasn't Daniel's mother. Jane Doe's name was Hanna Birch.

"I ran her through our missing persons database." His voice was tight. "She vanished about six months after my mother. Same general area."

"I don't understand." Reni looked up at him. "What about the dress? The fabric was a match." Wrapped up in a bafflement that echoed Daniel's was the selfish knowledge that she'd been granted a reprieve. For now at least, she might not have been behind whatever had happened to his mother.

"I don't know, but a twenty-point fingerprint match can't be disputed."

"True." Her mind changed directions. Why was the victim buried with his mother's dress? If it had been an off-the-rack design, she might be able to convince herself that two people had bought the same one. But this was handmade. So another dress had either been made with the same fabric, which was possible, or it was the same dress.

"Maybe they can extract DNA from the fabric," she said. "Evangeline was talking about a new wet-vacuum method."

"That was my first thought too. It's a long shot, and I honestly don't know if I can get funding approval, but I'm going to try."

Her heart went out to Daniel. There would be no closure for him, not yet. "I'm sorry."

"I've spent the past twenty-four hours trying to come to terms with my mother's death, even though it wasn't a surprise. I'm a detective. I know how these things typically turn out. I guess the good news is that she could still be alive." He didn't sound convinced. Reni wasn't either, but she made a sound of agreement.

"Bo doesn't know about any of this, does he?"

"He knows about the recent body found in the desert, but I haven't had a chance to tell him about the dress, which, as things turned out, was for the best."

"It would still be good if you could talk to someone about it."

"I'm talking to you."

That made her feel both honored and uneasy. She didn't know how much comfort she could give anyone. "As we know, kids don't see things clearly sometimes," she said softly. "My reality, the reality of my childhood, was false for the most part. My memories aren't accurate. And adult memories aren't accurate either. As detectives, we know how much memory changes between field memory and distant memory. Emotional memory and logical memory. But I can still feel the love I had for my father and the man he never really was. And that love is real even though I want to deny it."

So much time had passed since his mother had vanished. It could be hard to find, but she'd like to get her hands on character testimonies and neighbor interviews. Maybe bank records. Had she been in debt? New behavior patterns.

"Your love for your mother and her love for you were real," she said. "Are real. And when we take our age and mix it with innocent emotions and the superheroes of our lives who happened to be our parents, things get really confusing."

He took a deep breath and nodded. "I know, but I can't stop searching for answers. The results were so unexpected." His face was pale. "I keep thinking about the dress. Did Benjamin Fisher save it to put it with another victim?"

"My father wasn't known to collect trophies." Daniel knew that. But it was possible he'd had a trophy stash they'd never found. And all this was assuming Daniel's mother had actually met Benjamin Fisher. She decided to tell him about the memory of her mother in the dress.

"It might not even be real recall," she warned once she'd related the story.

"Actually, it could explain some things. He saved my mother's dress, your mother put it on, he freaked, and then buried it with the next victim."

"That could be it. I'm sorry." She'd still like to do some digging of her own. And she would. Once they got to the bottom of the Carmel Cortez murder.

"Suppose your memory is false," he said. "How else could my mother's dress have ended up with another of Fisher's victims?"

"Maybe your mother knew this victim. Maybe they were friends."

"I'll research that. See if I can find a connection. Talk to her family, if possible. Now that the FBI is involved, I expect them to make the initial contact." He looked ready to drop.

"Right now, as impossible as it seems, you need to get some sleep," she said. "I'll call a cab for myself."

He pulled a set of keys from his pocket. With a clatter, he placed them on the desk in front of her. "Take my vehicle."

"You sure?"

"I'll catch a cab to Headquarters tomorrow and meet you there."

"I'll swing by here and pick you up."

She left.

The day had been full of welcome and unwelcome surprises.

Now she had his keys and was getting into his SUV, with plans to pick him up in the morning. It was beginning to sound like a partnership, which was something she didn't think she'd ever wanted again. Next thing, he'd be morphing into Ben Fisher and she'd be trying to kill him.

CHAPTER 33

A call woke her.

Reni had made it back to her home in the desert, showered, and fallen into bed. Now, only half-awake, eyes closed, she mumbled a hello into her phone.

"I had a dream," the caller said.

It took Reni a moment to recognize Gabby Sutton's voice. Once she did, she sat up and turned on the lamp.

"It might not mean anything, but your visit has my brain spinning."

She was whispering, and Reni imagined her hiding somewhere, maybe a bathroom or the patio so she could talk without waking her husband.

"I dreamed about that night," Gabby said. "The night of the attack. You were in the dream. You were an adult, but everything else was the same. I remember thinking it wasn't really happening because you were a grown-up and not a kid. You know how dreams are, how they're half-real and half-nonsense. But anyway, there was someone else there. A second person. Someone who yelled and told you to come back to the car."

Dreams weren't memories. Dreams were often an unconscious need to work through something, and Gabby had a lot to work through. Reni was trying to figure out how to tell her to go back to sleep, when she shared information that made Reni's heart race.

"The man was crying. He said something about breaking his heart. And he called you Little Bird. No, Little Wren. That was it. In the dream I thought he meant *wren* with a *W*, but maybe it was a shortened version of your name."

Being a very logic-driven child, the nickname had annoyed Reni. She'd pointed out many times that her name didn't have a *W* in it.

"I don't know if it means anything," Gabby said, still unaware of the impact she was having.

Reni got out of bed and tugged a hooded sweatshirt over the T-shirt she'd slept in, awkwardly swapping the phone from one hand to the other as she dressed.

"Also, after you left, I started wondering if I'm in danger," Gabby said. "Do you think I should be concerned? Is my family at risk? I haven't told my husband about your visit, but maybe I should."

That said a lot about Gabby's relationship with her husband, and Reni felt bad that such a traumatic day hadn't been shared. "It might be wise to talk to him." She also understood the need to build a protective wall around yourself.

"I've always tried hard to keep my past from touching this life."

Gabby was giving her the saintly version of the story. Abuse came wrapped in different packages, and indifference to a partner's pain was one of them. "It's already impacting this life just by having happened," Reni said gently. "And I think everybody in your family should be vigilant. Just aware, that's all I'm saying. The only way you'll be in danger is if someone thinks you know something. And nobody has come after you in all these years. We'll keep this confidential, and we'll keep your name out of the press," she promised. "Of course, take typical precautions. Set your security alarm. Don't park in unlit areas. Don't walk alone after dark."

"I haven't done those things since that night."

Reni was getting a glimpse of Gabby's painful world since the attack. She wasn't sure how she would have dealt with the aftermath, although until recently she'd made it a point to step into her fear and not turn her back on it.

"Sorry to wake you."

"Never worry about that."

They disconnected and Reni moved barefoot through her house, the concrete floor cold on her feet, just another thing she took comfort in. Cold concrete. She passed her pottery shelves, the bowls and cups dry and ready for the kiln. It seemed months since she'd thrown them, but it hadn't been that long ago. In the kitchen, she made a cup of tea and took it outside, where she sat on a metal spring chair she'd picked up at a swap meet. It had a seat that bounced gently if you chose to go that route and activate it with a push.

Wondering if Gabby had heard of the nickname somehow, she tucked her feet under her, pulling her sweatshirt over her bare knees, cradling one of her own mug designs in her hands as she tried to recall details of that night, this time including the information Gabby had just supplied. It was no help. But there was a Milky Way above her head and a pack of coyotes howling in the distance. More comforts.

Feeling calmer just being home, she took a sip of tea and considered calling Daniel with this new information, but decided to send him a text message he could ignore or sleep through, telling him to call when he woke up.

He called immediately.

"Is that some kind of white-noise coyote app?" he asked. "I like the rain one, but that seems a little distracting."

"You really need to spend more time in the desert. It's real coyotes."

"I'm sure I'd enjoy being surrounded by what sounds like fiends from hell."

She laughed, then told him about Gabby's phone call.

"I hate to say it," he said, "but dreams mean nothing. I think you're both grasping."

She would have thought the same thing if she'd been him.

"There's no telling where the information that hits our dream state comes from," he continued. "She might have seen something on TV before she went to bed, or our visit could have been enough to produce a new narrative. I tend to think dreams are mainly our subconscious trying to make sense of the day we just had. I've never once had a dream re-create real life."

He was basically paraphrasing Reni's earlier thoughts. "Ordinarily I would agree with you about most of that. But there's only one person who's ever called me Little Wren." Maurice, who'd been there for them through everything. Birthdays, holidays, everything. Maybe he'd been there for Ben Fisher too.

CHAPTER 34

Stragglers were still hanging around on the street the following morning when Daniel and Reni visited Maurice. The crowd was made up of media and residents alike, but for the most part the scene felt and looked like the carnival had packed up and moved to the next town. Reporters didn't linger the way they used to, especially if they weren't getting an exclusive. It was all about the mad scramble to break a story to the people swiping fingers across their phone screens.

Reni rang the doorbell.

She found it near impossible to think her beloved family friend and neighbor might have somehow been involved in the events that had taken place years ago. But Gabby's information, combined with discovering that Maurice had frequently visited her father in prison, in secret, made things look bad for him. And cast more serious doubt on everything connected to her childhood.

She and Daniel had already decided she'd be the one to introduce their reason for being there. They hoped Maurice would be more responsive to her. Once inside and seated in the kitchen like last time, she got to the point. "We want to go over the events that took place the day my father was arrested." Words she'd never have expected to speak to Maurice, especially now. What a strange and newly unsettling turn this was taking.

Always a great host, Maurice placed cups of coffee in front of them. His hand shook. "Thirty years later?"

"We have new information that might be relevant to the case," Daniel explained. "We just want to go over events again to see if everything still tracks."

"I can't remember where I was last week, let alone that long ago."

"It was a special night," Daniel reminded him. "Your neighbor was arrested. I'd think something like that would stick in your mind. Like when we think of big events in history."

Maurice lowered himself into a chair. His hair was wet. He tended to take a lot of showers, and right now he smelled like aftershave. It was a scent she remembered from childhood. Her father had worn it too.

"We went to an art opening," he said. "All three of us. You went too," he told Reni. "The artist was someone from San Francisco who made sculptures out of felt. We thought it would be okay for you to go, but when we got there, we found out most of the art was of genitalia."

"I remember an art show, but not the felt sculptures."

"Something to at least be thankful for. Your mother, being ahead of her time and the bohemian feminist she was and still is, thought it was fine for you to be there, but it made me and your father uncomfortable. I think you and I hung around in an area with food and drinks while your parents took in the exhibit rooms. I probably imbibed a little too much. Then we all went home. It was an early evening. I always wondered how that night would have ended if the exhibit had been something you could have enjoyed too."

He might not have realized it, but blame was once again being put on her.

"That would have been an early night for you," she said. "Did you go anywhere later?"

"In those days I could cram a lot into a single day," he admitted. "But I just went home. Like I said, I'd had a little too much to drink at the art show. I drank too much back then in general. Part of my identity, I thought. I had to give it up when my liver started protesting."

Reni remembered. "The morning after my father was taken away, you came over," she said, hoping to ease him into revelations while at the same time aching and hoping he had some logical explanation she hadn't thought of. "My mother was hysterical, but you were so calm, and helped get us through it all. You answered the phone and dealt with reporters and the sympathy flowers that began arriving." Oddly enough, that memory was a good one.

His eyes welled up. "We've shared some tough times."

"The attack would have taken place after you returned from the art opening," Daniel said, circling back. "Do you remember anything that stood out about coming home? Did you all ride together? Was Ben acting strange?"

"Ben drove. And I didn't notice anything odd about him."

"Did he drop you off at your house?"

"I think he parked in the driveway and I just walked across the lawn, but my memory is fuzzy. I think Rosalind asked if I wanted to come in for a drink, but I don't think I did. Sorry. I can't give you any more information."

Without endangering Gabby, Daniel twisted the story. Not a lie, but an implication that another person had been in the park. "We have an eyewitness who has stepped forward. That witness puts you at the scene of the crime."

The color drained from Maurice's face, and he unconsciously gripped his own throat. "That's preposterous. A lie. And you believe this person? Why didn't they come forward years ago? None of this makes any sense." He turned to Reni and looked so hurt she almost fell back on an old desire to make him happy, draw him a picture, say something funny.

"We're just following leads," Reni said, feeling compelled to add, "but if you were there the night of, it would be easier for you to come forward now. It would help your case. You might not even be considered an accessory depending upon the level of your involvement."

194

"Are *you* the one pointing a finger at me?" Rather than being pacified by her attempt to persuade, he attacked. "Sometimes I wonder if you just wanted the attention. I wonder if you were really there at all. The story you told about helping your father didn't even come out until after his arrest. Your mother never knew anything about any of it. She would have done something if she had."

Reni recoiled. It wasn't like Maurice to attack her. He'd tapped right into her own doubts, just mainlined them.

"But I understand," he added. "What happened with your father could have caused a kid to go a little crazy."

She'd recently told Daniel that kids got things wrong all the time. Had she heard the stories of what had happened so often that she'd placed herself right in the middle of the crimes? No, Gabby had seen her there. She'd saved Gabby's life. How easy it was to slide into self-doubt. Self-doubt was the thing she found the most cruel and pervasive. Everybody needed answers. But the gulf between what a person wished and the actual truth could sometimes be vast. She wanted Maurice to be innocent because she couldn't bear the thought of another person she loved being involved in something so terrible. And so she battled logic and her own desire for a tolerable outcome.

"This isn't about Reni," Daniel said.

She hadn't known him long, but she could tell he was struggling to keep his voice level and his anger in check. Knowing he had her back and that he'd just steadied her in a moment of self-doubt, and not for the first time, made her feel grateful for his support in the midst of such a dark moment.

"She was there," Daniel said. "And if you were her friend, you wouldn't be trying to deflect and gaslight her right now."

Maurice got a little teary again. "I'm sorry."

Reni was about to cut him some slack because she needed to believe he wasn't deeply involved, but his next words were a chilling reminder of why they were here.

"I'm sorry, Little Wren."

They might not have camera footage or physical evidence yet, but his involvement in the game was indisputable. At the very least, he'd been in the park the night Gabby escaped. So, why didn't Reni remember him? She had no recall of what happened after Gabby's escape. The more immediate question: Did Maurice have something to do with Carmel Cortez's death?

Outside, Daniel called the sheriff's office and arranged for someone to keep Maurice under surveillance. Then he looked at Reni and said, "I'm sorry. I know he's your friend."

"Thanks." She appreciated his understanding of how hard this was for her.

"What do you think he's doing in there?"

"Calling my mother."

CHAPTER 35

Maurice watched them leave. Once their car was gone, he sat down heavily in his favorite chair, an overstuffed thing with a garish print he'd picked up at an antique shop in LA.

He'd always known this day would come. He'd actually been surprised it hadn't happened thirty years ago. But Ben Fisher, despite his weaknesses, was a loyal friend. He'd never mentioned Maurice's name to anyone. Maurice wasn't sure he himself would have been as generous if he'd been the one arrested. Maybe, if he were covering for the right person. He understood love and how it could twist you, how it could make you do things you'd normally never do. Just for love, expecting nothing in return.

He'd gone over this moment in his head many times. What he'd do. What he'd say. But those mental trial runs had never included Reni. Seeing her sitting in his house, knowing what she'd gone through . . . He couldn't confess in front of her. Maybe if she hadn't been present, he could have told the guy, Daniel. But he wasn't even sure about that.

In this crucial moment, he could admit his whole life had been a series of avoidance moves. Why not go out the same way? Never speaking of what he'd done, and certainly never looking again at the faces of the people who'd trusted him the most, Rosalind and Reni being the most significant. But also his brothers and other relatives. Friends in the community.

He'd already taken a shower that morning, but he was sweating. The kind of sweat that was primal and came from a place of deep fear.

He took another shower. Even used a clean, dry towel. Wasteful, but what the hell? Then he put on his favorite suit, handmade at a little shop in Palm Springs. Cost him a pretty penny, but it had been worth it. He added a tie and his best dress shoes. In his office, he unlocked the safe and pulled out a box and his will. He placed the will in the center of his desk. He opened the box and laid out several items, displaying them like museum pieces. Painful things to see, honestly. Then he retrieved the last item from the safe, a handgun. He was preparing to sit down when he had a thought.

The hummingbirds.

Pausing his plan, he set the gun aside, made his way downstairs, and opened the refrigerator where he kept the sugar water. He filled the red feeders, and while he was outside, he took a moment to enjoy the feel of the sun on his face.

Little things.

Back in the kitchen, he opened a bottle of exotic craft beer. He wasn't much of a beer drinker. It gave him gas. But he liked to have a variety of drink choices for visitors. Back upstairs, he sat at his desk and drank the cold beer. Then he loaded the bullets into the gun.

Rosalind had one just like it, purchased at the same time from the same shop. They'd been responsible and had taken lessons and gone to a firing range together. Rosalind ended up being a terrible shot. He hadn't been much better, and they'd both laughed until they cried when the paper silhouette revealed no holes to the head or heart. Funny to think they'd originally bought the guns for protection. From whom, he didn't know, but the lurking press could make anybody nervous. Now the weapon would have a new and unexpected purpose. It seemed right.

He had to admit he was more into the idea of ending his life with drugs. Of just going to sleep and not waking up. But he hadn't planned well. He had no stash of prescription painkillers saved.

He sat down at the desk and looked across the room at one of his favorite paintings, done by a young local artist. He'd loved supporting talented kids, and they'd loved him back. He'd done a lot for the community, and people were going to be surprised when they heard about his death. Some might even miss him.

His cell phone rang. Surprise. He hadn't been aware of putting it in his pocket. Seemed ridiculous to have it with him now, considering the circumstances. But he pulled it out and saw the caller was Rosalind. God, he'd loved her. He sighed and silenced his phone. Then, a few moments later, he silenced himself.

CHAPTER 36

Sometimes a person just reached the point when the need for sleep could no longer be ignored. Reni had hit that wall. Several hours after the visit with Maurice, she returned to the desert and was heading for the bedroom when her mother called.

"I'm worried about Maurice. His car is in the driveway, but there are no lights on in his house."

Rosalind must not have heard about their visit to Maurice's earlier. That in itself seemed strange because Maurice told Rosalind everything.

"I tried to call him," she continued, "but he didn't pick up. He always picks up when he sees it's me. I have a key to his house. Do you think I should go in?"

Maybe it was nothing, maybe he was out, maybe he'd run away. *His car is in the driveway.* "No. Call 911." Reni grabbed a jacket. "I'm on my way." When she was in her truck heading toward Palm Springs, she dialed Daniel's number.

"I'll meet you there," he said.

At Maurice's, an emergency vehicle was on-site, along with two police cars. She spotted Daniel's SUV, no one inside. Rosalind was in Maurice's front yard, distraught, dressed in pajamas and a pale robe, her hair a mess, her face without makeup, all care about her appearance forgotten in her concern for her friend.

"It's bad," she sobbed. "It's terrible. He's dead. Dead!"

Reni's breath caught and her knees went weak. She got a text from Daniel that reinforced her mother's report. *Don't come inside.*

A neighbor appeared and attempted to comfort Rosalind. Battling shock, Reni walked swiftly toward the house, following the sound of voices. Through the living room and up the stairs to the main bedroom and adjoining office. Daniel was there, along with emergency personnel, their blue gloves bloody. Photographs were being taken, and a detective was drawing the layout of the room. Daniel saw her, came striding across the room, put his hands on her shoulders, attempted to turn her around and send her back out the door. Wordlessly, she pushed past him. And stopped.

Oh, Maurice.

Dear, dear Maurice.

This was her fault.

Dressed in a suit and tie, he was slumped forward in an office chair, a pool of blood on the floor near his feet. He was wearing his favorite shoes.

Just feel this leather! It's so soft!

In the center of the desk was a blood-spattered will. More interesting were several items, all neatly displayed. Necklaces, panties, earrings, bras, cut hair bound with elastic bands.

Here were the trophies.

CHAPTER 37

The nucleus of neurons that governed Reni's master circadian clock was out of whack. One moment it seemed months had passed since Maurice had killed himself. The next, it felt like hours. Sleeping and meals were no longer things she thought about. Some kind friends brought food to her mother's house, but did not step inside. They might have been afraid, or they might have wanted to give them space. Daniel visited, sometimes to sit quietly with them, sometimes to ask questions about Maurice.

She was sorry they hadn't found Daniel's mother, but the FBI was still involved in the search and teams were still digging in the desert. It could happen.

She'd told Daniel she was done. She needed to help her mother, who'd just lost her best friend, and she had to take care of herself. And anyway, with so much controversy surrounding her, it was best for her to step away. She was glad her job with Homicide, if it could have ever been called a job, was over. Since Maurice's suicide, she'd chosen to stay in town at her mother's house, sleeping in her old room, waking up in the middle of the night confused, painfully aware of Maurice's absence in the house next door. But Rosalind seemed to be coping, and Reni planned to leave later that day. It was not a healthy place for her to be.

And once again, much like the emotions she'd felt surrounding her father after he was arrested, the pain of losing Maurice was twisted up with his role in the murders. He hadn't left a suicide note or any written explanation of the depth of his involvement, and she questioned whether he'd actually helped her father kill his victims. That seemed so unlike Maurice. But she could see him helping to bury bodies and maybe hiding Ben's trophies.

If only she'd been a little more cautious with questioning him. If only she'd stuck around, maybe even spent the evening with him, talked to him. But her head had been reeling and she'd just wanted to feel peace for a few hours.

She and her mother spent the immediate days after his death just getting through them. One minute leading to the next to the next. Somewhere in that period of lost time she made a numb call to Gabby Sutton, knowing she would have heard the news. As painful conversations could sometimes turn, the subject of pottery came up, and Reni once again promised to make something for her.

Now, according to the calendar, only a few days had passed since Maurice had been found at his desk. It seemed like weeks. Reni and Rosalind were in the kitchen, three newly purchased hummingbird feeders on the table, ordered online because neither wanted to face the world out there and the mob of media clogging the streets. Reni stood at the stove, gas flame turned off, stirring a pan of sugar water with a wooden spoon. The tile was cool under her bare feet, and a breeze moved through the patio doors, delivering the scent of orange blossoms, along with a slight undertone of bad air. Growing up there, Reni had never noticed the ever-present dash of smog that pervaded the city. It wasn't until she'd moved to the desert that she'd come to realize the particular aroma that made her think of home was actually pollution.

She put the spoon aside. "I think it's cool enough."

Maurice's house was still a crime scene, cordoned off with yellow tape. Investigators, including Daniel, came and went as Rosalind obsessed about Maurice's hummingbirds. From their backyard they'd noticed the empty feeders and had seen hummingbirds zipping around, looking for nectar. Their focus had gone from the horror of their lives to a call to action, something they could do that would undoubtedly have a positive outcome.

Rather than buying packaged nectar, they'd made their own using white sugar. They'd learned from experts. Maurice and her father had been adamant about making it themselves, often discussing the dangers of red dye and unclean feeders, fussing and fretting over the birds that had come to depend on them.

The contradictory elements didn't escape Reni. Men who preyed on humans but carefully cared for the tiniest of birds. Maybe those things had nothing to do with each other, or maybe it had given them both comfort to know that even though they'd taken lives, they'd also helped sustain the tiny creatures.

As with everything that had to do with birds, she'd been sucked into her father's ornithological orbit. He'd taught her all about hummingbirds long before she started grade school. Once there, she was able to proudly and pompously spew information to either bore or amaze, depending upon her audience. She still remembered that their wings, beating anywhere from twelve to over eighty beats per second, created the hum humans heard. And she knew they had a heart rate of over twelve hundred beats per minute. And the highest metabolic rate of any homeothermic animal. Most only lived three to five years, so none of the birds currently visiting Maurice's feeder had ever been fed by Ben Fisher, but it was likely he'd fed their relatives, because birds tended to return to the place where they were born and fledged.

Filling the red feeders wasn't a two-person job, but they made it one. Call it an act of combined comfort-seeking. Rosalind held a feeder over the sink as Reni slowly filled it with the clear, sweet liquid. As she poured, she thought about the public response to Maurice's passing. The city was in shock and mourning. So was she. It would take some time to sort this out. She wanted to hate him, but couldn't find that emotion. What did that say about her? That she was flawed?

Maurice had been loved and admired by many, and his presence would be missed. Some refused to believe he'd had anything to do with the murders. Even after the gun he'd used to kill himself had been found to be the same weapon used on Carmel Cortez. She must have discovered his connection to the crimes, and he'd killed her to keep her quiet. But what about Ben leading them right to the grave? He must have known. Maurice must have told him. Had it all been a way for Ben to get back at the relationship Maurice shared with Rosalind? The way Maurice had almost stepped into his shoes?

Maurice's admirers wanted to believe he'd been framed. Reni had found herself with some of the same thoughts and had even briefly wondered if his death was not suicide. But the video footage from the apartment complex where Carmel had lived revealed Maurice walking toward Carmel's apartment. The desk clerk had identified a photo of Maurice. And by using trajectory mapping, criminologists were able to prove Maurice had killed himself.

Maurice's home security cameras didn't reveal any visits other than the one from Daniel and Reni. When that information was leaked, Reni was once again the target of suspicion. Even having Daniel as an alibi hadn't been enough to dissuade people from creating their own story in order to save the reputation of a loved man.

She was used to being seen as the evil one. She was immune to it, but she hated being right in town, next to the gawkers and haters, the curious. She didn't want the Fisher misery to be anybody else's entertainment.

"Damn birds," Rosalind said, putting the filled feeder down and picking up an empty one.

Rosalind wasn't really talking about the hummingbirds, but rather what they represented. Reminders of others existed in the most mundane and ubiquitous of things.

Once all three feeders were ready to go, they carried them outside, to their own backyard, and hung them on hooks her father had installed long ago. The plan was to lure Maurice's birds to their yard, thus providing the food the little ones had come to rely on.

"What are you going to do about your pottery logo?" Rosalind asked as they eyed the newly hung feeders, both of them wondering how long it would take for the birds to find them.

The logo was well-known. From now on, whenever Reni stamped the bottom of a cup or bowl, it would remind her of the day her father had brought her along on his little outing to bury a victim in the desert.

"I haven't decided."

"I've never wondered about Maurice," her mother said, obviously unable to stop thinking about him. "And now I can see that was stupid of me. He and your father were such good friends. And yet I loved Maurice. I still do."

"Me too."

There was no starting over for most people. That was a misconception. Unless a person's memory could be erased, there were no fresh starts, only progression. Even if you burned down a house where bad things had happened, the house would still be there in your mind, regardless. Several times in the past few days Reni had imagined going to the desert and painting over the bird she'd scratched in the rock that day. Using some kind of paint that perfectly matched so no one would know it had ever existed.

But she would know the bird was there, under the paint.

That seemed worse. To know it was there even though she couldn't see it. It would be an echo of her life. Two men she'd loved, her father and Maurice, carrying around such darkness and lies, hiding behind eyes and skin and clothing and smiles and their books about birds. There had been too many secrets. Like she'd told Daniel, children made their own reality. That's how they got through the darkness.

"What should I do about the award ceremony?" her mother fretted.

Reni had forgotten about the event being held in her mother's honor. What a weird thing to contend with or to even have to think about right now. Reni's choice would have been to just not show up. "Call the coordinator and let them know you aren't going to be there. They'll understand." And would probably be relieved not to be honoring her now. Rosalind's best friend and her husband, both behind despicable crimes.

"I think I want to go. I haven't done anything. I deserve it. But I want you to come with me. I don't know if I can do it alone."

What torture. For both of them. "I will." She couldn't let her mother face it alone.

"I had a thought last night," Rosalind said. "What would you think about going somewhere for a day or two? To get away from the press and the neighborhood?"

That was a good idea. Getting out of town, even for a night. But Reni was fixated on returning to the desert. "Maybe Grandma's house."

Rosalind made a miserable face. "I don't like being off the grid with no cell service. I don't like to be out of touch in case a young woman needs a place to stay."

Her mother's house would never shelter abused women again, Reni was pretty sure of that. But let her think young women might call. Let her think her name hadn't been removed from the organization's call list. Time would pass and no one would come, and her mother would quit waiting. Maybe she'd turn the guest room into a space for something else. A hobby? Or maybe she'd finally move far away, past the mountains and the fields of wind turbines, to another city. Unlikely.

"I haven't been to the cabin in so long," Reni said. "We should see if it's okay. When were you last there?"

"It's been years. But I have to be back by Saturday night for the ceremony."

They might both find it healing.

"I was really thinking about a nice hotel somewhere," Rosalind said. "On the ocean. We could sit on the beach and watch the sunset like we used to. I'll bet I'd get cell service on the beach."

"Let's go to the desert," Reni said, warming to the idea, feeling a spark of interest. "It will have much better sunsets." The cabin, without her grandmother, would be sad, but it might also give them some peace. And Reni suddenly needed confirmation that her life with her grandmother had been real. She had a flash of memory, her mother at the cabin, a pair of scissors in her hand. "Bring your scissors and you can cut my hair," she said, pushing aside a vague feeling of unease. "Any style you want."

The haircut seemed to settle it.

"Look." Reni pointed. A little friend had already found the feeder. She recognized the purple markings. And thanks to her father, she knew it was a Costa's hummingbird that could be found in Palm Springs year-round.

A short time later, Reni left the house, driving slowly through the mob of people. Most seemed respectful and stepped aside, eyes downcast. Some glared, and one woman gritted her teeth and threw Reni the finger.

None of it reached her in a deep way. It was all just behavior.

CHAPTER 38

The next day, dressed in jeans and a faded T-shirt, sleeves rolled up, Reni hefted gallons of water into the trunk of her mother's car, then retrieved her backpack from her cabin, where she'd spent the night for the first time in days. With the pack in the trunk, she rechecked her supplies. Protein bars, jacket, beef jerky, hat, extra sunglasses, bandanna, sunscreen.

"You're really prepared."

Standing behind her, hands on hips, Rosalind looked like a celebrity in her pale scarf, huge sunglasses, white jeans, and a chambray work shirt. On her feet were leather sandals, but Reni had spotted a pair of sneakers in the trunk.

"I never go into the desert without enough to survive at least a few days," she said.

"A vacation should be something that relieves stress, not causes it. We shouldn't have to worry about survival. But I'm going to get my revenge. I plan to give you quite the trim."

Reni tugged her hair over her shoulder, smoothing it with her palm, surprised to find she felt a little sad at the thought of telling it goodbye. She hadn't expected to care. But her father had loved long hair and ponytails. That was where her unease was coming from. Cutting it would be a good thing.

Slamming the trunk closed, knowing her mother would be happy to relinquish the wheel, she said, "I'll drive."

Like many newer models, Rosalind's car had a keyless ignition system. Once her seat belt was fastened, Reni dropped the fob in the cup holder and pushed the start button on the dash and they were on their way. With the air-conditioning blasting, they listened to music while Joshua trees flashed past the windows and the landscape opened and closed. Almost two hours on a real road, followed by another forty minutes on dirt, through deep sand that threatened to trap them, the terrain more suited to vehicles with higher clearance. Reni straddled the wheels over washouts as her mother gripped the handle above her door and said something about not remembering the road being so bad. True. It had fallen into disuse and probably hadn't had any maintenance since Grandma Beryl's death.

When they got to the property, the cabin looked forlorn and Reni felt bad about not visiting sooner. They got out, shut the doors, strode toward the building. Temperature about eighty, wind blowing the chimes hanging from a rafter on the wide porch.

"No broken windows," Reni said. Always a worry in the desert. It wasn't unusual for thieves to break in, looking for vintage goods, or squatters to take up residence in remote buildings.

Her mother unlocked the door and shoved it open with a shoulder. "I guess that's something."

It was stuffy and hot inside. Like most homesteader cabins, it had a cement floor, brick walls, and a fireplace. Mostly an open space, with a small bedroom to one side. In the living area were a couch and oil lamps.

Hard to believe Reni had spent her first few months of life there. Of course she had no memory of it, but she liked to think the rustic cabin was why she loved the desert so much.

They went about opening windows, propping up the wooden frames with sections of yardsticks that had been cut for that purpose. Fresh air rushed in. While the cabin cooled down, they unloaded the car, stacking their belongings on the porch, including the water and

Reni's backpack. Rosalind dragged a small suitcase to the cabin, the wheels leaving a trail in the sand. She set the case near the door.

Inside, Reni turned on the kitchen faucet, surprised when water spit out. Many remote places with no well or city water had outdoor tanks that were filled a couple of times a year. She didn't know how long water could last in a tank before it evaporated. Forever? Unlikely in the summer heat. Then she spotted a free weekly entertainment magazine for Palm Springs. "How did that get here?" Maybe squatters *had* been in the cabin.

Rosalind's eyes widened in surprise, then narrowed in puzzlement. "I don't know."

Reni picked up the magazine and thumbed through it. Some art events were circled, one of them sponsored by Maurice. "Did Maurice come here?"

"He might have had a key," Rosalind said.

Reni checked the date on the magazine. The week of Maurice's visit to the prison.

"You and I came here to get away from everything." Rosalind shook her arms as if shaking off water. "Let's don't think about him. I'll cut your hair and we can watch the sun go down."

It would be good to get it over with, and cutting it might bring a sense of relief. After grabbing a towel from a cupboard, thinking she needed to let Daniel know about Maurice's visit to the cabin, Reni bent over the sink and wet her hair, wrapped her head, then carried a wooden chair outside and placed it on the porch so she faced the valley. She removed the towel, flipped back her hair, and sat down while her mother plucked a pair of scissors from her bag.

Rosalind moved into position, planting herself behind Reni and combing out her wet hair. "I used to give you trims here," she said. "You and your father."

"I don't remember." The comb moved across her scalp. Another set of chimes played in the distance.

Rosalind pulled Reni's hair into a ponytail and secured it. "There's no sense in letting this go to waste," she said. "I'll give it to a place that makes wigs for cancer victims. Hair for the Children." With no hesitation, never asking Reni if she was ready and sure, she began cutting alarmingly close to the back of Reni's head, the scissors struggling to get through her thick hair with a sound that was like no other . . .

"It's always interesting how hard it is to cut through a ponytail," Rosalind said as she made the final slice and passed the hair, held together in a band, to Reni.

Reni stared at the hair in her hand, an echo of the trophies that had been laid out so carefully on Maurice's desk.

How does this dress look on me?

Reni's heart pounded and her mouth went dry. "How many ponytails have you cut in your life?" she asked, managing to keep her voice neutral, glad her mother was standing behind her and couldn't see her expression.

"Too many to count."

How does this dress look on me?

Ponytails too numerous to count.

Reni had no idea how much time had passed when her mother announced she was done. Could have been seconds or minutes or hours. She felt her remaining hair. Chin length, blunt ends. She handed the ponytail to her mother, and Rosalind laid it on top of her suitcase, the hair not yet dry enough to pack. So reminiscent of the ones on Maurice's desk . . .

Reni searched her mind for the kind of conversation that would have taken place if things had been normal. "I'm glad we came here." She seemed to be watching the scene from a distance, mouthing words from an awkward script.

"Me too," Rosalind said.

The hair. The water. The magazine. It had nothing to do with her mother, right?

The chimes kept chiming.

"We should play Scrabble," Rosalind said. "I think there's a board in the bedroom closet."

Do you still play Scrabble?

They used to play it here, as a family. "I'll check," Reni said. Searching for it served as an excuse to get away and collect herself.

Inside, she caught her reflection in the oval mirror near the door. It was the same haircut her mother had given her as a child. The same haircut she'd had when she coaxed poor Gabby Sutton into the woods. Not strange, right? The pageboy was her mother's signature style. For some reason, maybe because she'd practiced on Reni so often, she'd become very skilled at it.

On a high shelf in the bedroom closet, Reni spotted the lonely Scrabble game. The lid wasn't completely closed. She pulled the box from the shelf, placed it on the bed, and opened it.

Birds of the Desert.

Her heart seemed to stop and start again.

Her hands were bigger now, no longer the hands of a child, but she recognized the book in a tactile way. The soft bend of the cover, not paper but not heavy cardboard. The size, something small enough for an adult to tuck into a jacket pocket, or even jeans.

It practically fell open and a scent drifted to her. Something so exclusively of the desert that it almost made her weep. Creosote bush. A small cutting tucked into the gutter where the spine was sewn, taking her directly to a page and picture she remembered.

A falcon. She'd sounded out the word that day so long ago.

The book had large folded maps that were also attached to the spine, the paper delicate now from living in the impossible heat of the Mojave for so many years.

She carefully opened one of the maps.

It was supposed to show specific habitats, but she suspected it had been used for another purpose altogether. Just to be sure, she checked two more maps. All of them had the same small dots of various colors. She reached blindly for the wall.

Do you still play Scrabble?

This was how her father had kept track of the graves. And this must have been why Maurice had been here. To hide the book. Ben might have instructed him to do so that last day Maurice visited him in prison. And yet it hadn't really been hidden. Not *that* hidden.

Do you still play Scrabble?

Ben had wanted her to find it, maybe because it hadn't been possible for him to remember the location of all the graves. But then why hadn't he just told her where the book was the day he jumped? Because it might have still been in Maurice's or her mother's possession? Or maybe the book had been insurance. Maybe he'd held the information back in case things didn't go as planned. But also, he loved games and he would have derived pleasure from imagining this moment. He'd given her the clues. She just hadn't been paying attention.

"Reni?" her mother shouted from outside. "Did you find the game?"

The game. "Y-yes!" Without taking her eyes from the book, she thumbed through it again and spotted her mother's handwriting on the title page.

It had been a gift.

To my darling Benjamin in memory of our many adventures.

Under it were colored dots, along with a list of women's names. Some names Reni recognized.

She was pretty sure she was looking at a color-coded key for the maps, indicating where each specific woman had been buried.

To my darling Benjamin in memory of our many adventures.

The names of the missing women were also written in her mother's handwriting.

CHAPTER 39

Thirty-two years earlier

Reni was obsessed with birds. All kinds of birds. Everybody said she'd gotten it from her father, and that was true. She thought about birds a lot, and she even dreamed about them. She loved to go through the book he took to the desert, and she'd draw her own versions of the birds she found inside.

She never drew on the wall. She always drew in her drawing tablets. She had a lot of drawing tablets, and her father said she was quite the artist, like being an artist was a good thing. So she drew even more. On scraps of paper her parents left around the house. The backs of envelopes. She liked how white and smooth envelope paper was. She drew in tablets with and without lines. Big tablets. Little tablets. When she was done, she'd tear out the pages and scatter them through the house for her parents to admire. She also gave some of her pictures to Maurice for his art collection. That's when he started calling her Little Wren.

At some point, she began drawing birds with two heads. She didn't know why, but one day she just had to do it. The two-headed birds became a topic of conversation in the house. Her parents would laugh about the drawings as her mother attached them to the refrigerator with magnets.

The two-headed birds were eventually followed by people with two heads.

"Should we take her to a child psychologist?" her mother asked one night as the three of them sat in the wood-paneled living room. Her father was smoking and grading papers, while her mother drank a mixed drink and flipped through a pretty magazine, sometimes holding up a page and asking if they liked the outfit. It was usually a skinny lady in a bright dress.

"*I'm* a psychologist," her father said.

"But you don't specialize in children."

"That's a ridiculous idea. Can you imagine what she might share?" To Reni, he asked, as smoke from his cigarette curled into the lampshade, "Why do all your birds and people have two heads?"

"I don't know." Reni was lying on the floor with her crayons, creating a whole family of two-headed birds.

"Two heads are better than one," her father said. He and Rosalind roared with laughter. Reni didn't get the joke.

After a while, her father stubbed out his cigarette and put his stack of papers aside. "Do you want me to help you draw a bird that really looks like a bird? A bird with one head and feathers that aren't every color in that box?"

She liked her two-headed birds, but she also liked it when they drew together, so she said okay and climbed onto his lap.

"Crayons wouldn't be my tool of choice," he said, "but I'll make do."

He started with a circle. Then he added a beak and a few sweeping lines, followed by feathers and eyes and feet. "Go ahead and color it in, then see if you can do it yourself."

His birds weren't nearly as fun as her birds, and she didn't want to copy his drawing. "I'm tired of this."

"At least *try*," her father said. "You haven't even tried." He wasn't mad, but the love was gone from his voice. "If you want to be good at something, you have to work at it."

Rosalind sighed.

Reni slipped off her father's lap, lay down on the floor, and struggled to do exactly what he'd done. Draw a bird with one head.

"That's better," he said when she was finished. "Try again."

Rosalind let out another sigh, louder this time. Ben gave Reni a secret wink. He sometimes said Rosalind had ants in her pants. Reni was pretty sure if she really had ants in her pants, she'd be jumping around the room.

She drew another bird, trying harder this time. It was worse than the first one. "I don't want to draw birds anymore." She pushed the crayons away. "I like *my* birds." Birds with bright colors and wings in the wrong places. Birds with two heads.

Her mother tossed the magazine aside. "What a boring night. Do you two realize how boring you are?"

"Maybe we should do something," her father said. "Scrabble, maybe?"

"Oh God. I'm so tired of that," Rosalind said.

He looked at Reni. "Do you have any ideas?"

She didn't like the game anymore even though her father promised the girls who played were actresses. Like the war enactment they went to once, and the plays she saw at the college where her father taught. People screamed and there was fake blood, but they got back up and smiled once it was over. She also knew there were some things she was just too young to completely understand, like the ants. But it made her sad when the love left her daddy's voice. She wanted it to come back, all the way back, so she thought of something that would make both of her parents smile. "Can we play the other game?"

CHAPTER 40

Standing in the cabin bedroom, Reni turned the pages. There were so many dots. Thirty? More?

Her mother had been in on it. Maybe even the mastermind.

She slipped the book into the back pocket of her jeans and pulled her T-shirt over it. She felt hollow and numb, and for a long time couldn't form another thought.

"Reni?" her mother shouted again from outside.

She left the game on the bed and walked back through the cabin. It was dark inside, the open door a frame that led to blinding sunlight and the chimes that rang madly, like warning bells. She tried to find the memories of her childhood, more specifically memories of her mother and the part she played in the killings, but couldn't. They were there, but just beyond her reach.

The chimes chimed.

And her heart broke.

And her mind continued to deny what was right in front of her.

Outside, her mother had placed a small wooden table between two chairs. She'd opened two bottles of beer.

"I don't want to play Scrabble," Reni said, dropping into a chair, reaching for a beer, drinking it, her mind as yet unwilling to process the horror of her discovery in the bedroom.

The sun was setting, and it was beautiful. Back in Palm Springs, hummingbirds with purple feathers on their heads would be gently sipping from the feeders she and her mother had hung together, a mother-and-daughter project. She thought about how Rosalind had flown to get her when she'd had her breakdown. Just packed her up and took care of her. She *was* a wren, after all. A little broken wren who'd needed her mother's help.

The beer bottle was suddenly empty. With no memory of finishing it, she set it aside. Numb, she willed her mind to return to the lesser horrors of hours ago rather than the new and bigger horrors of her mother's involvement in the game. As the chimes chimed, she directed her gaze toward the horizon, focusing everything she had on the pink sky that grew and spread and was beginning to turn red.

"Let's go for a walk," Rosalind suddenly said.

Yes. Reni liked that idea. One last walk together.

All those colored dots.

So many of them.

They moved side by side, their shoes stirring up little clouds of dirt, Rosalind's toes, with their red nail polish, turning gray from the dust, Reni's heart breaking a little more with each step. She couldn't hold back reality, and she suddenly understood how people cut themselves because it seemed like more pain was the only thing that might stop what she was feeling.

They reached a place where the land dropped steeply, a cliff almost. Below were large boulders, the shapes softened by wind and sand. No sharp edges anywhere, the rocks worn smooth. The sun going down, the blush in the sky, the scent of creosote, and her mother beside her. It brought a memory rushing back. They used to do this too. All of them together. A family.

They sat down, side by side, on a large flat rock still warm from the day. Yes, this had been their magical spot. Even her mother had tolerated it. Reni wanted to hold this moment, this last moment before the world turned upside down again.

"It's so beautiful," Reni said, a sob catching in her throat. Sunlight illuminated distant peaks surrounded by dark mountains and ghostly mountains and mountains that appeared and disappeared, seeming almost from another time and place. Moody, changing moment to moment, finally fading and vanishing as if never having been there at all.

As she watched the horizon, her mind began to unlock, making her look at the reality of her life and what had happened. She'd been a damn good profiler. Had she always known? Deep down? Had it been something even her adult mind hadn't been able to face? Or had her child's mind done such a remarkable rewrite of events that she'd never even suspected?

Good job, Reni!

Her mother reached out and stroked her hair. That loving touch had such a new and sinister meaning now. Such physical contact had always seemed an effort for Rosalind. Ben had been the one who'd kissed her and hugged her with unselfconscious enthusiasm. "You and your father always loved it here."

"But you didn't."

"Not really. I tolerated it."

But it was a good place to dispose of bodies.

What was the next step? Tell her mother they had to go home? Drive to Palm Springs? Or stay the night and try to get more information from her? Reni wasn't sure she could do that. Even now, she wondered how her mother couldn't see that she knew, because everything had changed in a matter of seconds back there in the cabin. She'd gone into the bedroom one person and had come out another. She was generating silent screams of denial that surely her mother could see and feel.

And yet they sat together hugging their knees, watching the sky put on a show. A mother-and-daughter adventure.

"Maybe we shouldn't stay the night," Reni said abruptly. "I think you were right. It's just not the place it used to be."

Rosalind laughed. "You won't get any argument from me about that."

It would be best if Rosalind dropped Reni off at her cabin. Once her mother was on the way to Palm Springs, Reni would call Daniel and he could bring Rosalind in for questioning under the pretext of needing more information on Maurice.

None of it made sense, but then killing almost never did.

"I do love this place," Reni confessed.

Rosalind reached over and touched Reni's hair again, this time tucking a strand behind her ear. She seemed pleased with the cut.

Another memory hit. Rosalind standing in the kitchen, wearing the red dress, with scissors and a ponytail in her hands.

The sun was gone. "Let's go," her mother said, getting to her feet. "Let's go home."

In a daze, Reni struggled to her feet . . . and felt her mother's hands on her shoulders.

There was nothing to grab, nothing to hang on to. With an odd sense of relief at the turn of events that wasn't entirely unexpected, Reni flew through the air. This must have been how her father had felt when he jumped. Graceful, almost poetic, pockets of cold air hitting her skin. The fall itself lasted only a second or two. When she hit bottom, she heard a crack, and then the pain drove everything from her mind.

CHAPTER 41

At first there was only pain and the moaning that went with it. The kind that obliterated personality and stamped a body with excruciating agony. But gradually Reni became aware of herself, enough to know she was sprawled on her back, her limbs twisted. *Just like my father.*

They'd both flown, but he'd succeeded in escaping. She hadn't. Unlike with him, there didn't seem to be a lot of blood. That could mean she was bleeding internally. Some secret dark damage sucking the life out of her.

As her brain attempted to evaluate her injuries, her sense of self and the situation grew from a pinpoint, opening up until she heard the sound of the wind, felt the radiant heat from nearby rocks, felt the ground under her, tasted the blood in her mouth. Had she bitten her tongue when she hit, or was there something more fatal in her future?

She tried to move, gasped, and held very still, taking shallow breaths.

A shadow fell across her.

This was it. The curtain was closing. But then she heard her mother's soft voice, and for a moment she felt a rush of relief. She wasn't alone. Someone who loved her was with her.

And then she remembered.

The water and magazine, both indicating the cabin had been used recently.

The bird book.

The push.

Her mother tugged at Reni's contorted leg, attempting to straighten it. Reni screamed, and her mother stopped.

"I think you've broken something, dear heart."

Reni squinted up through a red haze. Through clenched teeth she whispered, "Wasn't that the plan?"

"How can you say such a thing?" Rosalind looked concerned. Maybe she was having second thoughts about her actions.

"Get help," Reni rasped.

"I will, sweetheart. I will. Don't try to move."

Instead of leaving for that help, she began walking in slow circles. At one point, she bent and picked up something. Reni turned her head slightly, enough to recognize her phone in her mother's hand.

"I do want to take this opportunity to explain a few things," Rosalind said, poking at the phone as she talked. "This was all your father's doing. I made the mistake of telling him I sometimes fantasized about killing. Someone, anyone. Just to see what it felt like. I mean, haven't we all wondered such a thing even though most won't admit it? He told me he'd actually helped your grandmother kill your grandfather. I'm not sure if it was true. I suspect he was trying to impress me. That was before we were married, and you know how guys are. They pretend to be something they aren't until they get you. Then they just fall back into their old annoying ways."

She settled herself on the ground next to Reni, knees together like someone posing for a photo shoot. The pale scarf on her head, an affectation, billowed like it had a life of its own, an eel against the blue of the ocean.

"You know how he was. Kind of a phony." She picked up Reni's hand and placed a finger on the phone's home button. When that finger didn't work, she tried Reni's thumb and seemed satisfied with the result, giving Reni her limp hand back as she scrolled.

"After we'd been married awhile, I called his bluff and challenged him to actually kill somebody. And then I got busy with other things, you for one, and forgot about our conversation. But I remember so clearly the night it happened. I was attending a gala with Maurice, and your father was babysitting you. I got home late, you were in bed, and he had this grin on his face that I'd never seen before. His eyes were so alive, and he was so electric. I honestly thought he was on something, but it turned out he was high from a kill. He didn't tell me what was going on until we were done having the best sex we'd ever had. Sorry, I know kids never want to hear about their parents' sex lives, but there was a sexual component to the kills. While we were lying in bed and I was marveling at his stamina, he told me what he'd done, said he'd gotten the idea to use you as bait. I wasn't happy about that, but he assured me you didn't see anything, and that you had fun and thought it was a great game."

Reni *had* loved it. Something special she and her father had done together. And she understood what her mother meant about how alive he'd been afterward. It was exciting to see him that way.

Looking at the phone, Rosalind paused her scrolling. "Oh, I hate this. So unfortunate that you've been in touch with Gabby Sutton. I wanted everything to be resolved, and it just keeps going. I really did want to get on with my life without this hanging over my head."

Fear for Gabby evoked a response. "Don't drag her into this. She doesn't know anything."

"She might. I was there that night. After the attack, I tried to coax her into the car. Like a Good Samaritan, but she ran."

Her mother in the car, and Maurice. Reni had managed to block it all out.

Rosalind went silent as she read, then pulled her attention from the phone and back to the story she was relating. She seemed to want Reni to know what had happened, as if she was proud of it. She had nobody to share with now that Maurice was gone.

"He told me the dead girl was in the trunk, and he wanted me to look at her. We went to the garage and there she was, wrapped in plastic.

When I asked him what he planned to do with the body, he said, 'Take it to the desert.' He said there was a whole remote land where nobody but the coyotes would find her."

She let out a deep sigh. "I thought about going to the police. I really did. This was somebody's daughter. But I also felt responsible for what he'd done. And I had a reputation to maintain. I couldn't be complicit in a murder, and I didn't want the world to know I was the wife of a murderer. So we got up early the next morning and all three of us came to your grandmother's cabin. You stayed inside with her while your father and I disposed of the body. Of course his mother knew nothing about it. She just thought we were there to explore."

She glanced at the phone again. "I wanted to just dump her anywhere, but he's the one who suggested recognizable landmarks. I don't know why. Maybe he thought it was more respectful. Maybe he thought we might need to know someday. Maybe he thought he would have to hang it over my head if it came down to it. But anyway, we chose a beautiful spot. And let me tell you, digging a deep hole in the desert is not easy. I said we shouldn't leave the plastic behind. Just the body. It seemed more natural that way."

She tucked the phone into the pocket of her shirt. "It was fun. I'm sorry, but it was so exciting. Days went by, and then weeks. We read about the missing girl in the paper, and we saw it on the local news. We would look at each other and giggle. But then time passed, and the excitement wore off, and people quit talking about it. And we got bored and began to crave that rush. We decided to do it again. But neither of us wanted you hurt, honey. In fact, I'm the one who told him he needed to quit taking you along."

The pain killed Reni's ability to mentally react, but she managed to ask, "Did *you* ever kill?" For some reason, she still wanted Ben to be less guilty even though she knew he wasn't.

"No."

Very possibly a lie. "Maurice?"

"He thought he was protecting us, and he was. Carmel Cortez might have had information that would make us look guilty." She pointed to herself, then Reni. "He helped us over the years. You. Ben. Me. He never knew the extent of our obsession. He loved you and he loved us. He knew sometimes you begged to play the game, and that we did it to make you happy."

At least a partial lie. Reni closed her eyes tightly as a fresh wave of pain washed over her, then forced them open again. It was getting dark.

"I told him he had to help us protect you."

"Did you kill him?"

"Of course not. He was my friend. Maurice was what your father called a helper bird."

She meant birds that didn't reproduce, but instead helped others in the family raise their young. "That's cruel."

"You know your father. He had to find a bird analogy in everything. All things considered, Ben was a good father."

"How can you possibly say that?"

"He took care of you when I couldn't. Did he ever hit you? Spank you? Sexually abuse you? No."

"He used me for bait."

"You enjoyed it."

She was too weak to drum up adequate anger, but she whispered, "I was too young to know what was going on."

"Exactly. After your father was arrested I missed it all, but there's a reason more men than women kill people. We don't have the strength to dispose of the bodies."

"You had Maurice."

"He could be reluctant at times."

Was it possible her mother was the one with the obsession? And she'd dragged Reni's father into it? Two killers with the same obsession would have been rare. But a man like her father, kind and eager to please, would have been sucked into something that was practically a cult, a cult of two. Three if you included Maurice.

"I'm going to die out here," Reni said to herself, feeling nothing but resignation and relief.

"Oh, darling. I'd never let anything happen to you."

Did she want Reni to think she was coming back with help, or was she in deep denial about her actions?

Rosalind looked up at the sky. "It's going to be dark soon. Do you need anything before I leave?"

Reni's survival skills kicked in and she found herself making a practical request. "Water."

"I'll bring you some. And when I get back to town, I'll call for help, and tell them where you are."

Lying again. "Don't do this."

"*Shh. Everything's going to be all right. Just close your eyes and take a little nap, and when you wake up someone will be here for you.*"

Similar to words Reni now remembered hearing in the park, in the car, spoken by her mother.

"And when I get back to town, I'm going to contact your friend Gabby and see if she'll meet up with me, well, you, so I can give her the gift you planned to make for her."

Reni forced her mind back to the present. How could she stop this, broken as she was?

"Maybe we could even get together at a park. Memory is a funny thing. I'm concerned about what seeing you and talking to you the other day might have stirred up. She remembered Maurice, and she might eventually remember me."

"Don't," Reni begged, searching for something that might convince her mother such action was unwise. "You can't do it without being caught."

Rosalind began walking out of the canyon. As she left, she spoke over her shoulder. "This is steep. Your rescuers are going to have to be careful. I'll be sure and tell them that." She paused and turned around. For a moment, Reni thought she might have had a change of heart.

But no.

She had no heart. And oddly enough, Reni found it reassuring to finally be able to acknowledge that. So many things had never made sense. The bond between them that had always been forced. How her mother had never suspected her father of murder when they'd shared the same bed. And yet someone might even wonder how Reni, a cop, had never seen it. But this was what all behavioralists knew: An idea, a notion, love, hate, formed in childhood, was hard to redirect because it was so ingrained and so accepted as normal.

"You were very loved," Rosalind said with a serene smile. "Your father adored you. I adored you, but you had his heart like no one else. I want you to know that."

Adored you. Past tense. With those final words, she left, vanishing behind a towering boulder.

Nobody was fooling anybody. They both knew she wasn't coming back and she wasn't bringing help. And Gabby Sutton was in grave danger.

CHAPTER 42

Rosalind had sensed something was wrong the second Reni joined her on the cabin porch. Poor girl had tried to cover it up, but a mother just knew these things. She'd been given no choice, but it made Rosalind feel good to know she'd left her daughter in the desert she loved.

Rosalind had told the truth about a lot of things. She did love her daughter. She just couldn't allow the world to know what she'd been doing behind the curtain. There were two Rosalinds. The one admired for her charity work, and the other who was a little too drawn to murder.

People might be surprised to find that she'd never hurt any of the girls staying at her home. That was unthinkable. Those girls needed her and would continue to need her. It was gratifying to help people, to rescue them, to save their lives. She liked caring for the weak and helpless. It made her feel good about herself, but motherhood hadn't been for her. Motherhood held a promise of a fulfilled life, that promise dangling out there as the blessed event that would make a person whole, complete. But in reality, it was *hole* not *whole*. Like punch a hole right through you until everything leaked out.

The garbage that people spewed. *I didn't know what love was until I had a baby. I didn't understand what true selflessness was until I had a child. I didn't know I could love another human the way I love my little Jimmy or Fanny or Margaret.*

Lies, lies, lies.

No one had coerced her into having a baby. Yes, Benjamin had wanted children. She'd known that before they married. And having a kid seemed the natural progression of life. First comes love, then comes marriage, then comes Rosalind pushing a baby carriage. She'd been brainwashed, inundated with images of the false glamour of mother-hood. All the magazines and TV shows portrayed women having babies.

A baby crawled out of you and suddenly you were supposed to be a saint. Mothers couldn't cuss or get drunk or have sex. Mothers couldn't be creative or outrageous or attractive.

Back then, postpartum depression wasn't on her radar. She'd known about it the way she'd known about the possibility of birth defects. They were things that happened to other people, and worrying about such rarities while pregnant wouldn't help anything or anybody. She wasn't sure it would have mattered if postpartum depression *had* been a concern. She didn't even know if it had been her problem. She believed in depression and hormonal imbalance. But the root of it, the damn root of it that absolutely nobody talked about, was that when an infant was born it took your soul. Nobody wanted to talk about *that*. But there it was. Her spirit, her zest for life, pushed right out of her birth canal. She'd decided that was why some people ate the afterbirth. She should have eaten hers. She had recurring dreams about doing just that. Eating it raw and feeling herself reawaken as she consumed it. Sometimes she dreamed she was in a hospital, searching for the afterbirth, going down hallways, looking in dark rooms at labeled jars on shelves. She would find a jar with her name on it. But in the end, as was typical of quest dreams, she couldn't complete her mission. After opening the lid, she'd catch a whiff of formaldehyde and recoil.

Two days after Reni was born, they brought her home. This little red foreign thing that squirmed and cried and peed.

Rosalind couldn't stand to look at her.

At first Benjamin tried to get Rosalind to nurse the baby, but she was afraid the child was going to suck the last drop of her away.

Rosalind took to her bed, where she stared at the wall, memorizing every flaw in the paint. The only time she had any real thought was when she fantasized about getting rid of the infant. Maybe forgetting her in the back seat. Or driving the car into the ocean and jumping out at the last minute to swim to shore. She imagined the aftermath and the public sympathy.

She never said anything to Benjamin, but he must have known, because one day his mother showed up at the house. She and Benjamin packed a bag, and an hour later the child was gone. Over the next few days Benjamin put away all reminders, and there was no talk of the kid.

Rosalind left her bed and gradually began to tend to herself again. Brushing her teeth. Washing her hair. She and Benjamin went for walks the way they used to. One day someone asked where her baby was and she screamed, "I don't have a baby! Do I look like someone who has a baby? I'm a strong, independent woman! Not a baby slave!"

Benjamin took her home.

She cried a lot.

He was a psychologist, and he thought he could solve her problems, but he didn't understand she had no problems. The *baby* was the problem.

He talked her into going to see a friend. A psychiatrist who medicated her. She gradually returned. Never full-blown Rosalind again, but at least a shadow of herself.

Months later his mother showed up with a baby that could sit up with very little support. And it wasn't as pink or red as it had been, and it didn't seem as much like an alien that needed to be smothered. She could look at the child without feeling as if she were looking at some pale-pink representation of her own pathetic soul. And with Benjamin's help, she began to see the child as a person.

"Children are for us," he told her. "They complement our lives. We don't owe them anything. They are here for us, not the other way around."

"Could we eat it if we wanted to?" she'd mused. Kidding, but maybe not kidding. "If we didn't know what to prepare for dinner?"

He laughed. "I wouldn't advise it. Someday you'll be glad to have her around. That's my prediction. And for now? Don't worry if you don't like her."

She clung to that way of thinking.

Once she no longer felt responsible for every breath the child took, it got easier. And once Benjamin came up with the game, she began to enjoy motherhood. It became a plus rather than a minus, and it brought her back from oblivion. She wasn't the old Rosalind. Motherhood had taken that person away forever. But she was someone better. Someone clever and mischievous, but also artistic and kind and respected by people in the community.

CHAPTER 43

It was funny, when Reni thought about it. People were always advised to let others know their schedule when heading off to the desert. Whenever Reni planned to trek to remote areas, she'd send her mother a text to tell her where she was going and when she'd be back.

Over the years, Reni had wondered about her mother. How could Rosalind have missed Ben's behavior? The euphoria that came after a kill, the clothing, the blood, the odor of that unique sweat that often accompanied an act of murder. How did a person miss the signs? As an investigator, Reni had found it baffling. She'd even studied the behavior of those living in the same orbit. Relatives, people who often shared the same bed with a killer, professing ignorance when there should have been signs. Would have been signs.

Until now, she'd decided her father had simply not projected anything. Somehow. While that answer had seemed a stretch, it was the only one she'd been able to come up with. Which of course she now knew was the wrong answer.

Her mother had known.

Her mother had been involved. Her mother might have had blood on her clothes and smelled of that unique odor, and had been high on the euphoria of a kill herself. The depth of their depravity made it especially hard to process. Involving a child. Making her part of it. Other families went camping. Reni's family killed. The family that slayed together stayed together.

That last thought was a clue that Reni's brain was misbehaving, no longer sorting her thoughts in order of importance. Right now she had to focus on staying alive. Getting back to civilization. Telling the world what she knew. The monster, because at the moment it helped to no longer think of Rosalind as her mother but instead as the beast, had to be exposed and stopped.

She forced herself out of her head and into the world enough to take in her surroundings. The brilliant blanket of stars above, a beautiful and magical thing to behold. A half-moon on the horizon.

She managed to prop herself against a rock. The pain of sitting upright was worse than the pain of lying down, but she couldn't stay there. This was the desert: the temperature was dropping quickly and would be in the forties soon. Later, when the sun rose and the temperature rose with it, she wouldn't last long without water. It was dangerous to stay where she was, and dangerous to wait for help that might never come.

She shifted her body and imagined shattered bones moving in a container of skin. But she wasn't any worse than she'd been an hour ago, which meant her original concern of internal bleeding could be put to rest. Or if she was bleeding, it was a slow drip.

Her pain threshold was average, and it told her to stay put. She had to override that desire. When she'd fallen, she'd heard a crack. Something was broken. She just wasn't sure what. Ribs? One ankle was swollen. Maybe sprained. Maybe worse. Her breathing seemed okay except for the panting and gasping she hoped was more to do with pain.

The plan was to drag herself up the steep incline—a mini mountain—and crawl back to the cabin. Hopefully her mother hadn't thought to collect the supplies they'd left on the porch.

The act of rolling to her knees caused blinding agony. She held very still and waited for the stabbing to subside, each beat of her heart driving the pain deeper.

Movement could and probably would cause more damage, but she had no choice. The alternative was dying there. Perfectly acceptable if she didn't have important things to do, like making sure her mother didn't kill again. Making sure she didn't try to contact Gabby.

Time was sketchy and she no longer had her phone, but she guessed it took at least twenty minutes to drag herself up the steep incline. When she reached the top, she looked in the direction of the cabin and could make out the building's dark shadow. On her hands and knees, she crawled toward it.

The gallons of water, along with her backpack, were still on the porch where she'd left everything. Her mother's suitcase was gone. She dug out a small flashlight, turned it on, and held it between her teeth as she worked to fill her personal water container from one of the jugs. She checked her pack for supplies. Sunblock, glasses, hat, energy bars, and beef jerky. All things she would need. She had to consider weight and what she'd be able to carry for miles. Certainly not a gallon of water. In the end, she took only her personal bottle and a single gallon container with half the liquid poured out. She would hike now, in the dark, with the moon and stars for light.

Until this point, she'd been on her hands and knees. Time to see if she could stand.

She dragged herself to one of the wooden chairs. A sob escaped her. Just one. That was all she would allow. With one hand, she slowly levered herself up, leaning hard against the building, breathing shallowly as waves of pain crashed over her. Once upright, she entered the cabin, stripped a blanket from the bed, and wrapped it around herself. Her grandmother's walking stick, the handle worn smooth, was in the corner near the door. She'd use it for support.

She guessed it was around ten p.m. when she left, backpack over her shoulders. She gripped the walking stick tightly, each step sending a bolt of pain through her.

It was ten miles to the highway. If she walked a half mile an hour, it would take her until tomorrow evening to reach it. When she got there, if she got there, she hoped she could flag down a vehicle.

All she thought about was putting one foot in front of the other. A kind of self-hypnosis, a meditation similar to what she'd learned while throwing pots on the wheel. Sometimes she dropped to her knees, the blanket around her. Sometimes she dozed briefly before waking again.

As the night progressed, getting to her feet got harder. In the open there was nothing to cling to except the walking stick. She'd fall and lie on the ground, not wanting to move because everything, even breathing, was knives and fire and broken pieces of herself. Eventually she'd get up and follow the faint road that nobody used. At one point, a false dawn sent a rush of elation through her, but she quickly reminded herself daylight would bring an even bigger challenge: heat. Then the real dawn came, and birds sang. She didn't feel as alone.

Distance traveled? No idea.

Right direction? Fairly certain.

After the sun rose, Reni stopped long enough to apply sunblock to her arms and face. The blanket became her shade when she bothered to drape it over her head. At one point in her semi-oblivion, she thought she spotted something in the distance, center of the road, back the way she'd come. She blinked and tried to focus. An animal. It took a few steps, sat down. Took a few more.

Coyote?

Didn't move like one.

Jackrabbit?

Didn't seem like a rabbit either.

A dog? Yes. Maybe.

It crept close enough for her to confirm that it was indeed a small dog, maybe twenty pounds, matted hair. Feral? Seemed unlikely with how near it was to her, but starvation could tame most wild things.

She dug in her bag, found the remaining piece of jerky, and tossed it at the dog.

It was gone in one swallow, the animal sniffing for more.

Even though the jug was almost empty, she poured water into the tiny lid, put it on the ground, and stepped back. The dog slinked closer, drank. She gave him what was left in the gallon container, each bend causing waves of pain and dizziness. "Where'd you come from?" He was so matted, it was hard to tell what kind of dog he was. Poodle mix?

She returned to her journey, and soon reached a point where she could no longer lift her feet from the ground. Instead, she dragged them, stirring up dirt and sand so thick it coated her lips and settled between her teeth. In a stupor, she fumbled for her backpack, intending to pull out a tube of lip balm. The pack was gone, forgotten somewhere along the way.

She looked behind her. The desert stretched for miles. No sign of her belongings, but the dog was still following her. She turned the other direction. More of the same.

Nothing to do but walk.

Or fall down.

Reni woke up on the ground in a pile of pain. From somewhere in real life or a dream came a soft rushing sound. A shadow moved over her and she spotted a circling bird. The sound was wings.

The bird was real. Maybe.

CHAPTER 44

After Maurice's suicide, Daniel had deliberately allowed Reni space, but now, as he sat at home on his first Saturday off in weeks, he gave in to the urge to check on her, partly because he felt responsible for dragging her back into a nightmare even though without her and her relationship with Maurice they might never have known about Maurice's connection to the Inland Empire murders.

His call to Reni went to voicemail so he tried Rosalind. She answered and told him her daughter had gone back to the desert. No surprise, and actually just what he'd been worried about.

"I hope you'll respect her privacy right now," Rosalind said.

He would. After he talked to her and reassured himself that she was okay. As okay as a person could be given the horrific situation.

It was forty-five minutes to Reni's if traffic wasn't bad and Highway 62 wasn't closed, which happened from time to time due to flooding, earthquakes, and haboobs, those nasty walls of sand and dust that moved in like dense clouds, making travel, and even breathing, near impossible.

He gassed up his SUV at a little desert station that sold cacti and succulents. He picked one out for Reni. Inside, he grabbed a few snacks, paid for his haul, then hit the road again, passing fields of white wind turbines that decorated the landscape, creating a surreal mix of technology and nature. Twenty minutes later, he was driving up the bone-jarring dirt road that led to Reni's house.

Her truck was there.

He knocked. No answer.

He tried doors and windows.

Everything was locked up tight.

She might have gone somewhere with someone, but in the short time he'd known her she'd never mentioned any friends or associates. She'd been through so much since the day he'd first shown up and pressured her to be part of his quest. How much could a mind take before it broke? And his big concern—was she a danger to herself? That was at the heart of his worry. Her mental state. Being alone in the desert right now seemed the worst possible choice.

Coming to a decision, he retrieved a set of tools from his vehicle, picked the lock on her cabin, and opened the door. Out of habit, he braced himself for the whiff of a dead body. He smelled nothing but clay.

He moved through the house, spotting her tent near the door, noting the tidiness of the made bed, the small bathroom with nothing that seemed out of place. Same with the kitchen. No half-eaten food, no cell phone or purse or bag on the table. Nothing spoke of foul play, or something happening unexpectedly. And yet his heart pounded in an unsettling way, and it was a while before he realized he was being sucked back to the morning he'd found his mother gone. She was there, and then she wasn't. And he realized Reni had become important to him. Identifying the reason for his overreaction was enough for him to get it under control, at least a little.

Outside, he circled the cabin. It was small, constructed of gray cinder blocks on a concrete slab. The picture window overlooked the basin. Once he'd gone over the whole place, which didn't take long because of the size, he locked the door and wondered about trying to contact Gabby Sutton. Had Reni possibly reached out to her? As he contemplated the wisdom of such a move, he got a call from Gus Waters, the deputy coroner investigator.

"You know that old university study we discussed?" Gus said. "It took some work, but I was able to get permission to share highlights of the original files with you. And I'm glad I checked it out, because it ends up some of the information I gave you was incorrect. That can happen when a participant's identity is protected. Anyway, I just uploaded the pertinent material to your database."

Daniel thanked him, got his laptop from his vehicle, and settled into a metal chair in front of Reni's house. Using his phone's hot spot, he was able to log into the VPN and access the uploaded file Gus had been talking about.

He clicked the icon on the screen and was surprised to see two sets of brain images, from two different people. He thought he recognized the ones he'd viewed at the morgue. The same blank spaces in the pre-frontal cortex, the area that controlled morality. To his untrained eye, the other brain didn't look normal either, but the gaps weren't as severe as the ones in the images from the morgue.

One of the sets belonged to Benjamin Fisher. The other was attached to a last name he at first didn't recognize. Then it hit him.

He was looking at Rosalind Fisher's maiden name.

Both she and Benjamin had participated in the study. Maybe they'd even met there. And the highly unusual brain pattern didn't belong to Benjamin. It belonged to Reni's mother.

CHAPTER 45

Gabby received a text message from Reni. She had a piece of pottery for her and wondered if they could meet in a park in Riverside, the town where Gabby had gone to college and Ben Fisher had taught psychology. Not *the* park, but all parks were hard for her. She didn't do parks. When Gabby balked, Reni pointed out what Gabby's therapist always told her: Sometimes facing the thing you fear can render it powerless. It would just be trees and jogging trails. Just a beautiful park.

And she trusted Reni.

Days ago, she'd been terrified to meet her and had almost said no. But when Reni had come to her house and they'd talked, it felt as if they'd known each other forever. And they kind of had. They'd experienced the same trauma and had lived through it. Maybe Gabby's life after the attack had been a life of shadow, but they'd both survived. So returning to the town where she'd been attacked could be the next step. If Reni thought it would help, then Gabby was willing to push herself out of her comfort zone.

But she wasn't ready to tell her husband what was going on. Instead, she put on a red dress and black tights and said she was meeting a friend for the afternoon. Her husband never asked too many questions, which meant she'd never had to tell too many lies. Today he just seemed relieved that she was feeling motivated enough to get out of the house.

But bravery was a funny thing. It could fluctuate and vanish if you looked away too long. Several times on the way to Riverside, she had to pull over. If she saw a rest area, she stopped. If she saw a sign for a gas station or Starbucks, she took the exit. A few times during the drive, she thought about calling Reni for a pep talk, but always decided against it. She wanted to be brave. She didn't want to lean on anybody. She wanted to be more like Reni.

In town, she followed the GPS instructions to the green area and jogging trails. She was a little early. She'd factored in extra time, and there were no other cars there. Her heart pounded and she blamed it on the coffee. She parked in an empty lot, made sure her doors were locked, then tried to control her breathing, checking the clock on her phone repeatedly, only to find very little time had passed since her last view.

She finally heard a sound.

In the rearview mirror she saw a big white car. It pulled up beside her, a woman at the wheel. The woman lowered the passenger window and leaned across the seat. Gabby fought the urge to leave her own window up, and lost. She hit the down button—and felt herself mentally tumble into an unsettling sense of déjà vu. She shook it off.

"I'm Reni's mother," the woman said. "Rosalind Fisher."

Of course. Rosalind Fisher. Benjamin Fisher's wife. Could this be any more surreal? Gabby would have recognized her immediately if she hadn't been so on edge. Rosalind was known for taking in and helping abused women. When Gabby first heard of Rosalind's work, she thought she might have been trying to make amends for the things her husband had done.

"I'm so sorry, dear," Rosalind said, "but Reni had an emergency and couldn't make it. She didn't want you to be stuck here waiting."

Gabby frowned at that lack of logic. Why had she gotten mixed up with these people again? "She could have sent a text."

"She was going to, but knew you were on your way and I was going to be in the area anyway, so I said I'd bring her gift." She got out of the car and came around to Gabby's door. She was dressed in what Gabby called casual chic, a popular style with women her age from the Palm

Springs area. White jeans and sandals, big jewelry that made noise when she moved.

"Reni has done remarkably well with her art therapy," Rosalind said. "I don't know where she'd be right now if she hadn't turned to it. But anyway, she told me all about the gift she made specifically for you."

Gabby knew pottery took a long time from start to finish, and she'd only met Reni a few days ago. Probably not enough time for a custom piece. But if they wanted to pretend the present had been made specifically for her, she wasn't going to be ungrateful.

"It's in the trunk and it's pretty heavy." Rosalind made an apologetic face.

"Right." Gabby got out. Together the women walked to the back of the car, where Rosalind popped the trunk open.

"Oh, the box must have slid to the back," Rosalind said. "Can you reach it?"

A fresh wave of uneasiness came over Gabby, but she leaned in and was reassured to see there was indeed a cardboard box in the trunk. Unable to grab it with both feet still on the ground, she leaned in deeper, one knee inside the trunk, one foot still on the ground.

Unbelievably, the supporting foot was kicked out from under her. Hands shoved and she tumbled forward into the trunk. Before she could react or process what was happening, she felt a hot stab of pain in her back, between her shoulder blades. That pain was followed by a sucking sound. She twisted around to see a bloody knife high in the air above her. Behind it, Rosalind Fisher's contorted face. Gabby screamed as the blade descended and struck her again, this time in the neck.

A sound. Maybe another car.

The trunk slammed closed.

Footsteps followed, then the thump of the car door. The vehicle rumbled to life and vibrated under Gabby, backing up, then shooting forward. Gabby pressed a hand to her neck, attempting to slow the blood flow as she dropped into full survival mode.

Trunks had emergency escapes.

She spotted a glowing lever above her head. With slick, sticky hands, she pulled. Nothing happened. She pulled again. After several weak attempts, she remembered her phone and checked the pockets of her dress. She'd left it in her car.

Rosalind headed home with Gabby in the trunk. She planned to park in the garage and check to see if the woman was still alive. If she was, she'd tape her mouth and wrists and hope she lived until she could get her to the desert to dump her. No way could Rosalind remove a dead body from the trunk without help; Gabby Sutton would have to get out on her own. Then Rosalind would kill her. But right now Rosalind had to focus and prepare for her Community Service Award dinner.

CHAPTER 46

Daniel rang the doorbell. It was Saturday evening, and he'd driven straight from Reni's to Rosalind's house. He was trying not to let what he'd just learned about Rosalind mess with his head and cause him to see evil intent where there was none. Even if the tests were accurate, they still meant nothing without dark deeds to back them up. According to the research, even the most alarming results could be overridden by a positive childhood. And he knew nothing about Rosalind; his focus had always been Benjamin and a little bit Reni. Besides, the brain was still a mysterious land. Yesterday's theories could very well be debunked tomorrow. He just wanted to find Rosalind, look her in the eye, get her story and more information on Reni's possible whereabouts.

"She's not home."

He turned to see Josh Perkins standing in the Fisher yard. News crews were still staking out the house, and his journalist friend was one of many waiting for a scoop.

"Have you seen Rosalind?" Daniel asked.

"She was here earlier today," Josh said. "Returned for a couple of hours, then left again. According to the *Palm Springs Gazette*'s event calendar, she's being honored tonight with a community service award at the Palm Springs Conference Center and Art Institute."

"Thanks." Daniel moved toward his SUV.

Josh fell into step beside him. "Got anything for me?"

"Not right now, but I might have something soon."

Thirty minutes later, Daniel arrived at the conference center. The street was wide and ended in a cul-de-sac. Nearby was an empty lot of cacti and the ubiquitous creosote bush. The harshness of the day was fading and would soon be replaced by a beautiful desert night. In the parking lot, he tried calling Reni again. Like before, it went straight to voicemail. "Call me when you get this." His voice revealed a sense of urgency he was still struggling to contain.

He wasn't dressed for a fancy event, but he typically carried a change of clothes for emergencies. Outside his vehicle, not into the idea of waiting around for the event to end, he slipped a tie around his neck and put on a black jacket. At the door of the center, they asked for his name. He flashed his badge instead. "I'm looking for the guest of honor. Rosalind Fisher."

He was given a table number. Daniel flipped his leather case shut.

Dinner was long underway and the room was a roaring wall of noise, brightly lit with contemporary chandeliers. He spotted the number stuck in a metal clip in the center of a table near the stage. An arm went up and a hand waved. He hoped it was Reni, attending the dinner. No, it was her mother, pushing back her chair and getting to her feet, looking pleased to see him.

CHAPTER 47

Pain was Reni's friend. It was the one thing, maybe the only thing, that kept her conscious and moving, each anticipated step a jolt that started at her heel and bolted to the top of her skull.

After a confusing period of time that felt both endless and short, the day was fading. Once total darkness fell and she hadn't yet reached the road—what then? She'd given it her best shot. As she considered lying down, she spotted shimmering lights in the distance, blinked a few times in an attempt to focus. It was the sun reflecting off moving vehicles.

Her goal was renewed.

Get to the highway.

It was farther than it looked, and darkness was almost complete by the time she reached blacktop. Once there, not a single car in sight now, she braced the end of the walking stick on the center yellow lines and began to shuffle west, where the sky was still hazy and pink, and the road rolled and unrolled, furled and unfurled, turned and unturned, in and around the landscape of mountains near and mountains far, the shimmering beauty reminding her that the desert would outlive them all, even as it embraced the dead and murdered and buried.

The lines under her shuffling feet were comically long. The length of a semitrailer. How was that possible? So long. *Really* long. She was so engrossed in the length of the lines that she failed to hear an approaching car. A horn honked behind her, breaking her concentration.

She swayed and staggered to the side of the road. The walking stick hit a soft patch of earth. She pitched forward and collapsed just past the solid white line, pain so familiar and ceaseless that the increase of it barely registered. Rolling to her back, she weakly lifted both arms in the air as if she'd burst through a marathon banner.

The car blasted past.

Air sucked one way and the other, lifting her hair, then slapping it against her face hard enough to sting. Brakes engaged and tires squealed as the vehicle came to a full stop. She craned her neck.

Doors opened and people walked toward her. From where she lay, she could see shoes and bare legs and cowboy boots and a floral dress. Trendy clothing. Kids. Once they were closer, she guessed them to be in their early twenties. Two males, one female, all with long brown hair. They began talking as if she couldn't hear them.

"What should we do?"

"I think she's hurt."

A flashlight app suddenly and rudely blinded her. She squinted and put up a hand, palm out.

"She's got blood on her face."

"Should we call the police?"

"My phone doesn't have any bars."

"We can't just leave her here."

"I don't want her in my car. She could be a murderer."

Points for that. Not a bad thing to be aware of.

"Give her some food and water and let's go."

"No."

That was the girl.

"We're going to miss the show."

"You know how we were talking about things we regretted not doing? Like those moments when we didn't step up and act when we should have?" the girl asked. "This is one of them. This is the kind of thing I want to get right and not think about twenty years from now with regret. I'm not leaving her here."

"It's my car," one of the guys said.

"Then go on without me. We'll hitchhike. I might get to the show or not."

"You're the singer."

"And I'm not leaving without her."

One of the guys finally spoke directly to Reni. "Do you need help? Or are you layin' there on purpose? We can leave if you want to be left alone."

"She's not there on purpose," the girl said, irritation in her voice. "Look at her."

"Think she's homeless?"

"Or maybe one of those crazy people who lives in the desert and walks to town for supplies a few times a year," the other guy suggested.

"Get that light out of my face," Reni croaked, her mouth so dry she could hardly talk.

What a surreal collision of worlds. Hipsters, and whatever she was. A turtle crawling out of the desert. It seemed like she'd been wandering for a lifetime. "What day is it?" she asked.

"Saturday."

A little over twenty-four hours had passed since her mother had left her to die.

"We're on our way from Las Vegas to Pioneertown." The kid completed that by saying they were opening for a band she'd never heard of. From his voice she could tell he wanted her to be impressed.

"Help me up."

Nobody moved.

"Go on," the girl said.

The two guys grabbed her under the arms.

"I think maybe she pissed herself."

Very possible.

"She needs an emergency room," the girl said.

Reni wasn't going to argue with that.

They eased her into the back seat. Pain had become such a constant that Reni didn't even gasp when she sat down and felt something shift in her body. The girl circled and slipped inside with Reni while the two guys climbed in front. One of them asked, "Is that your dog?"

She looked out the window. Sitting near the car, staring at them, was the matted dog. She was too exhausted to try to explain, so she just nodded.

The dog got in front. The driver groaned. "He smells worse than she does."

Doors slammed and tires spun over sand and gravel as they pulled onto the two-lane road, high beams on, cutting west. Music played loudly.

The girl popped the top on a beverage and offered the can to her. Reni couldn't read it in the dim light.

"Energy drink," the girl said. Then, "Give the dog some water," she told the guys.

Liquid of any kind was good. Reni drank the whole can. She heard lapping from the front.

"I used to date him." The girl gestured toward the driver. "But I don't anymore. Have a brownie." She held out a container. With blood- and dirt-caked fingers, Reni fumbled for a brownie.

"They have pot in them. It might help."

So California.

Reni took a bite. And another. When she was done, she rested her head against the seat. She hadn't forgotten her mission. With eyes closed, she said with authority, falling back on her old FBI persona, "Somebody search for Gabby Sutton of Yorba Linda, call her, and give me your phone."

"I found a Jerome Sutton." He read the address.

Gabby's husband. "Call it."

Moments later, a phone was passed to her from the front seat. She put it to her ear, hoping to hear Gabby's voice at the other end. A man answered.

"I need to talk to Gabby," Reni said, eyes closed.

"She's not here."

"When will she be back?"

"She went to meet someone for coffee." He sounded worried. "She should have been home hours ago."

"Who was she meeting?"

"Who am I talking to?" Understandably cautious.

"Reni Fisher."

He made a strange sound. "I checked her calendar. She drove to Riverside to see you."

CHAPTER 48

Two minutes after arriving, Daniel was a guest at Rosalind's table. He'd come hoping to talk to her in private. Instead, the mayor took the stage and the ceremony began. The list of accolades was long, and people began shifting restlessly in their chairs. Rosalind finally accepted her award, a piece of crystal with engraving on it. Dressed in a white pantsuit and red heels, she smiled for the cameras and held her prize high.

She'd been taking in young women for thirty years. Had any of those women gone missing? Or was he following the weak trail of tests performed by some mad scientist who was no longer even alive? Never in Daniel's own investigative research had any of the crimes suggested Rosalind's involvement. And if she had been involved, why hadn't Ben spoken up?

His thoughts were interrupted when the tenor of the event changed and people turned to check out a commotion in the back of the room.

The waitstaff was attempting to stop someone from entering. It wasn't until the person broke free and was moving down the center aisle that Daniel recognized Reni. His first reaction was one of relief that she wasn't missing. Or worse, dead. That response was quickly replaced by concern. She was injured. Maybe seriously.

And her hair was short. Why was her hair short? That question took up too much space in his brain considering everything else going on. But even if her hair had still been long, he wouldn't have immediately known who it was. She looked like someone who'd clawed her way out of a grave. Her face and clothing were caked with dirt and what appeared to be dried blood. And she wasn't moving with her typical long strides. Her steps were slow and deliberate, her full focus on the stage.

Rosalind stopped talking, her face frozen as if someone had hit pause at an unfortunate spot. Daniel became aware of the absence of sound. The deafening roar of the ill-designed room was gone. Left behind were a few scattered clinks of silverware hitting plates as unaware staff continued to do their jobs, heads down. Eventually the silence told the story of something amiss, and all work ceased.

For a moment it seemed as if there were only two living, breathing people in the room. Reni and Rosalind. Everyone else felt like cutouts or placeholders or people who'd gone blurry and out of focus as the energy and emotion of mother and daughter collided.

Reni took the stairs to the stage, each step a struggle.

Daniel pulled out his phone and called for an ambulance.

"I'm glad . . . I could be here for this," Reni said in a whisper that snagged on each inhale. She was taller than her mother, and she had to bend into the microphone. "I was afraid . . . I wasn't going to make it." She took the piece of crystal and read it. "Rosalind Fisher, Community Service Award."

Once Daniel was off the phone with the 911 operator, he started moving toward the stage.

"The thing is . . ." Reni's eyes closed for too long, and a couple of times she latched onto the podium to keep from falling. At the same time, she seemed incredibly strong and powerful. "My mother is so much more than you realize . . . and I . . . I want to publicly acknowledge that here today." She paused, took a stabilizing breath, and continued, "This award should really say . . . Inland Empire Killer."

The audience gasped in unison, and any uncertainty Daniel felt about Rosalind's involvement vanished with Reni's public accusation. With those condemning words, Reni threw the award down on the stage. It exploded, and shards flew. People screamed.

No hesitation from Rosalind. "You poor dear," she said. "You poor dear." Her calm in the face of such questionable behavior drove home how much she'd always been there for Reni. Even here at her own event, she was watching out for her daughter, thinking about her, rather than herself. At least that's what she was trying to portray. And Daniel was pretty sure not a person in the room doubted that Reni had lost her mind.

There was a new flurry of sound near the back of the room, then waves of conversation riding emotions of relief as three uniformed officers poured through a door.

As if she'd just noticed the other humans, Reni looked around, searching for an anchor, her eyes locking on Daniel, who'd made it to the foot of the stage. The strength he'd noted earlier wavered. Doubt seeped in. He saw confusion in her face.

Have I made an error in judgment? Am I wrong about everything?

He spoke Reni's name quietly, eye to eye, as if they were alone. "You're doing fine," he said. "Don't doubt yourself."

She heard him and nodded.

Where had she been, and what had she been through? And did Rosalind have anything to do with it? Daniel wanted to ask, but chaos was still alive and well in the room. Some of the people who'd been transfixed scrambled away. Others continued to gawk. Outside, ambulance sirens screamed, then went silent. Doors burst open again, and the emergency medical team appeared toting heavy cases.

Daniel helped Reni down the steps. She was shaking, and her breathing was quick and shallow as if each inhalation hurt.

Despite the confusion, Reni was efficiently loaded onto a gurney. Daniel stayed beside her as they wheeled her from the building. In the parking lot, she asked them to pause so she could talk to a young woman standing beside a car covered in bumper stickers. A scruffy dog watched from the front seat. Daniel was trying to figure out who they were and what they had to do with Reni when he spotted Rosalind scurrying away.

Reni had just publicly accused her mother of being the Inland Empire Killer. An accusation alone wasn't enough to arrest the woman, but he wasn't letting her out of his sight.

"I'll meet you at the hospital," he told Reni, then sprinted off.

"I'm going to follow the ambulance," Rosalind explained when Daniel caught up to her.

The layers of Rosalind Fisher were revealing themselves. Now that he knew at least some of the truth, he was able to recognize what had escaped him before. Whether she'd actually killed or not, he was looking into the eyes of a sociopath. And she had no plans to drive to the hospital.

He held out his hand for her keys. "I'll drive."

The trick was to not give away his own agenda. He decided to employ the kind of persuasion someone like her might respond to, making her the martyr and hero of her personal story. Which she'd always been in her own mind. Even her social work spoke to that. "You've had more than your share to deal with today."

"You should think about growing a beard." With distracted annoyance, she gave him her keyless fob. He tucked it into his pocket.

Saturday night and traffic was heavy. Daniel took a back way that wound through residential streets. There were more stop signs on the route, but fewer lights. He didn't want to push too hard and spook her, but he asked a question any rational person would ask. "What was that about back there?"

"With Reni, you never know." Rosalind sighed, and even that sound of motherly resignation and concern now felt sinister. "Her reality is skewed. I'm sorry I haven't been able to help her more."

"Sometimes it doesn't matter how much we do," Daniel said with just the right amount of sympathy. "Some people can't be helped."

A faint sound intruded, something he couldn't lock in on. Was it far away? Nearby?

Nearby.

Tapping.

Coming from the trunk of the car.

The reality of what he was dealing with connected like a punch to the stomach. He hadn't expected the evidence he needed to be so near. At the same time, Rosalind turned on the radio and cranked up the volume to mask the noise.

He pulled to a screeching halt in the middle of the road and threw open his door. Music was blasting, some nineties rock ballad that added another layer of weird to the scene. "Out!" he told Rosalind. "Now!" He wanted her far from the car so she didn't try to drive away.

She got out.

He hit the trunk button. The lid flew up as he raced to the back of the vehicle. Lying inside, curled on her side, was a woman, her wrists and mouth bound with duct tape, a shovel beside her. She looked dead, but she'd come around enough to alert him. Yet none of those things hit him as hard as what she was wearing.

A red floral dress.

He faltered. His knees went weak, and a wave of dizziness washed over him. Through a roar of blinding emotions, he reached for the fabric with a shaking hand.

The trunk lid slammed hard against his head, pitching him forward. Then something slid past his face. He staggered upright in time to see Rosalind swing the shovel, connecting with his skull. His ears rang. Stunned, he stumbled, almost caught himself, fell, his head striking the blacktop. Blinking, trying to focus, he managed to unsnap the holster at his waist. While the music continued to play, before he could pull his weapon, she was on top of him, grabbing him by the jacket, slamming his head into the street.

CHAPTER 49

Like a boxer revived for the next round, Reni opened the car door before the vehicle came to a complete halt. A half block away, her mother's sedan sat in the middle of the road, trunk and both front doors open.

After seeing Daniel leave with Rosalind, knowing he was in danger, she'd refused the ambulance and rejoined the band kids in order to tail him. Now she planted her foot on the ground and pulled herself from the car. "Call 911 and get out of here." She wanted her new friends far from danger.

The young guy behind the wheel hesitated, then threw the car into reverse as Reni moved toward the horrifying scene of her mother bashing Daniel's head against the ground, Reni's own pain dulled by fresh adrenaline rushing through her body and her concern for Daniel's life. All the while, music blasted from the car, making the scene look like a staged social media event or flash art.

"Stop!" she shouted. "You're hurting him!" The familiar words, the words of a deep and troubling and horrifying memory, came from her unbidden.

Rosalind looked up in surprise, then scrambled to her feet.

Daniel's face was bloody. So much blood. No movement. As Reni came closer, she saw a body lying in the trunk and let out a sob. Gabby Sutton. Dead? She looked dead. And Daniel just a few feet away? Also dead?

"It's over," Reni managed to say. "You can't cover this up."

Rosalind nodded. "It's time to quit pretending everything is fine. Parents want to protect their children, but you should be locked up so you aren't a danger to others. I'm sorry, honey, but I'm going to have to tell them how you lured Gabby to the park, and how you killed your partner. This can't go on any longer."

She was convincing. *So* convincing. Reni found a familiar cloud rolling over her as she felt herself succumbing to Rosalind's gaslighting.

"I didn't do any of those things," Reni said with hesitance. Along with the brain cloud, pain was creeping back. After the exertion of the past few minutes, her body was beginning to give up again. It might be easier to accept what her mother was telling her. She was weak, confused. And maybe it was true. Maybe it was all true.

"I know it's hard, and I know it's bewildering, but you can trust me," Rosalind said. "Like you've always trusted me. I'm your mother. Let me take care of you. Come here. Get in the car. I'll drive you to the hospital."

From a distance came the sound of sirens.

Alarmed, Rosalind pushed the shovel into Reni's hands, circled the car, got into the driver's seat.

But the vehicle didn't start and her mother didn't drive away.

Daniel must have had the fob, and he wasn't close enough for it to activate the ignition.

Reni looked from Gabby to Daniel to the shovel in her hand. It would seem so obvious when the cops got there. Reni, guilty.

Don't doubt yourself.

Time seemed to jump and Rosalind was back out of the car, now with a gun in her hand, her eyes full of panic as she was forced to confront the truth of the situation. She might not be able to charm and lie her way out of this.

Reni remembered the gun her mother held. Rosalind and Maurice had bought matching ones. They'd even taken lessons.

With a shaking arm, Rosalind pointed the weapon at Daniel. She probably wanted to ensure all witnesses were dead. That seemed to be her strategy and the drive behind her behavior, even going back to the death of Carmel Cortez.

Reni played into her mother's need to look innocent. "Every gun has its own individual signature," she said quickly. "He's already dead. Don't leave evidence behind. Let's go. We have to hurry. You and me. To the desert." She put the shovel in the trunk next to the body of Gabby Sutton, and slammed the lid. "I know you think you're alone now, but you aren't," she said, searching for words that would tap into Rosalind's current state of frantic fear. Make her think she needed Reni the way she'd needed Ben and Maurice. "I'll help you bury the body. Just like Daddy used to do. Just like Maurice. Let's go to the desert."

"Oh, honey." Rosalind appeared relieved as she spread her arms wide. "Let me give you a hug."

Reni inwardly shuddered as she stepped without hesitation around Daniel, partially shielding him, and walked into her mother's evil embrace. Now was the time to grab the weapon and pull it from Rosalind's grip, but Reni's sight began to fade, a blackness creeping in. She felt her mother shift, felt the absence of Rosalind's arm, felt the gun between them, jabbing into her belly.

Reni blinked, clearing her vision enough to see her mother lean back and look into her eyes and finally speak the truth: "You sucked the life out of me, little bird."

A gunshot exploded, deafening because it was so close. Reni waited to feel hot blood running down her stomach, waited to feel the burn of lead in her gut. She felt neither of those things. Too near death to process sensation?

Rosalind frowned. The gun she held clattered to the ground. Her lips parted, and a dark, round circle appeared on her forehead.

Reni tried to hold her up, couldn't. Rosalind's body went limp and dropped straight to the ground. She landed on her knees with a crack of bones, then toppled backward with a snap. Reni looked over at Daniel. He was lying on his back, eyes closed, gun in his hand, a spent shell casing beside him.

"Not dead," he whispered faintly.

From the car speakers, a chorus soared.

CHAPTER 50

Thirty minutes later the street was blocked off, generators were powering floodlights, crime-scene techs were placing plastic evidence numbers, and ambulances waited to carry the injured away. The body of Rosalind Fisher had been bagged and was in the coroner van.

Daniel had surrendered his gun and was sitting on the bumper of an ambulance, blanket around him, his head wrapped in a bandage, while emergency personnel monitored him. No matter the circumstances, standard procedure for all officer-involved shootings required the weapon be secured as evidence and the officer put on short administrative leave while the department conducted an internal investigation.

Gabby and Reni were both on gurneys, getting IVs established before transportation. Gabby's vitals were weak, but the fact that she was still alive and had been aware enough to signal for help gave Daniel hope that she'd recover from her injuries. She'd hung on this long. Not far off, two cops were taking the statements of the young adults with the dog, who'd reappeared after everything went down.

As the EMTs wheeled Reni past him, she put up a hand and told them to stop.

"I'm sorry," Daniel said, talking about her mother. "I didn't have any choice." No need to speak Rosalind Fisher's name. He could see Reni understood.

"Check . . . my back pocket." She rolled slightly, enough for him to see a small paperback protruding from her jeans. He pulled it out.

A book about birds. Was she delirious?

"Maps," she muttered, eyes closed. "Look . . . at the maps."

He riffled through pages, found the maps, unfolded one—and his breath caught. Dots everywhere, a lot more than in the crude drawing Ben Fisher had made.

"Look at the title page," Reni said.

He turned back—and saw it contained an index of names and dates, all written in small, neat cursive. Many of the names he recognized as missing women who were suspected to have been victims of the Inland Empire Killer.

"Rosalind's handwriting," Reni said faintly. "She was part of it."

His heart slamming, he scanned the list for his mother's name, didn't see it, scanned again. Not there. He went through the pages, quickly at first, then slowly, hoping, hoping . . .

But he found nothing.

Did the book mean both Reni's parents had killed? Had Rosalind been in charge and had Ben Fisher carried out her orders? Or had they been equals? He didn't know exactly where Maurice fit in. Maybe he'd been in unfortunate love with one or both Fishers. Whatever the situation, Ben and Rosalind would go down in history with other infamous murdering couples. Homicide fans would rank them in the top ten, along with killers like Gerald and Charlene Gallego, Ray and Faye Copeland, Fred and Rosemary West.

The big question: Would Reni be okay? Until now, she'd been able to draw from the darkness of her past and use it to drive herself forward. Maybe she could do so again. Maybe discovering the truth about her mother would set to rest those strange and nagging feelings that could hover in the background and foreground of life. The sense that something didn't fit. Daniel had experienced enough of them to understand their gossamer quality. Maybe those would stop for her. Maybe the unease that could descend on a person in the middle of the night would visit less frequently, or not at all.

And yet his own life quest hadn't ended. His mother was still missing.

CHAPTER 51

A cracked pelvis, broken rib, and sprained ankle.

The rib and ankle Reni had suspected, but she'd been surprised to learn of the cracked pelvis. In speaking of her survival instincts, doctors tossed around words like *amazing* and *resilient*. She'd just done what had to be done.

After a group consult, it was decided surgery was not required. Due to location and size, the hairline fracture was expected to heal on its own with no complications. She'd have to spend several days in bed, followed by a predicted twelve weeks until full recovery. Doctors were notorious for presenting patients with the best-case scenario when it came to time frame. She added a couple of weeks to their numbers. The words *full recovery* were what mattered.

Daniel and Gabby were also expected to be okay. Daniel had visited her room several times already while tethered to and pushing an IV rack, his face pale and battered, lip swollen, stitches above one eye, head bandaged. On his fourth visit, he came dressed in street clothes, no IV.

"They're releasing me," he announced, cruising the room, looking at cards and flowers from strangers. He found a box of chocolates and asked if she wanted one.

She shook her head. "Help yourself. They're from Gabby's husband. He brought her here in a wheelchair for a short visit." While the husband hovered anxiously over his wife, Gabby had related how Rosalind had lured her to the park. Despite everything that had happened, the attack seemed to have brought the couple closer together. Reni was glad Gabby would have the support she needed at home.

Daniel eased himself into a chair, the care he took a reminder that he was still in pain himself. "I'm sorry about your mother," he told her again. It must have been weighing heavily on his mind. "I messed up."

"You saved my life."

"I could have stopped her earlier. I opened the trunk and saw the red dress that reminded me of my mother's, and I allowed myself to be distracted. I lost track of everything. Where Rosalind was. What she was doing. It didn't have to happen the way it happened."

The fact that he could regret taking the life of someone like Rosalind Fisher said a lot about him. "We aren't superhuman," Reni said.

He looked at her with a wry expression. "You sure about that? Because the word around here is that you are."

"I'm just a desert rat." Going forward, it wouldn't be easy. She'd grieve for the loss of things she never really had, and for the false life Rosalind had presented to her. But she also felt a sense of hope.

Someone knocked on the open door.

It was the girl from the highway rescue, the one in the band. Turned out she had a name. Indio. She smiled a mischievous smile, stepped in, and pulled her sweater aside to reveal the little dog that had followed Reni on her trek.

He wasn't ugly. That was Reni's first thought. In fact, now that his brown and black hair had been clipped and washed, he was rather handsome, although very thin.

"I took him to the vet, and they groomed him. We were surprised to find he had a chip. He's three years old, and his name is Edward."

Edward was a suitably regal name.

"He belonged to a guy who died six months ago." She made a sad face.

"He's probably been roaming ever since," Reni said.

"That's what the vet thought too. Poor thing." Indio stroked him. "I can't have a dog right now because I'm going back to college in the fall, but I wanted to check with you before I take him to a no-kill shelter or send out a social media blast to see if anybody's interested in him."

"Bring him here." Reni patted the bed. She didn't know how she was going to take care of a dog when she wasn't even sure how she'd care for herself right now, but she'd figure it out. "He's coming home with me."

CHAPTER 52

In a remote area of the desert known for some of the darkest skies, Reni and Daniel walked, Daniel carrying folding chairs and wearing a backpack, Reni, still healing, clutching blankets to her chest, Edward following at her heels. Just a few hours earlier she'd finished throwing a bowl for Gabby, and stamping the bottom with her new business name, Desert Dog Pottery, along with an image of a dog that looked a lot like Edward.

Daniel had spent the past weeks coordinating victim recovery operations with the FBI. In addition to overseeing the project, a large part of his focus involved contacting families of the missing victims as bodies were located. With the use of the bird-book maps, twenty graves had been found so far.

Reni knew he was trying to come to terms with his own lack of closure. She wished she could help. Maybe that was what tonight was about. He hadn't been that interested in coming to the desert, but the power of natural darkness and an expanse of sky that stretched from horizon to horizon could not be disputed. She hoped it might bring him at least a little peace, if only for an hour or two.

Placing the chairs side by side, they sat down and tucked their phones deep into their pockets so no light would escape. Proper night viewing required total darkness, and it could take up to thirty minutes for a person's pupils to adjust after turning off even a faint light.

It was easy to forget the earth actually existed inside the Milky Way galaxy that was visible above them. Such a crazy thing to think about. "See the shape in the center of that cluster?" Reni pointed even though he couldn't see her hand. "It's called the Summer Triangle. And the bright stars? Those are Vega, Altair, and Deneb in Cygnus." Boring information for many, and she understood she was forcing her obsession onto someone else. But she told herself it was okay because she had a motive.

Bad things were still happening in the world, and bad things had happened to both of them, but nature brought solace. Not that the bad things could be erased and forgotten. They couldn't. The murders. The evil. But she and Daniel were only specks in the universe. Stardust. While that might overwhelm some people, it brought her comfort. To know that once the bad people were locked up, once the victims were buried, once the bodies were found, once she'd cried it all out, this would remain. Strong, enduring. Even if she chose to return to work to the job Daniel had offered her, this would always be here waiting. And if she didn't return, he'd made it clear that he'd like to bring her in on a case-by-case basis.

They wrapped themselves in the blankets. Edward got on her lap, and they sat in silence for a long time. They could do that without it feeling awkward. She finally brought up the topic of his mother. "I'm sorry you haven't found her." Especially heartbreaking when he was providing closure for others but was unable to do so for himself.

"It's a struggle, I won't lie." The darkness seemed to make sharing easier for him.

"I've spent my life searching for her," he said. "It impacted my marriage. The obsession. Do I stop? I think I have to, but I don't know if I can. And oddly enough, I'm having a hard time figuring out who I'd be if I quit searching. My quest for her is my identity. I became a detective because of her."

"Can you imagine being anything other than a homicide detective?"

"No." An honest answer, but she could hear the pain in his voice for the loss of options and paths not taken.

"I understand. It's who you are now." Her own voice trembled with emotion at the thought of their different yet similar journeys. Like him, she'd been a shadow, a foot soldier, moving through the wake of someone else's life. But in her case, she was trying to find and correct and atone for the sins of others, while also attempting to define and untether herself from those very people.

She'd realized something recently. Something that had eluded her since the day she'd seen her father arrested and the world had fallen apart. It had been Ben and Rosalind's journey, not hers. It had never been hers. She'd just been swept along in the current.

She'd seen her parents' brain scans, and had naturally wondered what her own would look like. Right now she had no plans to get tested. She was slowly learning to trust herself, and had recently heard that her old partner had been arrested for taking bribes from criminals. His face morphing into her father's might have been her subconscious picking up on his untrustworthiness. Gut instinct and not logic. As for her father's ashes, they were locked up in a safe-deposit box until she decided what to do with them. She didn't want them in her home, but throwing them in the trash hadn't seemed a good idea either. Her grandmother's property was in the process of being donated to the Mojave Desert Land Trust, a nonprofit that acquired and protected land, and Rosalind's house would be put on the market soon.

"I honestly don't know how you do it," Daniel said. "How you get through the days."

"I cope by looking up and out. That's where I find help. Nature never lets me down."

Unlike Daniel, Reni was experiencing something close to validation now that she'd discovered the truth about her mother. Because deep in her heart of hearts, she'd always known the world hadn't been turning for her and her family in the way it had turned for others. Something had been off, even after Benjamin's imprisonment.

"You feel that?" Daniel asked.

"Yep." A ground tremble. Just a little one. Just a warning of things to come. Not today, but maybe tomorrow or next week or next year.

"Are you worried about a big one?" he asked.

"I'm more worried about evil people than I am about a major earthquake."

"Me too. Oh, man. Look." He let out a gasp. "Two o'clock."

"Perseid meteor shower." Curiosity and the ability to be amazed were essential for them both right now. When those responses slipped away, a person was in trouble. Awe was part of the human experience that couldn't and shouldn't be discounted.

"That's one of the most beautiful things I've ever seen," he said.

In the dark, Reni smiled to herself. He might become a desert lover after all.

ABOUT THE AUTHOR

Photo © 2018 Martha Weir

Anne Frasier is the *New York Times* and *USA Today* bestselling author of the Jude Fontaine and Elise Sandburg series. Her award-winning books, with over a million copies sold, span the genres of suspense, mystery, thriller, romantic suspense, paranormal, and memoir. *The Body Reader* received the 2017 Thriller Award for Best Paperback Original Novel from International Thriller Writers. Other honors include a RITA for romantic suspense and a Daphne du Maurier Award for paranormal romance. Her thrillers have hit the *USA Today* bestseller list and have been featured in Mystery Guild, Literary Guild, and Book of the Month Club. Her memoir *The Orchard* was an *O, The Oprah Magazine* fall pick; a One Book, One Community read; a B+ review in *Entertainment Weekly*; and one of the Librarians' Best Books of 2011. Visit her website at www.annefrasier.com.